CREWEL
AND UNUSUAL

CREWEL AND UNUSUAL

MOLLY MacRae

W★RLDWIDE

TORONTO • NEW YORK • LONDON
AMSTERDAM • PARIS • SYDNEY • HAMBURG
STOCKHOLM • ATHENS • TOKYO • MILAN
MADRID • WARSAW • BUDAPEST • AUCKLAND

For the Clinton County Area Arts Council,
the Johnson City Area Arts Council,
and the Vault Art Gallery in Tuscola, Illinois.
Your support and encouragement of local artists
nourish and enrich our communities beyond measure.

WORLDWIDE™

Recycling programs
for this product may
not exist in your area.

Crewel and Unusual

A Worldwide Mystery/March 2020

First published in 2019 by Pegasus Books Ltd.
This edition published in 2020.

ISBN-13: 978-1-335-29970-3

Copyright © 2019 by Molly MacRae

This edition published by arrangement with Harlequin Books S.A.

For questions and comments about the quality of this book, please contact us at CustomerService@Harlequin.com.

Harlequin Enterprises ULC
22 Adelaide St. West, 40th Floor
Toronto, Ontario M5H 4E3, Canada
www.ReaderService.com

Printed in U.S.A.

CREWEL
AND UNUSUAL

ONE

ARGYLE CAME TO greet me as I unlocked the front door
of the Weaver's Cat. He pounced on a couple of dry
leaves that blew in with me on the morning breeze and
then twined around my ankles, leaving a trace of tabby-
yellow on my pants.

"Just the accessory I needed," I said, stooping to
rub his chin. "Now we'll both look good in the front
window."

The Weaver's Cat was a beautiful place to spend time
in any season—surrounded by scads of skeins and colors and textures, in bins and on shelves and hanging
throughout the yarn shop—but fall edged out spring
and summer to be my favorite season for displays.
We'd brought upper east Tennessee's changing colors
indoors with wools in goldenrod, pumpkin, bronze, and
deep purple spilling out of baskets in the front window.
Roving in russet, mahogany, chestnut, salmon, and tomato hung from pegs to tempt spinners and felters. We
splashed every autumn color in the displays around the
shop but the brightest reds. We'd quietly tucked the
reds back in their bins, two weeks earlier, when Garland Brown died.

My late grandmother, Ivy McClellan, had introduced
me to Gar Brown during one of the summers I'd spent
with her in Blue Plum when I was a kid. He'd been a
contemporary of my grandparents, and he'd charmed

me and made Granny laugh when he said I could be the "Honorary Illinois Belle of Blue Plum." Gar had come to Granny's funeral this past spring, and when I'd made the decision to stay in Blue Plum and step into her shoes at the Weaver's Cat, he'd stopped by with flowers to welcome me and say it was Illinois's loss.

A banker, Gar had involved himself in the community throughout his career, and he'd been one of those people who grew busier and more involved after retirement. He sat on the Arts Council board, the library board, the mayor's landscape advisory committee, and the sheriff's task force on littering.

We were all shocked when hikers found him dead beside his pickup truck in a trailhead parking area on nearby Grandmother Mountain. The police said he'd surprised the person or gang responsible for a series of smash-and-grab car burglaries over the past few months at trailheads up and down the mountain range. When we heard the gang smashed a rock into Gar's head, Ardis, the longtime manager at the Cat, took the scarlets and crimsons out of our displays.

Neither Argyle nor I dwelled on the tragedy that morning, though. He lifted his nose toward the bakery bag in my hand. "Mel's mystery scones," I said. I'd taken a detour on my way to work and picked up coffee at Mel's on Main, the best café in Blue Plum. Along with the coffee, Mel had handed me the bag and asked me to critique her new recipe. She'd only told me the bag held scones but wouldn't say what kind.

"Classical music all right with you this morning, Argyle?"

Argyle didn't object, so I set the coffee and bag on the sales counter, turned on the radio, and switched it from Ardis's bluegrass station. To something sonorous with strings, the cat and I performed a serpentine paw-de-deux down the hall toward his food dish in the kitchen.

Argyle had hooked up with me after what must have been a fairly devil-may-care existence. I'd never found out where he came from, but he'd been happy to retire and become the next official cat of the Weaver's Cat. He lived in the shop, and the shop lived in one of three connected houses that were part of a mid-nineteenth century row house on Main Street. If you faced the row, we had the house on the left. That put us on the corner of Main and Fox Streets, giving us light from three sides.

Granny and Granddaddy moved into the house when they married. Granny, a weaver, spinner, and dyer, started the Weaver's Cat in a corner of the living room. Over time, the shop grew until it filled most of the rooms, and after Granddaddy died, Granny let it take over completely. Then she'd bought the little yellow house on Lavender Street and walked home there each night. And now I did, too.

In the kitchen, Argyle lifted his chin toward the top of the refrigerator and said, "Mrrph."

A damp sigh came in response, followed by, "So it took the cat to finally drag you in, did it?" Geneva shimmered into view on top of the fridge, looking as lively as a heap of forgotten dishrags and sounding like the ghost of...well, like a ghost.

That I knew what a ghost looked and sounded like still blew my science- and reality-loving mind away. Eight months ago, I would have looked for the hidden camera. Now I could tell this ghost's mood from her dismal sigh even before she delivered her snarky greet-

ing. But to say that she looked like a heap of dishrags
wasn't really fair. She wasn't as solid as a heap of anything. Looking at her made me want to blink or squint
my eyes to bring her into better focus. Neither helped.
Geneva looked no more substantial than gossamer-fine
lace seen through a rain-washed window, and sometimes just as sad. I liked her, though, and gladly called
her my friend.

"Good morning. How are you?" I smiled, ignoring
her doldrums. One of her favorite jokes started with
the line, *I'm not a morning person.* Then, depending
on her mood, she might laugh and say, *That's haunted
humor, because I'm not much of a person at all.* Or the
joke might end with her impression of Greta Garbo and
the line, *I want to be alone.* She did Elly May Clampett
better than Garbo, but the Garbo meant that Geneva really was in a funk.

"Have you noticed that I can't count on you anymore?" she asked. "You're so late this morning that you
barely have time to feed Argyle and none at all to clean
his litter box. He can't count on you anymore, either."

"Sorry about the box, old man. I'll do that as soon
as Ardis gets here. There's plenty of time for breakfast,
though." I tipped crunchy fish kibbles into his dish and
gave him fresh water. He rubbed his chin against one
of my shoes in thanks before digging in. "Look. I think
he's forgiven me."

Geneva *hmph*ed but followed me to the front room.
She floated to a favorite perch on the mannequin that
stood near the sales counter. The mannequin wore a
stylish knitted cape and hand-felted fedora, both in for-
est green. The fedora had a pheasant feather stuck in
a deeper-green ribbon circling its crown. One of our

customers had made the cape and hat. Geneva, drooping on the mannequin's shoulder, might have brought the jauntiness of the ensemble down a peg or two, but instead, her misty translucence turned a lovely sage color. Together they looked not quite festive but certainly interesting.

"You look nice on her shoulder this morning, Geneva."

She *hmph*ed again but sat up straighter and rested an elbow on the fedora.

I continued getting the cash register ready for the day, but when I looked up again, I saw Geneva leaning forward, her hollow eyes on the bakery bag. She took a few tentative sniffs, lifting her nose the way Argyle had. Then she left the mannequin and drifted over to the counter. She settled next to the bag, and that gave me the only hint I needed about one of the ingredients in the scones. I went to unlock the front door and flip the sign from "We're home counting sheep" to "Come in and knit a spell." When I returned to the counter, Geneva was obviously trying *not* to be obvious about her interest in the bag. I opened it, sniffed, and held it out to her.

"Ginger." It sounded like a prayer. She closed her eyes and hummed.

As much as I wanted to eat one of the scones, I held off so she could enjoy her ginger meditation. She had a serious relationship with ginger and few enough other pleasures in life. *In death,* as she corrected me when I slipped. I still didn't know much about ghosts. For that matter, neither did Geneva, except that she was one. Her memories of her life were as misty as she was, but she said the smell of ginger took her back to her mama's warm kitchen.

How she could smell ginger, though, I didn't know. She didn't seem to notice other scents, good or bad. It was the sad truth of Geneva's ghostly existence that she'd been dead for a hundred and forty years and hadn't successfully haunted anyone until I came along. She couldn't slam doors, drop vases, or do any of the other ghostly classics. She couldn't manipulate anything at all. In all the time since she'd died, no one had heard her voice, and no one had seen her misty form appear at the end of their bed.

Geneva and I hadn't met at the Weaver's Cat; we startled each other in an antebellum cottage, now a caretaker's house, at a historic site on the edge of town. I'd stayed in the cottage for a few days in the spring, when I'd come for Granny's funeral. I'd never believed in ghosts, and she'd spent those hundred and forty years undetected, watching the decades and the cottage's occupants arrive and move on, or pass on, one by one. With the advent of television, she'd also watched countless hours of whatever happened to be on. She'd been the proverbial fly on the wall, not even able to annoy anyone by buzzing in their ears. She'd been a ghost of a ghost, and it was no wonder that she wasn't always the most cheerful of souls.

The string of camel bells at the door jingled, and the first customers of the day came in. They were a couple of women I didn't recognize. Tourists, maybe. The mountains around Blue Plum were as pretty as a quilt, and Blue Plum's red-brick storefronts and Victorian houses as charming as a tidily stitched sampler. Tourists loved the area, in any season, and the local economy loved them right back.

Whether the women were tourists or not, they hadn't been in the shop recently. They only made it to the middle of the room before they stopped. Then they turned in a slow circle, taking in the saturation of colors and textures around them, one of them with a breath I could hear at the counter. Granny had called that breath "the reverent respiration."

"Welcome to the Weaver's Cat," I said when she closed her mouth and smiled at me. "Are you looking for anything in particular?"

Looking dazed, as though they'd been hypnotized by a spindle whorl, the women shook their heads.

"Then I'll just give you a quick rundown of where things are and turn you loose. You'll find roving, wool, cotton, bamboo, ramie, and other yarns in the rooms downstairs. Other knitting, felting, crochet, and embroidery supplies, too. Spinning, weaving, dyeing, and quilting supplies are upstairs. Let me know if I can help you with anything at all, and don't mind the cat if you see him. He's customer- and yarn-friendly."

"Don't mind the ghost, either," Geneva said.

The women waved their thanks and started a more thorough tour of the front room, fondling and oohing and aahing as they went.

"I don't think I'll be bothering them much, do you?" Geneva didn't seem to expect an answer. She finished communing with the scones and floated back to the mannequin's shoulder. She rested her elbow on the crown of the fedora again and sank her chin into the cup of her hand. There weren't many sounds as mournful as the rhetorical question of a depressed ghost. Still haunt-challenged, only Argyle, Ardis, and I knew Geneva had followed me to the shop and now haunted it.

Before folding down the top of the bakery bag, I took a napkin and one of the scones from it. The scone was gorgeous. It didn't just have a bit of dry ginger in it; crystallized ginger studded the whole thing. Chunks of something else, too. Pear? To eat or not to eat; that was the eternal customer service etiquette question.

Geneva looked over at the women. "The coast is clear. Take a bite. The suspense would be killing me if I wasn't already dead."

I took a bite—tender, buttery, not too sweet. The chunks of pear hadn't just been baked into it. They were tender, too, and hadn't made the scone the least bit soggy. How had Mel done that? I kissed my fingertips and sighed for Geneva's benefit. The crystallized ginger made the scone fabulous. Geneva's shoulders rose and fell on an echoing sigh, and she smiled for the first time that morning. I wrapped the rest of the pastry in the napkin to finish later. Flaky, buttery, and the least bit sweet didn't mix well with fibers and fabrics.

"Why have you never named my friend, here?" Geneva asked.

I raised my eyebrows.

"The mannequin. While it's true she doesn't say much, she does support me in my times of need." She reached down and patted the mannequin's cheek.

I turned my hands palms upward and raised my shoulders a bit.

Geneva didn't mind carrying on conversations while other people were around. She wasn't the one who looked like a loon as she talked into thin air. I could avoid the loon factor by pretending to take a call on my cell. I'd also thought about wearing a bluetooth device on my ear, so I could be "on the phone" without the phone in my hand. I didn't much like that idea, though, and unless I wore my hair back, no one would see the device. But we'd developed a sort of sign language that worked, too, more or less.

"Have you developed an unattractive twitch," Geneva asked, "or was that meant to be a shrug?"

I started to answer her with a look, but one of the customers glanced over. I took a cloth from the shelf behind me and pretended the counter needed cleaning.

"I'll think of a name," Geneva said. "I'm good at names."

I continued wiping the counter but raised my eyebrows again.

"Of course I am." Geneva sounded indignant. "I named Argyle. It's the perfect name for him, too. If you agree, take another bite."

I unwrapped the scone, toasted her naming acumen with it, and took a bite. Mid-chew, the women came to the counter. I swallowed and rewrapped the scone, making sheepish eyes.

Geneva *baa*ed loudly.

"I'm so sorry," I said. "A scone from Mel's on Main, just down the street. Irresistible."

"You've given it an excellent recommendation, then," one of the women said. "We're meeting friends there for lunch."

"And one of them told us you have vintage patterns," the other woman said.

"We do," I said. Granny had never considered anything out of date. I once overheard her as she filed away a pattern for a prom dress dating from the late '50s, telling it, *Someday your customer will come, and she'll be better than any prince.* "What are you interested in? Sewing, knitting, crochet, embroidery—"

"All of the above," the second woman said, the look of pattern lust in her eyes.

"You'll find a few of each with the new patterns, but most of them are in files in the dressing room off the front bedroom upstairs. I can show you—"

"No need. We'll explore along the way. You carry on with your scone."

Lovely customers. They browsed their way into the next room and I heard the electronic sheep at the back door say *baa*, letting me know someone had come in through the kitchen—Ardis. She came down the hall singing "We Are the Champions" loudly but in tune. Her decibel level and attention to key and notes tended to mirror the trouble she'd had getting her ancient daddy up and out the door. On weekdays, she took him to what she called geezergarten. The good people who staffed the place called it adult daycare. The windows weren't rattling this morning, and her choice of song made it sound like they'd had a good start to the day.

At sixty-three, and six feet tall in flats, Ardis wasn't a woman who bustled. She was more a force of nature. Sometimes a rock, sometimes a wave, and either one made up of strong will, loyalty, and a love for amateur theater. Also a hovering suggestion of honeysuckle, which managed to be pleasant and not cloying.

As a rock, Ardis provided stability (and sometimes proved immobile). As a wave, she might dance, she might buoy those around her and carry them along, or she might well up and wash right over anyone in her way. She'd retired from her first love, "bringing order and enlightenment" to the third and fourth grades at Blue Plum Elementary. In the years since she'd hung up her chalk and ruler, she hadn't lost sight of her calling to correct anyone who needed it. That strong-willed honeysuckle still rapped knuckles or, just as likely, smacked transgressors upside the head. She'd worked alongside Granny for as long as I could remember, first part-time, and then full-time as manager when she retired from teaching. I'd felt lucky when she agreed to continue at the Cat after I took Granny's place.

"Good morning," Ardis sang. She twiddled her fingers at Geneva and then moved past me at a bit of a slant, her nose leading the way. "Mmm, something in a bakery bag? But oh!" She spun around to me again. "First I need to tell you what I heard about Nervie."

Her news about Nervie had to wait, though, as the camel bells announced more customers. Ardis went to help a young woman pick out enough of our ever-popular self-striping sock yarn for half a dozen pairs. I rang up a generous gift certificate a man bought as a seventh-anniversary gift for his wife. Then the women who'd first come in the shop browsed their way back from looking through vintage patterns. They'd found issues of *Popular Needlework* from the 1960s, and I went to help them choose threads and materials for some of the projects. When we returned to the sales counter, Ardis was wiping her fingers and dabbing her lips. While she rang up the sale, I noticed it was the rest of my scone she'd eaten.

"Sorry, hon," she said when I mentioned it. "You know I eat when my nerves are on edge, and what I heard about Nervie—but here." She held out the bakery bag. "Put it under the counter. Keep it safe for later." She glanced toward the front door. "In fact, I'll remove my-self from further temptation. I'll nip upstairs and get—"

She'd already turned her back and started for the stairs, so I missed what she said she'd get. But if Ardis thought we needed it, we probably did. I put the bak-ery bag on a shelf and then bent to tidy the bottom shelf where several scraps of paper had missed the re-cycling box. The door jingled, and I missed something else Ardis said as she took the stairs at an unusually aerobic clip.

When I straightened, I stood face-to-face with Shir-ley and Mercy Spivey.

TWO

I EXAGGERATED. It only *felt* like the Spiveys and I were face-to-face. They'd actually stopped six feet from the counter.

Shirley and Mercy were Granny's twin cousins. Cousins at some remove, but not so far removed they couldn't occasionally find their way into the Weaver's Cat. They were indistinguishable from their toes—this morning in matching pink walking shoes—to the tops of their permed gray heads. Today they also wore pink sweatshirts and leggings in eye-killing pink camouflage that would work only if they were stalking a flock of lawn flamingos. The sweatshirts came down to within a few inches of their almost seventy-year-old knees.

Since moving to Blue Plum, I'd learned a couple of tricks to tell the twins apart. Mercy usually wore a dab too much of her unpleasant cologne, and Shirley wasn't as likely to jab people with her elbow. Otherwise, in looks and peculiarities, they matched as completely as their outfits. Despite being Granny's cousins, I hadn't seen much of them during my childhood visits to Blue Plum. Maybe if I'd gotten to know them better, I'd find safer ways to tell them apart. But braver women than I, women who'd known the twins all their lives, shied away from scrutinizing them too closely. Not so, Geneva. The twins delighted her every time she saw them.

She circled them now, much the way Argyle circled customers when he tried to beguile them.

"Good morning, Shirley," I said. "Good morning, Mercy. How's Angie?"

"Angie's fine. Keeping busy," said the twin on my left.

"Too busy," the twin on the right said. "Mel's given her extra hours. She seems to be holding up, but we hardly see her."

The last time they'd been in the shop they'd just heard that Mercy's daughter Angie was expecting, and they'd surprised us by binging on every shade of pink baby wool we had in stock. Angie was a bit younger than me and quite a bit more pleasant than her mother or aunt. Angie and I hadn't known each other during my childhood visits from Illinois. The removed nature of Granny's relationship with the twins kept us apart. Angie's partner, Aaron, was an odd-jobs man. As he advertised, the odder the better. For instance, Aaron was the guy to call if you found rattlesnakes in your house, a skill that no doubt helped him cope with Angie's mother and aunt.

Geneva left off circling and came to sit on the counter next to the cash register. She pulled up her knees, resting her chin on them, and wrapped her arms around her legs. It was really too bad the twins couldn't see her. Everyone should have an audience so rapt and adoring, hollow-eyed or not.

"We came to put a couple of bugs in your ears," said the right-hand twin.

"What kind of bugs is she talking about?" Geneva asked. "That one is Mercy, by the way, but you should avoid looking at me out of the corners of your eyes like that. It screams 'shifty shopkeeper.' Like this." She demonstrated. "Also," she said, whispering again, "wincing, as you did just now, doesn't inspire confidence."

"A couple of friendly news items," Shirley continued, "looking out for family as we always do." She said this with only the slightest hint of a simper.

"We know you're involved with those people in the Arts Council setting up shops in the old bank," Mercy said.

"Calling it the Blue Plum Vault," Shirley said. "Artsy-fartsy Council."

"Artsy-fartsy except for Garland Brown, may he rest in peace," Mercy said.

"I helped Joe Dunbar with some of the work he did on the building, but I'm not really involved," I said. And by *helped*, I mostly meant watched while Joe hammered and painted. *Renaissance handyman-about-Blue Plum* was my favorite way to describe Joe. He and I were a bit of a thing.

"But Nervie Bales is involved," Shirley said. "She still teaches a crewel class here, doesn't she?"

"On Friday afternoons," I said. "She's going to sell her embroidery patterns at the Vault."

"There's some question about that," said Shirley.

"There shouldn't be," I said. "She's a member of the Arts Council, and I've seen her over there. Her shop's on the second floor."

"The shop might be hers," Mercy said, "but the patterns—"

"Are *not*." Shirley got that in, then said *oof* after a jab from Mercy's elbow.

"In case you ever thought of selling her patterns *here*, we thought we'd warn you," Mercy said.

"Because you can bet your eyeteeth," Shirley said, "there's going to be—"

The elbow made sure Mercy got in the last word. "Trouble."

"How do you know?" I asked.

"Well now, we don't like to spread gossip," Mercy said.

"But speaking of embroidery," Shirley said, "do you know Belinda Moyer? She's going to be selling vintage and antique linens at the Vault."

"I know who you're talking about. We haven't met yet."

That gave the twins an opening to gush back and forth.

"You'll like her."

"You'll like her textiles."

"Handkerchiefs, pillowslips, tea towels."

"From the sixties and seventies. Considering your former profession, you might be interested."

I probably wouldn't be. Run-of-the-mill linens from the sixties and seventies didn't thrill me. The adjective *former* didn't thrill me either. I was *still* a textile preservation specialist—highly trained, able to leap tall test tubes in a single bound, and ready to wipe out weevil infestations with a trusty fumigation hood. But right after I lost Granny, I also lost my job at the Illinois State Museum, thanks to an intractably terrible budget. I still mourned my job, and I could almost certainly find another, but Granny left me the wonderful safety net of the Weaver's Cat and her little yellow house on Lavender Street. And Blue Plum felt very much like home.

Still, linens from the sixties and seventies? *Meh*. The twins must have seen that in my face.

"Belinda has older pieces, too, of course," Mercy said.

"Table runners," Shirley added. "One table runner in particular."

"Embroidered with silk," Mercy said. "The kind of thing our mama's mama and her friends were so taken with and so good at."

That caught my attention. They saw that in my face, too.

Shirley turned to Mercy. "Needle painting, don't they call it?"

"They do," Mercy said, looking at me, not Shirley. "Isn't that right?"

"Or art embroidery," I said. "Or Kensington embroidery or art needlework."

"You're so knowledgeable. It's a blessing, I'm sure," Shirley said.

"But it's not often you see a genuine piece so large and in such good condition," Mercy said. "You can almost smell the strawberries and the climbing roses. Stitched with single strands of silk thread—"

Shirley shushed her. "No more spoilers, in case we get her hopes up and then it sells before she has a chance to see it. Wouldn't that be a terrible shame?"

I'd seen the kind of smile that broke onto her face then. I'd watched my good friend Joe land wily brook trout. Those trout never stood a chance. Neither did I. A familiar warmth grew in my chest as I listened to their back-and-forth about the beautiful piece of embroidery.

"Belinda's there today," Mercy said, "arranging her wares. Displaying them to best advantage. You know how important that is."

"We told her that once you got wind of that table runner you'd want to see it," Shirley said. "Easy enough to run over there on your lunch hour."

"See the rest of her stock, too," Mercy said. "You won't be sorry. The door will be locked to keep wandering riffraff out. Belinda will let you in if you knock."

"We might have said you'd offer your opinion."

"Offer authentication. It would be a little plus for her."

"Whoa, wait," I said. "Doesn't she have that information?"

"She probably—" Shirley started to say.

"She does," Mercy and her elbow finished.

"But this would be the icing on the cake," Shirley said. "It'll be the sheen, dare I say the *glow*, on the silk."

"Oh yes, the glow," Mercy said. "And it isn't just *on* the silk. The silk itself glows. Forty-eight inches long, eighteen wide, and the *colors*." She put a hand to her heart. There was no questioning the sincerity of that gesture. I felt the echo of it in my own heart. "We'll call and let her know you're on your way."

"Think how nice it'll be for you two to meet," Shirley said, "with so much in common. Something positive to counteract whatever Nervie's up to with her lying ways."

Bringing up Nervie again almost brought me out of my textile haze. But an Art Embroidery table runner that had the twins swooning? Their mama's mama—my great-great-grandmother—had excelled at embroidery, and the twins did lovely work, too. So how could it hurt me to go take a look? How could I resist?

ARDIS FINALLY CAME back downstairs trailed by a young woman. They each carried two of our four-pound cones of rug wool nestled in the crooks of their arms.

"Like babies. Like delightful twins," Geneva said.

She draped herself over the cash register. "Our twins left too soon, and I miss them terribly."

"*I* don't," Ardis said.

"Pardon?" the customer buying the rug wool asked.

Geneva snickered. "A rookie mistake for the newly haunted to make."

"Sorry," Ardis said to the customer. "There's a little glitch here with the register, and I didn't finish that sentence. What I meant to say is that I don't know what got into me, because I forgot to tell you it's your lucky day. You get a ten percent discount when you buy four cones."

"That's wonderful," the woman said. "Thank you."

"You'll bankrupt the business if you give a discount every time you forget that you look nutty when you talk to me in front of the hauntless," Geneva said.

"I don't make that mistake often," Ardis said, handing back the woman's credit card but looking at Geneva. "And if I'd made it today, it would have haunted me all afternoon."

I bagged the cones, and Ardis went to hold the door for the woman. Geneva watched, silent. When Ardis came back to the counter, Geneva floated up to the ceiling fan and sat with her back to us.

"Nice sale," I said.

"About the discount—"

"No worries. It was a fine idea."

We heard a *hmph* from Geneva.

"Speaking of which"—Ardis nodded toward the disgruntled glitch on the fan—"did I hear someone scream a while back?"

"If you thought you did, then why didn't you run

back down the stairs as fast as you went up them when the twins arrived? You abandoned me."

She looked crushed. "I did, didn't I? I'm sorry, hon, but you know how it is. With those two, sometimes I simply can't."

"It boggles my mind, sometimes, how we can be related," Geneva said over her shoulder.

It was fair to say that fact boggled all our minds. We'd discovered that Geneva, who'd died in her early twenties, was Ardis's great-great-aunt. We couldn't tell if they looked anything alike. Geneva, indistinct at the best of times, wasn't…it might be kindest to say she didn't look herself. She'd watched, listened to, and sometimes mimicked Ardis since moving to the shop. But Ardis had only known about and "known" Geneva less than two months, and their similarities seemed to go deeper than acting skills or rubbing off on each other could account for.

"What did the twins want?" Ardis asked.

While I told her, she found the bakery bag under the counter. She ate the second scone without seeming to give it much thought. She licked her fingers without much thought, either. The scone tasted good enough that she licked each finger twice.

"I've never heard that about Nervie," she said. "It happens, of course, people calling someone else's patterns their own. I know craftspeople at shows who don't allow pictures of their work because they don't want anyone going home to copy it and sell it themselves. Stealing." She slapped the counter with the word. "If that's what Nervie's up to, that's what it is."

"If," I said.

"Well, exactly," Ardis said. "Did you ask the twins how they know?"

"They said they don't like to gossip."

"Absolute baloney," Ardis said. "But, Kath?" She waited until I looked her squarely in the eyes. "Don't let those two get you mixed up in any of their meddling. You have enough of Ivy in you that you could turn the twins into putty in your hands, if you want to. Ivy had her ways. Keep that in mind." She touched the braided bracelet on her wrist. She'd never asked how it worked. I wasn't sure myself, even though I'd made it for her. But I'd followed a recipe in one of Granny's private dye journals, and that bracelet let Ardis see and hear Geneva. Granny did, indeed, have her ways.

"You said you heard something about Nervie, too," I said.

"I nearly forgot. She's going to teach embroidery classes at the Vault."

"There *and* here? If not, that could cut into our business."

"*Will* cut into it," Ardis said. "She hasn't said anything to you about it?"

"No, and I haven't heard anything about classes of any kind being offered there. Joe might have heard something, but he hasn't said."

"Where is he?"

"Handy-manning? Fishing? Thinking about fishing? I'm not sure."

"So call him," Ardis said.

Joe and I might be a thing, but lean, loping Joe's employment was casual and his whereabouts often hard to pin down. Ardis liked Joe, though she more often called him Ten, short for Tennyson. Tennyson Yeats Dunbar.

He'd rechristened himself Joe before he hit high school. He'd been one of her favorite students at Blue Plum Elementary. But it irritated her that she couldn't pin down the nature of our "thingness" any more easily than she'd ever been able to pin down Joe.

I tapped in Joe's number, but the call went to voice mail. I left a message saying only that I'd see him later, eliciting further irritation from Ardis. "Well, it isn't like we have a monopoly on classes," I said. "I don't know where they'd have them, anyway. The old boardroom upstairs was the only space big enough, but they took down the walls and opened it for a gallery."

"Maybe they'll have them *in* the gallery," Ardis said. "Creative use of space in a place devoted to the creative arts. I should write ad copy for them. I should ask Nervie about the classes, too, but she beetles in and out of here so fast she's hard to catch."

"So call her," I said.

"Better in person."

"Take a lesson from Argyle," Geneva said. "Lie in wait and pounce on her. It's as simple as that."

"I like it," Ardis said. "As simple as having another scone, too." She picked up the bakery bag, then seemed surprised it was empty. "Well, they were delicious. Be sure to tell Mel. As for Nervie, I'll pounce carefully. She's been known to have a temper."

"Really?" I said.

"Old stories, anyway," Ardis said. "Did the twins tell you why they thought you needed to know about Nervie's patterns? What do you suppose they're up to?"

"What makes you think the darling twins are up to something?" Geneva asked.

"Because they're Spiveys," Ardis said. "It's what they do. Kath?"

"I didn't ask them why," I said, "and they didn't tell."

Ardis pointed her finger at me. "I repeat: do not let them get you tangled up in…in… I don't know what."

"I won't."

"As simple as that?"

"Simple as that."

"Good. I see Ivy shining in your eyes when you say that."

"It's nice to know I've got her with me when I need her. Do you mind if I run over to the Vault at lunch?"

"Say hi to Joe for me."

"If he's there. To see a table runner, too. Do you know Belinda Moyer?"

"I've known a few Moyers. I don't remember a Belinda." Ardis leaned closer, squinting at my face. "I know Ivy's still in there, but now your eyes have a look I haven't seen much of lately. This table runner—is it the call of the wild textile?"

"Howling like a wolf under the full moon, luring me away?"

"Away?" Geneva flapped down from the fan and threw her arms around the mannequin to gape at me over its shoulder. "Away where?"

"From all this." They followed my hand as I waved it vaguely at the displays.

Geneva had told me that watching life in the shop was better than most of the TV shows she'd been glued to in the decades before we met. Most of the shows, anyway; knitting needles and crochet hooks could never replace cop shows or her beloved Marshal Dillon and his six-guns and horses. But in the raspberries, oranges, and

burgundies of the wool, I saw responsibilities, obliga-
tions, and bills. Knowing Ardis, she saw those, too. And
judging by the pinched lines between her eyebrows, I
guessed she also saw the Cat's sturdy old walls and
wondered if or when I'd wake up and want to escape
them, or the Cat, or Blue Plum. Time for reassurances.

"Ardis?"

"Hm?"

"See the roving hanging on the wall? On the right,
there. Do you know what I see in that splash of fuch-
sia? Security and friendship."

Geneva floated over to the roving and leaned her
cheek against it.

"I've always loved that color," Ardis said.

"Me, too." Even through the gray filter of a ghost.
"My life is full. I have things to do and people I care
about. Right here. It's still full of textiles, too. They're
just mostly in a pre-woven, pre-knitted, pre-crocheted
state."

"They're in a state of limbo," Geneva said, "like
your favorite GFF."

"Ivy would be proud of you," Ardis said. "She was
proud of your career, too, though, and no one would
blame you for missing it. You had a good thing going."

"Now I have this."

"It doesn't have to be gone for good."

"Speaking of going." I checked my phone. "Time
flies. I'll go to lunch early, if that's all right. It's a pretty
day for a walk. A pretty day to see something pretty."

"Well, Joe's always been the better-looking Dunbar boy, but I'd call him handsome before I called him
pretty." She expected a laugh and accepted the one I

gave her more easily than the reassurances she needed every so often.

"Pretty Boy Joe has a ring to it, though," I said. "Ardis, don't worry about the table runner. Even if it's the most amazing, the most astounding, the most fabulous and historic piece it's been my honor to behold, I'll look, and possibly heave a sigh, but then I'll turn my back on it and come right back here."

"It's Ivy's steel that's glinting in your eyes."

I WONDERED IF anyone else saw Granny shining in my eyes as I greeted them on my way to the Vault. The old guys sitting on the bench in front of the courthouse, who spent more time reminiscing than keeping up on current events, called out, "Hey there, Ivy," when I passed. They saw her just in my size and shape. I waved back. I liked being recognized that way, but those were reactions to generalities. I liked Ardis's recognition better. Granny had known Ardis for years, and she'd let Ardis get closer than most.

Rachel Meeks, a loan officer at the new bank, waved when she saw me. She was trying to get a scarecrow to sit up on a hay bale by the bank's front door. Other scarecrows and corn shocks dotted the streets here and there, part of the town's "Feeling Festive for Fall" campaign to bring people, not to mention their dollars, to Main Street.

According to Granny, if a cuteness scale existed for measuring small towns, Blue Plum sat at the bug's ear end of it. That was a good thing, she'd explained to me when I was five. I'd agreed, picturing tiny, perfect firefly ears. I still agreed. I also knew I was lucky she'd built her business soundly enough that I could stay in Blue Plum and make a living. Cuteness and town campaigns didn't guarantee success to every business enterprise. The town had lost a car parts store a few years back, and several restaurants had come and gone, though Mel's on Main managed to hang in there. Mel felt lucky, too. She said it was the luck of the ladle and larder that kept her serving up soup and sandwiches. She glossed over the hard work and long hours she put into it but readily gave credit to community involvement as an ingredient for the café's longevity. Granny had believed in that, too. *It isn't just that Blue Plum supports us and so we support Blue Plum,* she'd say. *It's that we are Blue Plum. It's a simple as that.*

A block beyond the new bank, newsprint covered the four tall, arched front windows and front door of the old one. The transformation of the building from defunct bank to the Blue Plum Vault was still a work in progress, but it was about to become the newest business in town. Businesses, plural, to be accurate. The brainchild of the Blue Plum Area Arts Council, and Gar Brown in particular, the Vault was going to be a collection of small arts-related shops housed in the newly renovated and repurposed building. The big reveal would come at the grand opening on Saturday. After Gar's death, there'd been talk about changing the name from the Blue Plum Vault and Gallery to the Garland Brown Gallery. There was also talk about postponing the opening. Both were decided against. People saw the project as Gar's baby. He'd started as a teller in that bank, and he'd come up with the idea of calling it the Vault. Keeping the name and opening it on schedule was a tribute to him.

I went up the two limestone steps to the front door. It was locked. I'd expected that, and I knocked. And, as simple as that, Nervie Bales opened the door.

THREE

KATH? YOU ALL RIGHT?"

"Nervie. Hi." I hadn't realized how nervy I'd now feel around her. *Thank you, Shirley and Mercy.* I'd already talked myself out of worrying about her patterns—not my patterns, not my problem. And I could let Ardis do the pouncing about whether she meant to teach classes at the Weaver's Cat as well as at the Vault.

"You're probably looking for Sierra," Nervie said. "She's around here, somewhere."

I didn't correct her.

Nervie swung the door open. "You don't mind looking for her yourself, do you?" She relocked the door behind me and didn't wait for an answer, instead trailing, "Lots to do before the opening," over her shoulder as she disappeared.

Minerva "Nervie" Bales wasn't easy to get to know. She reminded me of a darter, one of the quick, tiny fish native to Tennessee's streams and rivers. Joe had introduced me to a few. He liked them, and I could see why. They were pretty little things, in their own fishy way. Nervie was pretty, too, in a way that suggested it didn't matter to her. I liked that about her, even if I didn't see her often enough, or long enough, to know if I liked more than that about her. She was probably in her midfifties, although I didn't know that for sure, either. She taught her crewel embroidery class at the Cat, but as

Ardis said, she beetled in and out so fast, I rarely spoke more than a few words to her.

A voice called something upstairs and another, more muffled, answered. Five of the shop spaces were located on the second floor, as well as the gallery in the newly opened-up area in the middle. I'd met a few of the merchants when I "helped" Joe with the finish work. Floyd Decker, a retired antique dealer, had taken one of the spaces on the first floor. He'd missed the business and decided to keep his hand in this way. Simon Grace was selling used books. I looked forward to prowling their shops. I'd met a metalworker, too, but couldn't remember her name. Her welding mask and blowtorch had made more of an impression on me.

Sierra Estep, whom Nervie assumed I'd come looking for, was almost certainly busier getting ready for the opening weekend than Nervie. Sierra was the newly minted MA in arts administration hired by the Blue Plum Area Arts Council to run the Vault. In the few times we'd talked, I'd learned that she topped me by three or four inches, loved leggings and tunic tops with bold patterns, dyed her long, straight hair cherry red, and could load a heavy roll of newsprint into her car without much trouble. She lived in an apartment on the third floor of the bank building. We'd by no means forged a deep friendship over those details, but we were on good terms.

Sierra wouldn't miss me, so I didn't go looking for her. I didn't look for Joe, either. He wasn't answering texts or his phone, which wasn't that unusual. He might be on the road between Blue Plum and Asheville. Or there were plenty of places, most of them small creeks with trout and darters, with spotty-to-nonexistent cell service. He liked those places. I liked textiles. I rubbed my hands and went looking for a table runner.

I didn't have any real standing at the Vault, for Nervie to let me in and turn me loose to wander. But, having been there off and on with Joe, I wasn't a total stranger. Joe had bartered the finish work in exchange for the smallest shop space, rent-free, for a year. He painted exquisite postcard-size watercolors and planned to sell them and hand-tied trout flies.

The first floor waited quietly. No need for anyone at the information and sales desk without shoppers. Sierra might be in her office down the hall toward the back of the building. I pictured her answering questions from one person on the phone while simultaneously typing answers in an email to someone else. She might have been relaxing over lunch in her apartment, but I doubted that.

The Arts Council, calling the venture a co-op, had rented the shop spaces to a mix of craftspeople and merchants. The spaces were carved out of the old bank floor plan, upstairs and down, some in the original offices, some in newly created alcoves, one in the vault itself. The doors had been widened to give the feeling of shops in a mall. None of the shops would carry a huge amount of stock, and the shopkeepers wouldn't all keep regular hours in their spaces. Customers would shop and pay at the information and sales desk on their way out. A few renters had moved their wares into their spaces over the weekend, and the rest were scheduled to move in over the next few days. If I was Sierra, I'd be anticipating fires right now and have my boots on, ready to stamp them out.

Smells hadn't settled into place at the Vault yet.

Paint, varnish, and new wood scents hung in the air. They were exciting smells, smells with promise, but also unfinished. They were one of the reasons for the staggered move-in dates. The last lick of paint had gone on the night before.

A hamburger with onions lingered in the air, too, making me hungry. I followed that scent trail up the stairs. Halfway up, someone on the second floor turned on a blare of country music. Then turned it up.

"Down!" someone above me shouted. "Turn it *down*! For—"

The last part of the objection was drowned out as the volume increased again, the twang and guitar threatening to rupture my eardrums. Then they stopped so abruptly I felt disoriented. Gingerly, I crept up the last few steps.

The open gallery space lay before me. To my left, a woman with braids around her head still cringed in a doorway, her eyes squeezed shut. Nervie stood in the next opening. Both women had their hands over their ears. Nervie's eyes were open, though, and she stared at a room directly across the gallery.

"Honest to Pete," Nervie said through gritted teeth.

"Sorry, sorry," a high voice called from the room Nervie had a bead on.

The cringing woman with the braids opened her eyes, gave her whole body a quick, shuddering shake, and went back into her shop. She might be the jewelry maker, an enamelist Joe had told me about. The braids matched part of his three-word description—braided, brilliant, quiet. I hoped her ears recovered.

"Honest to Pete," Nervie said again, this time louder and more clearly.

"You know I didn't mean it," came the singsong answer. The owner of the voice still hadn't made an appearance. In fact, she sounded farther away.

Nervie muttered something I didn't hear but thought I might agree with, and then she went back into her own shop. Neither she nor the enamelist had noticed me at the top of the stairs. I crossed the gallery space toward the suspect door and saw the broad backside of a woman as she leaned over a box. I knocked on the doorframe.

"I *said* I'm *sorry*," the woman said. She didn't look up from her rummaging. "I just got confused between the ding dang up and the down buttons. Silly updates. They're always messing with things."

I waited for her to take a breath then knocked again. "Hi. Are you Belinda?"

"You'd think I killed a cat, for cripe's sake. Oh." The woman still bent over, looked at me from under her right arm, and in the half nanosecond between her high-pitched *for cripe's sake* and higher-pitched *oh*, her face went from squint-eyed and complaining to wide-eyed and smiling. "Well, hey," she said, coming upright. "What can I do for you?"

"You're Belinda?"

"I can't imagine who else I'd want to be."

"I'm Kath Rutledge from over at the Weaver's Cat."

"Nice to meet you. Welcome to Belle's Vintage and Antique Linens." Belinda flourished a gesture toward the corner where a sign stood on one end. The ornate, scrolling letters weren't easy to read sideways. The sign obviously pleased her, though, and I took her word for what it said. Belinda was less ornate. She looked anywhere from mid-forties to late-fifties. Her poufy 'do didn't bring the top of her head level with my eyes.

I looked around the space. None of the shops at the Vault were terribly big, and Belle's was about the size of a small bedroom. Belinda had hung some of her linens and set others in folded stacks on white wire shelves. She still had boxes to unpack. Her vintage and antique linens skewed heavily to the vintage. I'd expected that. They'd be easier to come by. I didn't spy a fabulous table runner anywhere.

"What can I do for you, Kathy?"

"It's just Kath."

Belinda's smile receded a fraction of an inch, cooling a degree or two as it went. "You know we aren't open to the public yet, don't you?"

"I do, yes, sorry. I stopped by to see your table runner."

"And how did you get in? Did someone leave the door unlocked? *Again?*" Her voice rose in pitch as she aimed those questions out the door. Toward the other women? Toward Nervie? She seemed to be listening for a response from across the gallery. I was glad when I didn't hear one.

"Shirley and Mercy sent me over," I said.

"Say what now, Kathy?"

People usually reacted when the twins were mentioned, sometimes favorably. More often they jumped, a reaction Ardis called the Spivey spasm, so Belinda's blank face surprised me. Plus she'd added a *y* to my name again, a common enough mistake, but it made me wonder if she'd missed my gentle correction. Maybe she was hard of hearing?

"But I tell you what," she said, her blank face recovering and breaking out in another smile, "this'll be good practice for me. I cannot tell you how excited I am to be part of this new enterprise. Now, what can I show you?"

"I'm not really a customer—"

But she'd turned her back to shuffle through boxes and didn't hear me. I started to repeat myself when she turned around again. I meant to clear up any misunderstanding, but when I saw what lay in the box she held, I was helpless. Silk pansies in purples I could almost taste. *Oh, the pretty, dainty thing...*

"It's a handkerchief," Belinda said. "The amount of work that must've gone into it staggers me, and if I'd done the stitching? I couldn't bear to watch someone blow his nose on it."

I had trouble watching her toss the box aside. "Do you embroider?" I asked.

"Never had the time, but I've been collecting for years. I have a good eye for it, and I've been lucky a time or two. Or three or four. You liked that handkerchief, didn't you?" She looked over her shoulder at me, then didn't wait for an answer before rummaging some more. "So now take a look at this. If I can find it. I knew I should've labeled these boxes."

"Would you like help?" If she said yes, could I keep myself from shoving her out of the way and opening every box myself? She hadn't heard me, so I held myself in check.

"I don't suppose people really used most of these, or I wouldn't have them to sell. But that's what makes them rare and worth every penny. There now." She turned around with a piece of linen draped over her hands. "I believe this was meant to be a napkin. My luck abandoned me that time. I didn't find the full set."

Oh, but she *had* been lucky. Silk goldfinches—so

realistic they might have been painted by John James Audubon—perched on a spray of blue bachelor's buttons. The piece wasn't a napkin. It was more likely a pillow cover. Did she have any idea what she had? I couldn't help testing her. "What's the…" I wiggled my finger at a goldfinch. "The thread. It's so bright."

"Silk thread on linen."

I nodded.

"They called it Society Silk because ladies in high society sat around drinking tea while they stitched."

So she knew something, but she hadn't dug very deep into the history. She was right about the thread and linen and maybe even about the tea. But the women who'd stitched while they sipped hadn't called their lovely pieces Society Silk. That was a modern term and not completely accurate. I looked up from studying one of the dear little finches' feet. Belinda studied me.

"Do you have larger pieces?" I asked.

"One or two." Her answer came curt, cautious. Her head tilted like one of the goldfinches, sizing me up.

Had my testing gone too far? I knew a way to find out, and as long as I had her attention, I might as well try again. "Shirley and Mercy Spivey said you have a silk embroidered table runner."

The high voice kicked up a notch. "You know the twins?" Belinda squealed. "Aren't they the funniest things? You should've said so straight off."

Shirley and Mercy, funny? Geneva would no doubt agree. She would love the squeal, too, though my ears, not so much.

Belinda whipped around so fast I thought the goldfinches would take flight. She laid the pillow cover back in its box and rushed over to a table on the other side of the room. She lifted a layer of cross-stitched hand towels. When I saw the flat box she'd exposed, my heart quivered just a bit. The box was bigger than the one she'd put the pillow cover in, but not big enough.

"Shirley and Mercy are the ones who told me about the Vault," Belinda said. If she said something else, I didn't catch it. I'd been busy beaming a silent message to the table runner: *Oh, please tell me she doesn't have you folded up in there.*

"They introduced me to Simon, too. Do you know him? Selling the books? In the actual vault downstairs? That's a real nice touch. Primo location. More rent than I can afford, but that's where a cushy college job gets you."

Open the box open the box open the box. Let it out.

"Simon found a couple of big old books for me. Embroidery, appliqué, history, styles. All that razzmatazz. Some of it maybe even interesting. Come on over here."

She couldn't have stopped me.

And then she lifted the lid from the box and oh, the razzmatazz of it. I think angels actually sang. Shirley and Mercy, for all their faults, were absolutely right. The table runner's silk embroidery, what I could see of it, glowed. But the hundred-year-old linen and silk jewel was folded. Only I could hear the screaming in my head.

"It's a beauty," Belinda said. "Here, I'll shake it out so you can get the full effect."

"*Wait!* Sorry, why don't you spread it on the table instead?"

"Bossy, bossy. I see what you mean, though. Table runner. *Duh.*"

Her hands seemed to know, better than her words, that the table runner deserved a gentle touch. They spread it out, lifting and shifting rather than flapping and tugging, and I relaxed. A tad. She didn't give me room to help, and her back blocked my view.

"Have you thought about rolling your old pieces when you store them?"

"Move that box, will you?"

I took the box and tried again. Louder. "The twins have some beautiful pieces. They roll them, kind of loosely, instead of folding them." Because they'd picked up that caring-for-old-textiles tip from Granny. They listened to expert advice, even if they were ornery.

"They're a hoot. Now, Kathy, not meaning any disrespect, but look around. This is a small shop. I need to make the most of the space I've got. So, yeah, I fold. It takes up less room."

I should have dropped it. I couldn't. Kath Rutledge, friend of fibers everywhere, forging faithfully onward for their future. "Folding stresses the fibers, though. Eventually they break."

"And that's not my worry. All these things are for sale, and my goal is to sell them before 'eventually' arrives. Posterity is for those who don't have bills to pay."

"Your pieces might bring in more money if they're properly cared for." *Back off, Kath. She doesn't want your help.* Except Shirley and Mercy had said… "Shirley and Mercy said you might want help authenticating the table runner."

Belinda crossed her arms. "Do you want to see it or not?"

I did, so I shut up, and she stepped aside, her arms still crossed. I hadn't made a friend. I didn't care.

Forty-eight inches long, eighteen wide, Mercy had said. *You can almost smell the strawberries and climb-*

ing roses, Shirley had said. And there they were, climbing the whole length of creamy white linen, and I swear I really could smell them. And if I'd touched one of the roses, a petal would fall, and if I plucked one, a thorn would prick my finger and make it bleed. And oh, the colors, they almost took my breath. Scratch that. They *took* my breath.

Nervie, on the other hand, had plenty of breath. "It's a fake," she said from the doorway.

"Nervie, sugar, I'm so sorry." Belinda's singsong voice went so high it dripped from the ten-foot ceiling. "My mistake with the volume controls upset you more than I realized, and I guess it made me deafer, too." She wiggled a finger in her right ear and turned the ear toward Nervie. "Did you say something about fate?"

"If you want to pretend I did, that's fine," Nervie said. "You might even say it *is* fate."

A good time for me to bow out, I decided. "Well, I ought to be getting back, now." Big smile on my face. Optimistically inching past Belinda, who suddenly reminded me of a bristling hedgehog.

"There is nothing wrong with my linens," she said.

"They're lovely," I said. Now, could I actually get past Nervie? How could someone so small take up so much space? "Thanks for showing them, Belinda."

"They're made in sweatshops in China, Vietnam, and Laos," Nervie said. "Her 'vintage' is nothing but knock-offs. Her 'antiques' are anything but." Nervie put air quotes around *vintage* and *antiques* with the savagery of karate chops. She hadn't moved from the doorway, and though she didn't match the decibels of Belinda's earlier music mishap, her clear voice carried. Anyone on the second floor would hear her, maybe everyone in the building. "And as *fate* would have it," she continued, "Blue Plum's resident textile expert is here to expose you."

Waving my hands to dissuade Nervie from saying more wasn't my smartest move. They didn't shush Nervie, and they encouraged Belinda to boil over.

"I thought you were an early bird customer."

"I never—"

"I thought you were like those people who show up the night before a garage sale."

"Shirley and Mercy told me about your table runner and said you—"

"And you came waltzing in here acting like some kind of expert?"

"I only came—" I didn't finish because she'd dismissed me. She didn't care why I was there, didn't know who I was, didn't know what I was talking about, and she definitely hadn't been expecting me. Why, *why* was I surprised? *Spiveys*. I flinched and looked around—had I said that out loud?

Belinda didn't seem to care if I stayed or went, didn't care enough to go on about my dishonesty. But she cared plenty about Nervie's accusations.

"Well par-don me," she said in four percussive syllables. "Maybe I haven't been on the selling end of the business for long, but I know what I'm doing. I have a nose for knowing what'll sell. I've been buying at yard sales and estate sales in the mid-Atlantic and southeast for years, when we lived near DC and since I've been here, and I've been waiting for the right opportunity to come along. And that's what this is. I'm no fraud. I'm not selling fakes. They aren't all valuable, but they're all pretty, and some of them are beautiful. Even *she* can tell you that," she said, jerking her head at me.

I didn't object to her aspersion; I tried to shrink and be invisible.

"People *will* buy my linens," Belinda continued. "If nothing else, they'll cut them up and make the pieces into something else."

Cut them up? I barely suppressed a gasp. Nervie barely managed a single shoulder shrug. Belinda's bosom heaved with completely unsuppressed emotion.

"I'm pretty sure the table runner is real," I said quietly to Nervie.

"And I'm pretty sure I know my business better than you do," Belinda said to Nervie, not as quietly.

Nervie gave a slow blink that clearly said, *Prove it.*

Belinda's eyes narrowed.

Nervie raised her chin half an inch.

Belinda tightened her lips.

Showdown at the OK Co-op. Neither of them moved for a count of four, three, two...

Belinda nodded. "*Fine.* I can prove it. I'll show you what an *expert* can find." She stalked to the back of her shop.

I raised my eyebrows at Nervie. She ignored me. Invisibility accomplished.

Belinda moved her sign aside, grunting with the effort. Behind the sign, tucked into the corner, was a trunk, the kind that characters in books find in attics— a storyline forever believable to me, because so many good and true antique textile discoveries start with someone opening a trunk in a parent's or grandparent's attic. Belinda shot a look at us over her shoulder (or maybe just at Nervie) then bent to open the trunk.

"You can see this," she said when she stood up, cradling her treasure in her arms, "then right back in it goes. It's entirely extraordinary. It'll have a place of honor here on the back wall, but it's staying under wraps until I unveil it at the grand opening." She raised the piece over her head with her arms spread and let it unfold. "Feast your eyes on *this*, Nervie Bales."

What she had, what she held up so casually, so cavalierly, by two corners, was an Arts and Crafts tablecloth. Thirty-six inches by thirty-six, maybe forty by forty. If authentic, it was at least a hundred years old. Turn of the last century, give or take a decade. Brown linen—typical of that time and style—and embroidered in a jaw-droppingly beautiful pattern of Art Nouveau trees, squirrels, and acorns, all done in greens, blues, and browns. She was right; it was entirely extraordinary. *Exquisite.* The silk-embroidered table runner, with its strawberries and roses, blew me away. But this piece stirred me so much more. Any museum with a textile collection would love to own it. I wanted to live in it. I wanted to sit under one of those trees and hold the squirrels in my lap. I thought I might cry.

Nervie had nothing to say, and I couldn't read her expression. Impressed? Jealous? Foiled?

"You think you're an expert?" Belinda jerked her head at me, again, jerking me out of my Arts and Crafts woodland daydream. "Come tell me this isn't real."

Nervie and I both moved closer. Nervie stopped before I did, though, leaving a decent amount of personal space. I went close enough to rub noses with one of the squirrels. We didn't rub noses, though. I didn't touch it. I studied the linen, the floss, the stitches, the hem.

I stepped to the side to get a look at the back. When I sniffed it, Nervie gave in and came closer, too.

"What on earth did smelling it tell you?" Nervie asked.

"It smells right. It smells old." I pulled out my phone. "Do you mind if I take pictures?"

"I most certainly do. No pictures. Not before the opening."

"Never mind sniffing it or taking pictures," Nervie said. "You have to touch it."

"No, I—"

Nervie took hold of the tablecloth's edge, swinging it toward us. I stepped back.

"I don't want to add my fingers, the oil from them," I said. "Really. I don't need to touch it." Oils were only part of the reason I didn't want to touch it. Fear was the other part. Odd, but true.

"She thinks she's 'saving' it," Nervie explained to Belinda, using her aggressive air quotes again. "You aren't saving it from anything, Kath. It's for sale. We're touching it, and every customer who comes through will touch it."

"And I wish they wouldn't." That was true, but again, my next statement was only half true. "It's my training."

"What kind of asinine training is that?" Belinda asked.

I knew a dare when I heard one. I could rise above them, too. But Belinda and Nervie stared at me, and so did one of the embroidered squirrels. The one with tufts on its ears. How had the artist created such a look of longing on its tiny face? It was the squirrel I couldn't resist, and I reached my fingers out to stroke its ears and tail, its white tummy. Really, I let only the tips of my fingers brush against the squirrel. When they did, I felt an incredible peace wash over me. Nothing more. Thank goodness.

"It's wonderful." I sounded far away. "Where did you find it?"

Belinda's lips tightened again.

"How much are you asking for it?" faraway Kath asked. That was one of the problems with being in love with textiles and fibers—wanting to own every hank, ball, skein, length, and every entirely extraordinary tablecloth that, for whatever bizarre reason, made you feel drunk and in another world when you touched it.

Then, just like that, Belinda whisked the table-cloth away and folded it back into the trunk. When she slammed the lid, I snapped out of my Arts and Crafts euphoria. It wasn't a pleasant reentry.

"I see what you two are up to," Belinda said. "You're in it together. You're out to ruin my business."

"We aren't," I said, but Nervie and I both started backing toward the doorway.

"You're trying to bring down the value of my stock by saying I'm a fraud. You're trying to bring down the prices so you can get that tablecloth on the cheap."

Nervie and I backed out of the shop and into the gallery.

"It's in your eyes," Belinda said. "You want it."

She'd have to be blind not to see how much I wanted that tablecloth. And although she didn't come right out and say *you can have it over my dead body*, I'd have to be deaf to miss that message.

The woman with the braids—the enamelist—stuck her head out of her shop, then came out into the gallery and suggested we keep it down, with surprising calm, I thought. Nervie and Belinda snapped at her.

Sierra, the Vault's manager, came charging up the stairs and planted her fists on her hips. She was trying to look in charge and almost succeeding. Nervie punctured that power stance by being unimpressed.

"I wondered where you'd gone," Nervie said. "But that's okay. There's nothing left to see."

The enamelist looked at each one of us, singled me out, and thanked me for stopping by. Her sarcasm cut as deep as the ice in her blue eyes. Then she went back into her shop. That seemed to be the signal Nervie and Belinda were waiting for. Nervie walked past Sierra and down the stairs. Belinda put her phone to her ear and drifted back to her shop as though nothing had happened.

I looked at Sierra, shrugged, and said something I hoped would sum up what had happened and my feelings about it. "Yeesh."

Sierra might not have caught the nuances available in that word. "Joe's not here," she said. "How did you get in?"

"I knocked on the door." I looked at her arms now crossed tightly over her chest. "Do you want to know what that fuss was about?"

"It's over, right? So, no. On top of everything else in the past few weeks, I don't need anyone stirring those two up again. If you don't mind?" She gestured toward the stairs.

"Sure, sure." She didn't follow me, but I mumbled apologies on my way down anyway. She didn't hear my mumbles, and I didn't pay much attention to them either. I'd gotten stuck on that word *again* and all of its nuances. Stir those two up *again*? Poor Sierra.

Nervie had surprised me at the door when I arrived, so it fit that she caught me again on my way out. I felt just as nervy when I saw her waiting. She looked as though she had more to say, but I decided to preempt her. I didn't want to hear about her beef with Belinda, didn't want to be part of it. There would be no stirring from me to make Sierra's job harder. But at least we could agree about the tablecloth.

"You have to admit the tablecloth's fabulous, Nervie. Better than fabulous."

She nodded.

Excellent. She didn't smile, and the nod lacked enthusiasm, but maybe we'd found neutral ground. I took a chance and took one more step onto that ground.

"If you had to sum that tablecloth up in one word," I said, "what would it be?"

Nervie looked over her shoulder and then leaned close. "Stolen."

FOUR

IT'S THE ONLY logical explanation," Nervie whispered. "The only way Belinda Moyer got her hands on that tablecloth. She stole it." She closed the door in my face.

I didn't knock again.

I stomped my way back to the Weaver's Cat. I'd fooled myself. How dumb could I be? With each stomp I slammed a litany of *hows*, *wasn't*s, *hadn't*s, and *never*s into the sidewalk. *How* could the simple act of gawking at and drooling over embroidery turn into such a shambles? I'd *never* claimed to have ESP; *how* was I supposed to know that Nervie and Belinda had some kind of ridiculous rivalry going? I *wasn't* a Spivey tool, running around looking for the trouble they'd dumped in my lap. I *hadn't* swooped down on the Vault to avert that trouble like the Avenging Angel of Mercy and Shirley. I would *never* do that—and I would *never* listen to them again. *How* did they know so much about what was going on at the Vault, anyway? And maybe I wouldn't be so cranky if Ardis *hadn't* eaten my share of the scones. On top of all that, I'd taken my lunch hour to get involved in this mess and I *hadn't* had lunch.

The stomping helped. Angry toddlers would agree. So would Granny. *Get the mad out,* Granny used to say. *Beat it like a rug or ring it like the neck of a wet towel. Then stop and remember what you're thankful for.*

I stopped on the sidewalk in front of the fire station

and looked down at my feet. I was thankful for my running shoes. I might never run in them, but they were great stompers. I was thankful Joe hadn't been at the Vault. Maybe the ill will I'd stirred up wouldn't sift down on him and cause him problems. I was thankful I'd seen the tablecloth.

Stomping out of my system, I started walking and tried Joe again, thankful also that he finally answered. He told me he'd gone to Asheville to pick up an engine and was on his way back. The engine was for his brother, Cole. Cole, the older brother, got the better deal when their English literature-teaching parents leafed through their *Norton Anthology* to pick out baby names. He was Coleridge Blake Dunbar to Joe's Tennyson Yeats. I never heard either of the brothers complain about their names. But Joe had tried out a string of replacements starting in early grade school, and Cole had become a muscled and well-respected sheriff's deputy. So maybe they'd each rebelled in their own way.

"It'll be midafternoon before I'm back," Joe said. "Then I might watch Cole horse the engine around until he asks for help. If he's free."

"Are you eating something?"

"Hot Brown. Picked it up on the way out of town."

"To go? Kind of a mess, isn't it?"

"Kind of cold by now, too. I'm at the Sams Gap overlook. The colors are subtle and deep this year. Did a couple of watercolor sketches."

"Isn't there a trailhead at that overlook? Is parking there a good idea?" I was pretty sure I sounded as alarmed as I felt. Trailheads and people I cared about didn't mix these days. Gar Brown's body proved that.

"It's a busy overlook," Joe said. "Steady stream of

people in and out. Not the kind of place you'd pick to smash vehicle windows. And I sat on the rock wall right in front of the truck. Gar liked this view. He liked a good Hot Brown, too."

I liked a good Hot Brown, with its turkey, toast, tomato, bacon, and brown, bubbling Mornay sauce. "Eat a bite in his memory for me, will you?"

"I'll do that right this minute."

"Thank you." *A bite of warm food. An act we take for granted. Hot Brown sacrament.* "Have you heard anything new about Gar? Has Cole said anything?"

"Not much. It's keeping him busy, though. It's why I picked up the engine for him. So." He took another bite. I listened to him chew and swallow. "Something going on?"

Besides begrudging him the Hot Brown? I didn't sputter about the Spiveys or purportedly stolen tablecloths, being kind and not wanting to ruin the rest of his peaceful memorial lunch. I did tell him I might have ruined my chance for friendship with the enamelist. "She might want to pin me to the wall with one of her brooches."

"Martha? Hard to picture," he said. "I wouldn't worry about it too much. She'll like you when she gets to know you. It took Cole a while, but he came around."

"Halfway around, anyway." It was good to hear his laugh. "What about you?" I asked. "How long did it take you?"

"I'm smarter than Cole. It took him a while. It only took me half a while."

Mood improved, I walked on past the Cat and headed to Mel's for a spinach salad to go. I sent Ardis a text letting her know I'd be back from lunch a few minutes late. That amounted to distracted walking, though, and when I looked up from the phone, I saw Shirley and Mercy sitting at one of the sidewalk tables outside Mel's.

I stomped over, and when one of them started to greet me, I stomped that, too. "Belinda was *not* expecting me at the Vault."

"You didn't call her," one of them said—I flipped a mental coin and decided she'd be Mercy.

"You didn't either," Shirley retorted.

"We got a call from Angie," Mercy said, "and our good sense went right out the window."

Shirley threw her hands in the air to demonstrate their missing good sense.

"She's dealing with a difficult relative," Mercy said. "Looking for motherly advice."

"Mel said now's not a good time, though," Shirley said. "Lunch rush."

Knowing Mel's opinion of the twins, she would never think it was a good time for them to interrupt Angie at work, with or without advice.

"You saw the table runner, though?" Mercy asked. "What did you think?"

"She thinks it's fabulous," Shirley said. "You can see it in her eyes."

WE DIDN'T HEAR of any fallout from the fuss at the Vault over the next day and a half. Joe said no one mentioned it when he stopped in to put up more shelves for a potter and for Martha the enamelist. I'd decided to stay away until the opening on Saturday so there would be no more stirring—not even a soupçon—from me. When I told Ardis that, she said soupçons only measured ingredients, not actions. I told her that just showed how little stirring there'd be.

Joe still had finishing touches to put on his shop. Stock to transport and display, too. He didn't need my help with any of it. His bartered "smallest space" really was.

That gave me unexpected free time over a couple of evenings. I used it to contact former museum colleagues who might know about discoveries or sales of American textiles dating to the turn of the last century—or missing textiles, specifically pieces noted as missing but not reported to the police for one reason or another. My questions were stitched with delicate, vague details, asking for any slender tendril of information.

THE SHOP'S LANDLINE rang Friday morning while I was helping a customer choose between two crewel pillow kits. Ardis answered. After listening for a moment, she handed the phone to me. She took over with the customer, rubbing her ear. I understood why when I heard the high voice on the other end.

"I am *ashamed*," Belinda said. "And while I can't speak for Nervie, I speak entirely from my own heart when I say that she and I should *both* be ashamed for how we behaved the other day. Will you accept my apology?"

"Sure, I—"

"I spoke with Sierra *and* Martha, and I was *appalled* when I realized they both thought you were to blame for our fireworks display. I want you to know that I have tried to set them straight. And then Sierra set *me* straight about your background. You do hide your light under a bushel, don't you?"

"Well, I—"

"I had no idea. But I'm not surprised, either. I keep a few secrets of my own. Like my beautiful tablecloth. Won't it make a splash at the grand opening?"

"It's gorgeous. The table runner, too. I'm really impressed. How—"

"How was I lucky enough to find them?"

"I was going to ask how you're going to display them, but sure, I'd love to know where you found them."

"Ah, ah, ah. *That's* one of my secrets. And it'll stay that way because of that terrible word, the big C."

Oh my gosh. Cancer? Belinda had cancer?

"With all the *competition* out there, a girl has to be careful to protect her sources. I know you understand."

"Oh, right. I—"

"I *am* glad we had this chance to clear the air. I feel so much better, and I hope you do, too. And I hope I'll see you tomorrow at the opening. Bring all your friends, hear?"

"Wait!" I might have sounded desperate. "How *are* you going to display the tablecloth? You said you were going to hang it. It's just that it might be more fragile than you realize. You might—"

"You might want to give me *some* credit."

"I didn't—"

"And I didn't call to be lectured. Now, if you'll excuse me, I'll be obliged if you trust me to know my own business."

"Ooh, *burn*."

She didn't hear that because she'd already disconnected. I wondered if Belinda still felt better about calling to apologize. She might feel more like she'd picked a scab. I felt better, though. My stress level had risen, but my curiosity—that invigorating C word—had sky-rocketed. Belinda said she had to protect her sources. Did that mean there were more exquisite textiles where the tablecloth and runner came from?

"Who *was* that?" Ardis asked. "You're bouncing on your toes."

"Belinda of the beautiful embroidery. Something tells me we aren't going to be best friends."

"Which isn't upsetting you."

"Because I'm fickle and care more for her textiles."

THE ELECTRONIC CHIME on the Cat's back door said *baa* as I finished my lunch, and Debbie Keith came in. She *baa*ed politely in return, sounding more realistic than the electronic sheep. She *baa*ed to me, too, when she saw me at the table.

Debbie worked weekends and a few weekday after-noons for us at the Cat. She called it her hobby job. It let her wear the long jumpers and skirts she liked to sew and embellish that made her look like a model for the Swedish painter Carl Larsson. The job also helped with her cash flow. For her serious, day-to-day job, she wore jeans and steel-toed boots and raised Cotswolds—sheep that made Saint Bernards look wispy.

"Very expressive *baa*ing today," I said.

"That's my 'Hey, how's it going, mm-mmm, I smell grilled cheese' *baa*. So, how's it going?"

"Going well, and you know what I just remembered? Carl Larsson was an Art Nouveau guy. Arts and Crafts."

Debbie hadn't purposely set out to look as though she'd stepped out of a Larsson painting. She hadn't heard of him until Granny showed her pictures, and then she'd been tickled by the occasional reference. Today she looked blank, though, so I filled her in on my new love in life—Belinda's Arts and Crafts tablecloth. When I had Debbie saying "aww" over my description of the squirrels' tufted ears, the door said *baa* again.

"Oh, hey, Nervie."

Debbie echoed my "hey," and when it wasn't returned, she nodded toward the hall. "I'd better get. *Baa.*"

I chuckled. Nervie didn't. That was Nervie's way, though, and nothing wrong with it. That someone chuckled easily or not wasn't a tick mark on my gauge for likability. She usually dashed in and straight up the back stairs to the workroom where she taught her crewel class. Dashing was also her way, and why we often didn't exchange more than a few words. She didn't dash, though, so I started over with a smile I hoped was warm and relaxed.

"I want to apologize," she said. "For the scene with Belinda on Wednesday and for the impression Sierra got."

Apologize for the scene, but not for calling Belinda a fraud and a thief? I let that thought dash away and went with something safer. "Kind people think alike, Nervie; Belinda called to apologize this morning."

Nervie's right eye twitched, and she didn't go for the stairs. Ardis planned to pounce on her after the class. Maybe I could smooth the way toward the topic of classes and soothe Nervie's twitch.

"We feel lucky to have you teaching at the Cat, Nervie. Not everyone who stitches can teach, much less design patterns. How long have you been doing embroidery?"

"My grandmother taught me." *Twitch subsiding, good.*

"Really? I learned from my grandmother, too."

"Are you questioning my memory?"

Oops. "No—"

"The first word out of your mouth was 'really.'"

"I didn't mean—"

"It's all right." Her eye stopped, but her shoulder gave an irritated twitch. "I just get tired of people doubting me."

"What else do they doubt?"

"You're doubting that they doubt?"

"No—"

"That's fine, then. Now I need to get ready for my class." She walked—didn't dash—up the stairs.

A familiar *tsk* came from the top of the refrigerator. "Have you noticed how often you annoy people when you ask questions?" Geneva asked.

I went over so I could whisper and not be overheard by wandering customers. Or Nervie. "I only meant to point out we have something in common."

"You're like Deputy Dunbar that way."

"I absolutely am not!" Being horrified and keeping to a whisper didn't quite work. Joe's brother, Cole, was unimaginative, starched, and officious. He and I operated under a truce, for the most part, but in my mind he would always be Deputy Clod.

"I mean it only in the nicest possible way," she said.

"That doesn't make me feel any better."

"He is a top-notch law enforcement officer," Geneva said. "He gets people to react and say things they might wish they hadn't. Much like the sheriff."

"When have you heard Sheriff Haynes question someone?"

"I meant Sheriff Andy Taylor of Mayberry. I studied

many of his cases. He would be proud of the way your question hit a nerve in Nervie."

NERVIE DASHED AWAY again after teaching her class. We assumed she did, anyway, because after the last members of her class trailed through the shop, buying hanks of jewel-colored wool for their next projects, she was gone.

"And I missed my chance to pounce," Ardis said.

"I tried buttering her up for you, beforehand, but I kind of muffed it."

"And you haven't asked Joe?"

"No, because you were going to ask her."

"Tsk."

"Did you borrow that lovely noise from Geneva, or did she borrow it from you? Think about it, though, Ardis. The students bought more materials, right? So we know there's at least one more class here."

"Unless that class is going to be held at the Vault. And you know if they don't have to walk through the shop on the way in or out, they're more likely to shop somewhere else or online."

"Tsk."

LATE FRIDAY AFTERNOONS were a special time at the Weaver's Cat. That's when a subgroup of Thank Goodness It's Fiber (TGIF) met in the second-floor workroom. TGIF was the fiber and needle arts group Granny had started soon after she opened the Cat. The full membership of TGIF came together for short business meetings and programs on the second Tuesday evening of each month. Smaller special interest groups met at other times throughout the month. There were groups for weavers, spinners, and dyers. The crochet group always drew a good number. Lace makers had the smallest group—two.

On Fridays, the workroom rang with the clicking of knitting needles and whatever sound a speeding crochet hook makes. The members of Fast and Furious Fridays dedicated themselves to producing a thousand tiny hats for newborn babies by the end of each year. Since I'd been at the Cat, we'd discovered we had a talent for solving crimes as well as for speed-knitting, and Ardis dubbed us "the posse." Although only Ardis and I knew, Geneva was an enthusiastic member of the posse, too. I didn't and probably never would knit as fast as the others in the group. They were all kind about my efforts and said our goal was really more about friendship and service. They also didn't let me forget how few hats I contributed when we tallied them at the start of our meetings each week.

"Look at those precious striped beanies." Ernestine O'Dell patted the two hats I dropped on the table at the center of our circle of comfy chairs. Short, stout, and seventy, Ernestine was one of the sweetest people I knew. "You put a lot of effort in this week. Good for you, dear." She couldn't see much better than a near-sighted mole. She no doubt gave me credit for more of the hats in the pile than I deserved.

Thea Green, the director of the public library, set her straight. "That's two more than you did last week. Red-letter day. I'll make the two extra big."

Attendance at Fast and Furious was hit or miss due to busy lives and busy jobs. Five of the seven comfy chairs in our circle were filled that afternoon. In addition to Ardis, Ernestine, Thea, and me, the other regulars were Mel, Joe, and octogenarian John Berry. John had retired back to his family homeplace sometime in the past few years, after a career in the navy and then more years as a vagabond sailor. He knitted baby hats as precise and shipshape as he kept himself. Mel hadn't sat down yet. She was setting up refreshments on one of the Welsh dressers that lined two of the walls in the workroom. Her spiked hair was back to mustard yellow from the previous week's unsuccessful attempt at bittersweet orange. We valued Mel's membership because she knitted many and a startling variety of hats, mostly in food-related hues. She'd worked through a lovely range of melon and spice colors over the summer.

"Scones and coffee on the dresser." She took her seat, took up her needles, and started on the final rows of her hat du jour. We also valued her membership because she brought refreshments from the café.

"So, Mel," I said, "did Shirley and Mercy ever find a good time to spread their advice around the café?"

"Not in my café, Red, not on my time," Mel said. Only she called me Red. She said everyone else wanted to, but they weren't brave enough to be so obvious. My hair being less red than auburn, I'd decided she just liked the name and needed someone to pin it on. "The only advice Angie needs is to never let a stray relative carrying a pillow and toothbrush through her front door. It isn't her relative, anyway. It's one of Aaron's cousins. She followed a heartthrob up here from Gatlinburg. Much drama."

"There's some interesting shading going on in that hat, Mel," Ardis said.

"I'm way into pears this month. This is my attempt at 'ripening Bartlett.' Next up will be 'red Anjou.' I might take a stab at Comice after that and get that whole half-scarlet, half-golden green thing going." She looked around the circle of chairs. "Is this it? Is Joe going to be here?"

"Pears?" I ignored her question about Joe and put down my needles. Even if Joe had returned an engraved RSVP we knew he still might get waylaid by one thing or another. "Did you bring your pear-and-ginger scones?"

If I'd looked over at the Welsh dresser first, I wouldn't have asked. Geneva floated above the plate of scones in a haze of ginger vapor bliss. I went to join her. The scones were still warm. *Bliss.*

But before I took one, my phone buzzed with a text from Joe. I read the text. Stood there. Read it again.

Vandalism incident at Vault.
Belinda's tablecloth in shreds.

"You look like a ghost," Geneva said. "Try breathing."

Not breathing seemed better than sobbing.

FIVE

RATHER THAN PING Joe back and get the details in a spare, emotionless text, I called. Our conversation ended up being just as spare over the phone.

"Tell me."

"She came in to hang it," Joe said. "Found it in shreds. Everyone in the building heard her scream."

"Have you seen it? Do you think there's any hope?"

"I haven't, and it's hard to know. She's kind of…incoherent."

Joe was probably kind to put it that way. *I* hardly felt coherent; I could hardly imagine how Belinda felt. He said he'd text or call again if he heard anything more. I disconnected and closed my eyes, picturing the tablecloth, wishing I'd snapped photos even without Belinda's permission. *It's gone forever?*

"Breathing is one of the more interesting differences between a ghost and a living woman," Geneva said. "Take several more of them, please, so that we can maintain our life-and-death equilibrium. Living women, some of them, also keep their eyes open and on what's important."

I opened my eyes. Our noses almost touched.

"Me," she said. "Your eyes are beginning to cross, but you're looking at me. It's nice to know that I'm so important in your life."

I shivered.

"Shivering is another difference between ghosts and living people," she said. "Although I occasionally shiver, it's because of a different kind of cold. Did you just hear bad news? Bad news is something we all share. Curiosity, too. Here she comes."

Ardis came up beside me and put her hand on my shoulder. "Trouble, hon?" She kept her voice low. "I don't mean to pry, but Mel got concerned when you didn't immediately take one of the scones."

"The clue of the rejected ginger," Geneva said. "Mel is an excellent detective, even if her hair looks perpetually surprised by its whereabouts."

I went back to the group and told them about the tablecloth and what had happened. None of them had seen it, but like the good artists they were, they were appalled at its destruction. And like the bright, good friends they also were, they started asking questions. Most of my answers were shakes of my head.

"Did he, she, they damage anything else?" Mel asked.

"Do they know who did it?" Thea asked.

"I wonder what kind of person takes the time to ruin a thing so that no one can ever enjoy it again," Ernestine said. "I don't condone stealing, but if something's stolen, at least it still exists. But taking it away from everyone forever?" She shook her head and fussed at her knitting. It had uncharacteristically gone awry and needed frogging.

"Was this someone who wandered into the building?" John asked. "What kind of security do they have at the Vault?"

"I don't know. Joe probably does."

"I bet he does," Geneva, lurking behind my shoulder, whispered in my ear. She liked to call Joe my burglar beau, a name that exaggerated the circumstances under which she and I had met *him* at the caretaker's cottage. I was never sure if she believed the nickname. I hadn't seen or heard anything since then to make me think she should, and his brother the deputy seemed to trust him. But apparently it only took finding someone coming through a window once to raise questions.

"You talked to Belinda this morning," Ardis said. "So it must have happened after that."

"She had it in a box. In a box inside a trunk. Maybe she only just discovered it."

"That'll make it harder to pin down."

But we both looked over at the worktable where Nervie taught her crewelwork class.

My phone rang: Joe. Geneva came around from behind me so we were face-to-face again.

"I'm here for you," she said.

Even though I could see the others *through* her, being nose to nose with Geneva gave me a sense of claustrophobia. I made a quarter turn to get away. She followed, wringing her hands. Ardis, seeing my problem, came to the rescue. She went over to the sideboard, picked up a scone, took a bite, and waved it back and forth. She looked eccentric, but I loved her for it.

"You there?" Joe asked.

"Sorry, yeah. Is anything else damaged?"

"I don't know. Sierra called Cole."

I tried not to groan, for Joe's sake, although he knew my opinion of his brother. He understood it, and often shared it, but he was still a good brother. "I want to see it. If I knock on the door, will you let me in?"

"You won't have to knock. I'll be watching."

JOE, A MAN of his word, had pulled back a corner of the newsprint on one of the windows to watch for me.

The hush surprised me when I stepped inside. Quiet voices, soft footsteps. Had I expected wailing and gnashing of teeth? Probably not, but I stepped into a hush more like a church before a service, a setting waiting for an event to start.

The place did suddenly look ready to open. A lot of work had gone into that "suddenly," but the Blue Plum Vault now looked like the eclectic, artsy indoor mall envisioned by Gar Brown. Shop signs had been hung, and whiffs of polish hung in the air from the newly buffed terrazzo floors. Potted palms stood on either side of the front door and next to the information and sales desk. Our steps, as we headed for the stairs, didn't echo so much, their sound deadened by merchandise filling the shops.

More of the merchants were there, too, like actors with opening-night jitters. Joe nodded to the few stepping out of their shops to see who'd arrived. I recognized some of them—the potter, the bookseller, the pastel artist. I wondered which of them were there when it happened. What did they see or hear? *Who* did they see? Could any of them serve as witnesses? Did one of them know who killed the tablecloth? I wanted to interview all of them. Ask probing questions they couldn't escape or avoid answering. It's possible I was getting carried away.

I nudged Joe. "Is Cole here yet?"

He shook his head. I read that as, "Murdered tablecloths aren't high on my brother the esteemed deputy's list of priorities." But I still had that carried-away thing going on, so my interpretation might have been unfair.

Martha the enamelist saw us coming up the stairs. She beckoned, and we followed her into her shop. Lean Joe offered lean introductions.

"Martha, Kath, you've met?"

"On the wrong foot," Martha said. She held out her hand. It was warm, and her blue eyes were warmer than they'd been the day Nervie and Belinda erupted. She'd wrapped her braids around her head again. Her untucked work shirt matched her eyes.

"Martha helped calm Belinda down," Joe said.

"Self-preservation as much as anything," Martha said. She looked quickly toward the door. "Sorry. I really do feel badly for her."

"Does anyone have any idea what happened?" I asked.

Joe started to shake his head, but a look from Martha stopped him.

"That's what I wanted to tell you," she said. "Belinda's over there making accusations. She's still very upset. She might be… I don't want to say overreacting, because I don't know what I'd do if someone came in here and purposefully destroyed even one of my smallest pins."

I looked around at her display cases—full of colorful and highly smashable brooches, pins, pendants, and plaques—and hoped the tablecloth didn't mean the beginning of something awful. The tablecloth seemed so specific, though, and too hidden away.

"I think I'd be physically ill," Martha was saying. "But someone should tell Belinda she needs to be careful what she says."

"Shouldn't that be Sierra?" I asked.

"You'd think," Martha said. "And she was there. She called the police. But she has a lot on her plate."

Joe and I found Belinda in her shop, spitting mad—though quietly and not quite literally, thank goodness, because her anger at full, piercing volume would have been painful. Her quiet anger didn't look healthy, though. She sat in the back corner, on the trunk where she'd kept the tablecloth, her cheeks splotched with red, her eyes red, too. The shop, except for the empty space on the back wall, looked ready for the opening. Belinda looked as though she, personally, might be shutting down.

"Shock?" I asked Joe quietly.

"Can I get you anything, Belinda?" Joe asked. "Water?"

She answered, but her eyes and her voice were directed at the toes of her shoes. "I don't need water. I need the police. Sierra said she called the police. *I* called the police. I don't see them. Do *you*? Do you see Sierra? Do you see Nervie Bales?"

If Nervie were a cockroach, Belinda's question would have ground her into the floor.

"When the police get here, I will inform them of what's happened," Belinda said to that same spot on the floor. "If they want to postpone the grand opening until they finish their investigation, that's fine, but it shouldn't take that long. I can tell them who's responsible. I know it was Nervie, and I will insist they arrest her. Then I'll make sure Nervie is no longer part of the Vault. Sierra will have to kick her out; there's no question. You can't run a shop when you're in jail."

I moved closer—not too close—and sat on the floor. It's what I'd done as a child when I tried so hard to convince one of Granny's cats to sit in my lap. My quiet lap hadn't worked then, but I'd never given up, and I'd learned a few things along the way. If you tell a cat what *you* think it should do—purr, play, keep its claws in its paws—it won't be impressed. If you keep it up, the cat might bite. But if you speak softly, move slowly, don't ask too much of the cat, and don't insist on anything, the cat still might bite, but it might not leave a scar.

So I sat cross-legged and didn't tell Belinda she should be careful about what she said or who she accused or how loudly she demanded retribution for the loss of that stunning tablecloth. I just asked if I could see it. "Just to see if there's any way at all it can be mended."

The noise she made sounded exactly like one of Granny's unimpressed cats. But unimpressed didn't mean ready to bite, so I sat, waiting. Quiet Joe, wily stalker of skittish fish in small creeks, had blended into the background and watched. Belinda made a more resigned noise and hefted herself from the trunk. I wondered if Joe noticed if she used a key to open the trunk. Even if Belinda's back hadn't been to me, I might have missed that detail. I was too busy praying.

Then she put a deep, flat box in my lap, and I opened it. The tablecloth—the appliquéd oaks with their charming squirrels and acorns—had been reduced to a tangle of brown linen strips, threads sliced through, a few left dangling.

"So, what do you think?" Belinda asked with a sarcastic jab. "Do you see any hope?"

There was no point in answering. I didn't see any point in picking up any of the pieces, either. *No hope. No possibility of hope. They're all dead. I'm holding their coffin in my lap.*

"Getting oils from your fingers on it hardly matters at this point." Belinda stuck her hands in the box and stirred the pieces around, tossing some of them up like a dish of nightmarish pasta. And some of the strands looked...

"Sorry, Belinda. Let me just..." Were they singed?

"Let you just what?"

"Will you hold those pieces up again?" I pointed to where I thought the shreds with darkened ends had fallen back into the box.

If she'd said no, it wouldn't have surprised me. Instead, she shrank away from the box.

"What's the matter?" I asked.

"You tell me," Belinda said. "What did you see? Why don't *you* pick them up?" Then I heard her mutter something that sounded like *phobia*, and I sort of didn't blame her.

What am I afraid of? When I'd brushed my fingertips against the tablecloth the other day I'd only felt the peace and joy of that woodland. And pleasantly tiddly, as Granny would have said.

"It's just kind of a shock to see it like this," I said. *And what if I feel the violence of the attack on that peaceful scene?*

At the edge of my vision, Joe shifted his position, a move as good as asking, "Need me?" If I'd nodded, he would have been right there, whether the problem was in front of our eyes or part of something less obvious. He and I had a comfortable relationship, comfortable enough that we didn't worry about not sharing everything in our lives with each other. We'd connected in a way that surprised me, a way I didn't completely understand. No more than I understood the connection I'd been feeling with certain textiles since coming back to Blue Plum and taking Granny's place at the Weaver's Cat. Literally *feeling*, like feeling the peace in that poor departed tablecloth's oaks and squirrels. Joe, being a noticing kind of guy, knew something went on between me and cloth—not all cloth, and only occasional pieces of clothing. He didn't ask me to explain it. I couldn't have, anyway.

"I really don't understand you," Belinda said. "Did you come here to gape or help?"

Before she could take the box away, I took a breath, dipped into it, and lifted a dozen or so strips on my outspread hands. And...nothing odd happened. But that's what *was* odd—I felt nothing at all from those pieces except my own sadness over the destruction. The peace I'd felt before had trickled away through the raw edges and dangling threads. I didn't know where the "feelings" came from, and I didn't like them, but staring at the scraps in my hands, I knew why I felt nothing now. The tablecloth's soul was gone.

I found one of the ends that looked singed and rubbed my thumb across it. "It took so much time."

"Months. Maybe years," Belinda said. "I wouldn't have the patience."

I'd meant the destruction—methodical, deliberate, and thorough.

"That's enough." Belinda whisked the box from my lap and snatched the strips from me. "I don't have time for this."

I got to my feet and looked at Joe. He tipped his head toward the door. A good idea.

"I do thank you for stopping by," Belinda said as she hugged the box to her. "If the police ever show up, they can't put it back together any more than you can. But at least you were good for something. You snapped me out of my self-pity. The grand opening's tomorrow, and now I've got more work to do."

I nodded at the blank space on the back wall. "What were you going to put there if you sold the tablecloth?"

"*When*, not if," she said. The second part of her answer came with equal firmness, but not as fast. "That's my plan B."

"Do you think she has a plan B?" I asked Joe as we crossed the gallery space toward the stairs.

"I get the feeling it's nothing or all. Either she doesn't have one, or she has plans B, C, D, E, and on down the line. Did you learn anything?"

"Someone's got time and a temper."

"Nervie?"

"It's hard to see how. She had a class at the Cat all afternoon. Has Belinda actually told Sierra she thinks Nervie did it? Where *is* Sierra?"

And why did that question sound familiar? Because of Nervie, again. Wednesday lunchtime, when she and Belinda fussed at each other, Sierra had come running up the stairs, when they'd pretty much stopped, and Nervie's response to her appearance had implied she hadn't known where Sierra was or where she'd gone. It sounded like that in my memory, anyway.

Joe took my arm and steered me away from the stairs and toward the back of the gallery.

"Where are we going?" I asked.

"Shortcut. She's probably in her office."

"You've got a brain in your head, Joe Dunbar."

"So do you, but it's otherwise occupied."

Like the Weaver's Cat, the old bank had a second set of stairs at the back of the building. But if the back stairs were a shortcut to Sierra's office, why hadn't she come running up them the other day? *Because she wasn't in her office,* I told myself. *And that's no big whoop-de-do.*

We went past Nervie's shop and two more—a leatherworker and a potter, all stocked over the last few days. I pictured the shops poised and waiting, watching for their first customers. The smell from the leather shop waved for my attention, but a sky blue bowl in the potter's caught it first.

"I'll come see you tomorrow," I told the bowl.

"That's what I tell the browns and the brookies every time I leave a creek," Joe said.

During the building's banking days, the back stairs had been a staff convenience and not for public use. That hadn't changed in the remodel, and the door shutting off the stairs from public view didn't look any more inviting than a closet door. As we approached, we heard feet pelting up the stairs. When we reached the door, the feet reversed course and ran back down. And then came up again. As they reached the landing, I reached past Joe and opened the door.

Sierra, wide-eyed, stopped with one hand on the railing and the other to her chest.

Joe looked down the stairwell and then looked at Sierra. "You all right?" He pointed down the stairs, up, back down, and up again.

"Stress steps," Sierra gasped. "They keep me from freaking out. Are you on your way down?" She'd started jogging in place on the landing.

"We were on our way to see you," I said.

Her eyes got wider. She motioned us quickly into the

stairwell, motioned for me to close the door, and then whispered. "*Now* what?"

"Do you want to sit down?" I asked.

Still jogging, she shook her head. "Just let me know the bad news fast so I know if I have to start running all the way up."

The three of us looked up the stairs toward the third floor. I wasn't sure she'd make it.

"I thought you should know that Belinda thinks Nervie destroyed the tablecloth," I said, "and she's going to ask you to turn Nervie out of the Vault."

Sierra might not have heard anything beyond Belinda's name; she was too busy shaking her fists and silently screaming up to the third floor. When she looked at us, again, her eyes weren't so much wide as wild.

"Do you want to know what I'm stressing out about? You wanna guess? You don't need to. I'll tell you. It's *everything*. The grand opening. The vandalism. But it's mostly these *women* acting like middle school *girls*."

She looked about as young and gawky as a teenager herself. She looked nearly hysterical, too. I wondered if it would help her, show that we were there for her, if Joe and I ran up and down a few flights with her.

"This is my first professional job," Sierra said. "I know I can do this, and I know we can get past it. But you know what else I'm worried about? Gossip. If this gets out and gets twisted around with small-town gossip and small-town minds—" She stopped, looking horrified. "That was a *terrible* thing to say; I'm so sorry. You have to believe me. I don't feel that way about Blue Plum."

"It's the stress talking," Joe said.

"I'm appalled." She looked it.

"Stress speaks for itself," I said. "We know you don't feel that way."

She said, "Thank you," in a tiny voice, and then she closed her eyes and looked as though she was giving herself a good talking to. When she opened her eyes, she appeared calmer. "Here's how I'm going to go forward. I'll let the police handle the vandalism. I'll tell Belinda that's how it is and that she can't talk about the incident based on supposition, no matter how well-founded. If asked, I'll say that despite an unfortunate incident, the grand opening is going forward as planned. How does that sound?"

"Like wow," I said. "If that's how you presented yourself to the Arts Council board, when they interviewed you, then I can see why they snapped you up."

Even in the poor light of the stairwell, she looked pink and pleased. "You don't think if people hear there's a feud they'll stay away?" she asked.

Joe laughed. "It'll bring them in."

Sierra's phone rang. She didn't jump, a further sign that her nerves were back under control. Joe and I wouldn't have stayed and listened, except that we heard her say, "Deputy Dunbar," and she raised her eyebrows at us. Then she listened for a while, which confirmed for me that she was "talking" to Clod. Joe and I looked at each other, shrugged, and waited. Sierra waited, too, pursing her lips and batting at something in front of her face, or maybe batting at Clod droning in her ear.

"Sorry, what?" Sierra finally said.

Clod had asked her to meet him at the front door. We decided to keep her company.

"Have you had many people wander in while your

merchants moved their inventory in this week?" I asked as we went down the stairs.

"No."

"I just wondered, because Belinda said something about people forgetting to relock the door."

"*No.*"

So. I wouldn't be asking her about that again.

"There is something else, though." Sierra stopped abruptly at the bottom of the stairs. From the way she looked over her shoulder, I wondered if she might suddenly bolt back up them. "I didn't just call the police. I called the fire department, too."

"When?" Joe asked. "And why?"

"And shouldn't they be here by now?" I asked.

"Not the department, exactly," Sierra said. "Someone I know. Because I don't think...and I didn't want...but I wanted to be sure..." She definitely wanted those stairs.

"You looked at the shreds of the tablecloth, didn't you?" I said. "You saw singed edges."

"Burned. They were burned. Someone tried to set the place on fire and burn it down."

SIX

"WAIT, YOU DIDN'T think you should mention arson ahead of your worries over a couple of bickering women?" Joe asked.

"Don't patronize me, and don't belittle the power of bickering women," Sierra said.

Joe looked at me and said, "Huh."

I felt sure a lot could be unpacked from that syllable, but there wasn't time. Sierra steamed for the front door.

"Who do you think she called at the fire department?" Joe asked as we hurried to catch up.

"I see your 'huh' and raise you one. You know, there could be another explanation for the singed scraps."

"Huh."

At the door, Sierra peeled back the same corner of newsprint Joe had earlier. "He said he'd be waiting." She might have said something else under her breath, but I didn't ask her to repeat it. Then she returned to full volume. "I need fresh air. *Lots* of it."

She opened the door and went out. When she didn't close the door behind her (or slam it in our faces), we followed again. Sierra hugged herself, rubbing her upper arms. After her stress steps, the outside air probably felt chilly.

I didn't see Clod. But jogging toward us from the end of the block were Al Rogalla and Chief Inspector Bruce of Scotland Yard. Rogalla, who rarely answered to his first name, was an accountant and volunteer fireman. The Chief Inspector, who usually answered to Bruce and always to a dog biscuit, was a brindle Scottie.

"If she called Rogalla," Joe said quietly, "Cole will be delighted."

By "delighted" he meant "snarling with suppressed scorn." Clod and Rogalla had a long-running desire to one up, tear down, and drag each other through any-thing miserable—preferably involving deep mud—as well as a general loathing for each other. The rivalry had been going on since they were teammates in high school football twenty-five years earlier. Far too long, apparently, for either of them to stop and realize they probably liked each other.

"Do you think you can distract him?" I asked Joe. "Maybe I can ease Sierra's mind."

Hands in his pockets, ambling Joe Dunbar set off to waylay Rogalla and Bruce. Sierra looked as though she might join him, so I skipped around to get in front of her.

"Hey, Sierra?"

"What?" She moved sideways, watching Joe and Rogalla.

"The singed scraps."

"Burned," she said automatically, but it got her to look at me.

"Right. You're right. Burned. There's another pos-sibility for why someone did that. And if I'm right, it might make you feel at least a little bit better. It would mean no one tried to burn the place down."

"Okay. So what is it?"

"Someone might've been testing the composition of the fabric with a flame test. Depending on how a fabric burns, you can tell whether it's plant or animal fiber, or synthetic. You can get a pretty good idea, anyway."

"Why would anyone care?"

"A collector would. Or someone like me. Someone who wants to know if the fabric is what the seller claims it to be."

"By ripping it to shreds? Are you as crazy as the person who did that? Did *you* do that?"

"*No!*" The horror in my voice made both of us jump. I tried again. "That isn't what I meant. I'm saying that fabrics burn. Sometimes they melt. You can tell something from the way they burn, the way the flame acts, how it smells, and by what's left over."

If Sierra were any more skeptical, her nose would be permanently wrinkled. I could have warned her about her nose, or dropped the flame test explanation, but I decided to give it another try.

"Your blouse, Sierra—what's it made out of? What's the fabric?"

She plucked at the hem. "I don't know. Polyester? Cotton? I can check the label."

"Or if I put a match to it, we can find out immediately." In hindsight, I wouldn't throw a flip remark like that at someone worried about things catching fire. And if I'd realized Joe and Rogalla, the volunteer fireman, had ambled our way and stood behind me, I definitely would have chosen another way to get my point across.

"Are you threatening her?" Rogalla asked at the same time Sierra said, "You *are* crazy."

Without too much effort, I explained to Rogalla. Sierra, poor thing, sounded like she'd have to run up and down a building the size of the Empire State before she'd be herself again. Joe and Rogalla were doing a good job of bringing her around, though, so I left well enough alone. Then Rogalla handed me Bruce's leash, and the three of them walked down the block. Bruce and I looked at each other. He gave a few testing sort of tugs on the leash. I wrapped the leash a few times around my wrist.

"You can tell he's a new dog owner, Bruce, or he wouldn't have left you with me," I said.

Bruce thought that over and gave a firmer tug on the leash. Rogalla hadn't exactly inherited Bruce, but he'd adopted him a month or so earlier, after Bruce's former owner died. He eyed me now, possibly assessing my ability and agility. Between the tugs and some interesting shoulder and paw choreography, he appeared to be dancing closer to the conclusion he could best me. Any minute he might make a break for it.

"Come on, Inspector. I think we'd better go fetch your fireman."

They'd only gone as far as the green space between the old bank and the new post office. The grassy area was the last vestige of the front yard belonging to a house that lost its front porch view of Main Street decades earlier. The house, hemmed in by progress and commercialism, sat on a slight rise behind the bank and post office. Wide enough for a serpentine path, the strip of green also had a few benches and a picnic table. The current homeowners had donated the strip to the town. The town had named the space Postage Stamp Park. Some muttered, afterward, about the mayor holding out for calling it Dollar Bill Park, because the adjacent bank predated the post office, and the park's shape looked more bill- than stamp-like. Mayor

Palmer "Pokey" Weems had never been one to let mutters bother him, though.

Bruce didn't let mutters bother him, either. When we got to the park, he sat himself down, facing the wall of the Vault, and wouldn't budge. I kept a firm hold of the leash, in case he was bluffing, but otherwise he seemed more interested in the trompe l'oeil mural a local artist had painted on the wall as part of the renovation and repurposing. The artist incorporated several bricked-over windows and a bricked-over door into the mural, playfully giving the impression we were looking out the windows, shutters thrown wide, and could run through the open and welcoming door into a larger park that would forever be green and flowery.

Bruce and I looked over our shoulders. Joe, Sierra, and Rogalla sat on one of the benches under a spindly mulberry tree. Joe, being Joe, lounged more than sat—long legs out and crossed at the ankles, the back of his head cradled in his interlaced fingers, staring up at the sky. And did I see Rogalla patting Sierra's hand? Maybe. Bruce made a noise that sounded like *pfft,* and we turned back to the mural. It really was an astonishing optical illusion. From the way he stared at the mural, it was possible Bruce thought so, too. He kept making minor adjustments as he stared, though, as if each correction helped him figure it out. It reminded me of the way I sometimes turned my head a fraction to see if that would bring Geneva into clearer focus.

Into that scene of staring at walls, lounging, and possible hand patting, Clod finally arrived. He stopped at the foot of the path. His uniform, his posture, the look on his face, the uprightness of his Smokey Bear hat— everything about him said *harrumph*, with extra *R*s.

"Hey, Cole." Joe unlaced his fingers to wave one set at his brother over his head. The wave looked almost, but not quite, like a Three Stooges four-finger brush-off.

Clod gave a brother's minimalist acknowledgment. "Ms. Estep? Sorry to keep you waiting. I was unavoidably delayed. Shall we go inside?"

The three on the bench got to their feet—Joe, hands sunk in his pockets; Sierra looking calm and professional again; Rogalla hooking his thumbs in his belt. I'd seen him face Clod like that before and could never remember who he'd copied the pose from. Captain America and Mr. Clean both came to mind.

"Still nothing to report on Gar Brown's murder, Deputy Dunbar?" Rogalla asked.

"Nothing to report to you," Clod said. "Ms. Estep?"

Rogalla didn't let it go. "Lonnie said progress is slower than he'd like. He said that over breakfast this morning at the club. After a quick nine holes." He paused, as though Clod might need more time to read between the lines. Reading wasn't one of Clod's problems, but he didn't react to the dig. Joe had mentioned something about Clod and anger management sessions. "*Lonnie*," Rogalla went on, leaning hard on the name of Clod's boss, Sheriff Leonard Haynes, "wonders why you're having trouble identifying and locating the Saggy Bottom Boys."

"The who?"

"The smash-and-grab gang. Smash and grab, get it? S. A. G. Probably a bunch of unemployed, under-entertained, rural ne'er-do-wells, with jeans drooping halfway down their backsides. Saggy bottom."

"Sounds like you've got it all figured out," Clod said.

"Not me. Lonnie. He also wonders if you and your

colleagues take some of the leads you've received seriously enough. In particular, the tip about a liaison. A tragic tryst in the mountains. Find the other half of that equation, and you might learn something worthwhile. Not that I'm telling you how to do your job. Just a friendly word in your ear."

Whatever else I thought of Clod—and much of that "else" irritated me—I knew he was no slouch as a lawman. Ignoring solid leads didn't fit his profile. Ignoring Rogalla's comments didn't either.

Their posturing and Rogalla's baiting had gone far enough. Bruce kindly responded when I tugged on the leash. Together we went over, and I destroyed the symmetry of Rogalla's He-Man pose by handing the leash to him. He didn't say thank you, so I thanked Bruce.

"I felt we had a true meeting of minds, Inspector Bruce. Thank you."

Bruce ignored me, too, and looked back at the wall. This time he definitely saw something and let everyone know it. He danced around and ended up peering down the path farther into the park.

"Possum," Rogalla said. "Gotta be. They get him all stirred up. There, look at him."

Bruce had suddenly reared up on his haunches, front paws in the air.

"Those are his jazz hands. Definitely a possum. It's the only time he gets excited enough to wave his paws like that. Cute as the dickens, isn't it?"

Bruce toppled sideways, then righted himself, all four paws firmly on the ground.

"That's the trouble, though," Rogalla said. "Scotties aren't built for—" He splayed his hands to show what they weren't built for.

They weren't built for embarrassment, either. Bruce had lost interest in the possum and now stared at Rogalla. He gave a good impression of someone assigning blame for his clumsiness.

"Good dog," I said.

"Good nose, too. We're going in to sniff around," Rogalla said. "See if there's anything for Sierra—Ms. Estep—to worry about. See if we can give her some peace of mind before the place fills up with innocent bystanders tomorrow."

Sierra's professional look wavered.

"Sniff around for what?" Clod asked.

"Possible arson attempt," Rogalla said.

"I haven't heard or seen any reports on that," Clod said. "And I guarantee you I would have."

Rogalla's supercilious look wavered. "Well, erm, it's unofficial, as yet. Pending the sniff around."

"A credible report?" Clod asked.

I raised my hand. "I have a theory that doesn't involve arson."

Clod and Rogalla gave me identical looks, dismissive and annoying. Peace-loving Joe put a warm hand on my shoulder. I subsided, but I but didn't plan to forget.

Deputy and fireman went back to speaking civilly to each other over the top of my head. I put my hand over Joe's to reassure him I wouldn't jump up and bite either of them. A smile could have accomplished the same thing, but touching his hand felt nice. Besides, the only smile I could have pasted on would have been cheesy and wouldn't have reassured anyone. I worked at not grinding my teeth, because I wanted to hear what the two who were sworn to serve and protect, but continued to irk, were jabbering at each other.

"I'm going in more as a personal favor," Rogalla said. "The last thing Ms. Estep wants is to cancel or postpone the grand opening."

Clod touched the radio at his shoulder. "Do you need more manpower for a full search?"

"I'm thinking low-key, at this point in time," Rogalla said. "Keep it quiet. No alarms."

"Agreed." Clod's erect posture went into hyper mode. "Here's how it's going to work, then. You will follow my lead. You will not do or touch anything until I say so. If you find anything, you will report it to me. Understood?"

Rogalla gave a single nod. "Let's go."

"Ms. Estep," Clod said, "if you'll lead the way?"

No one thought to invite Joe and me along. I was kind of surprised they remembered to include Sierra.

"Never underestimate the vexation of a couple of boys with badges," I said, when we were alone on the sidewalk.

"Nothing's stopping us going in," Joe said. "I've got a few more things to do before tomorrow, anyway."

Oh-so-tempting, and Debbie could handle whatever traffic a late Friday afternoon brought into the Cat. "Then let's," I said. "A couple of things before we do, though. Have you ever heard anything about Nervie's embroidery patterns not being her own?"

He looked blank.

"My reaction, too. Okay. Had you heard what Rogalla said about Gar and a liaison? Could that be why he was up there? It's a lonely spot. It could easily be a lovers' lane."

Joe shook his head, as much dismissing the theory as answering my question. "Change of subject?"

"Sure."

"You brought about a miracle. You saw those two going through the door together just now—that's your work. By suggesting you knew something, and possibly knew better than either of them, you single-handedly caused them to stop butting heads and instead act together as a single butthead."

"You know how to tickle a gal's fancy, Joe Dunbar."

"Why, ma'am, I tell you what. If I had a hat like Cole's, I would take it off to you."

"If you had a hat like his, you'd use it for a bait bucket."

"Huh. I wonder if he's got a spare. Here's something else. I'll do you one better than your adage about boys and badges. Better than the power of bickering women, too. Ready? Never underestimate the power of a perceptive woman."

"Lacks punch." I punched my right fist into my left hand a couple of times, bringing back memories of a solid punch it once landed on Clod's nose. A completely uncharacteristic but very satisfying punch when he'd referred to Granny as Crazy Ivy. "Add persistent to your adage and I'll take it." I paused, then asked, "Did you notice that Sierra didn't say anything after Cole showed up? Not a peep."

"Hard to find an opening in all that testosterone to slide a word in. Not everyone has your skill and determination. She might just know it's better to let those two talk through their aggression once they get started."

"Has she lived here long enough to know that?"

"Probably not. Could be she's just into WWE and thought she'd get a show. Come to think of it, the Arts Council might want to consider that for a fund-raiser."

"If I've told you that you're brilliant any time recently, then I'm sorry, but that idea disproves it. Seriously, though, did Sierra say anything useful about the tablecloth while Rogalla patted her hand back there on the bench?"

"Useful how?"

"You mean he really was patting her hand?"

"It's the cherry red hair. He's helpless. It attracts him like a fireman to a flame. Useful how?"

"The way someone is who wants to help the police solve a crime."

"And you're interested because?"

"Because I'm a concerned member of the public."

He waited.

"And because it's like a locked-room mystery. If the building was locked, and the tablecloth lay safe and sound in a box, in a trunk, in the back corner of Belinda's shop, then who did it? Who knew where to find it, had the chance to get it and the time to slice it up, and also cared enough to do a flame test? And why put the poor mangled thing back in the box in the trunk in the back corner of the shop afterward? Why not keep it or toss it in a garbage can or Dumpster?"

"So again, do you see Nervie doing that?"

"I don't see how. I don't know. What if Sierra did it? Or Belinda."

"Huh."

"Yeah, huh. It's a puzzle. So, I'm puzzled. That's why I'm interested. I loved that tablecloth. I wanted to see it again. I wanted to visit it often. I wanted it, period."

Plus I had that perceptive thing going, I hoped. Definitely the persistent thing.

SEVEN

I EXPECTED TO hear Belinda's high voice before Joe and I reached the top of the stairs. We didn't. A low murmur of voices came from her shop as we approached and stopped when we stopped at the door. Clod noticed our presence before Bruce did. Chalk one up for the guy with the badge wearing brown and tan. The two brothers did their minimalist head nod.

"Ms. Rutledge." Clod didn't smile. He didn't growl, though, so chalk another one up for an excellent anger management counselor.

Bruce didn't growl, either. He looked preoccupied, not making eye contact with anyone. Rogalla stood off to the side, watching Clod and being as deferential as he'd promised to be. Belinda, her behind propped against one of the display tables, drooped like one of her vintage linens that needed to be aired and pressed. She stared at the floor, looking almost as sad and defeated as the scraps of her ruined tablecloth. Presumably we'd arrived in the middle of something Sierra was saying. She stood next to Rogalla, her arms frozen mid-gesture, chin lifted, her mouth still slightly open.

"Sorry," I said. "We didn't mean to interrupt."

"Ms. Estep was just telling us—" Clod started to say.

"What I told Joe and Kath earlier," Sierra said. "The incident, while unfortunate, won't keep the grand opening from going forward as planned, and unless there's evidence beyond personal dislike, we won't be hearing accusations."

"There will, however, be an investigation," Clod said. "I intend to look around and talk to your other co-op members."

Sierra's chin tipped a bit higher, but she nodded. Rogalla cleared his throat.

Clod, sounding pained, added, "Rogalla and the dog will accompany me."

Belinda continued staring at the floor.

Then Clod did something proving that deep down, under the badge and the uptight brawn, he was a Dunbar; he spoke gently to Belinda. "Ms. Moyer, you've given me your statement. I'll get it typed up, and at your convenience, you can come over to the courthouse and sign it. That doesn't have to be before next week. Now, the only other thing I need for you to do is show me the tablecloth. Then I'll leave you be." He scowled at the rest of us. "Everyone else will, too."

Assuming we were "everyone else," Joe and I moved out into the gallery, but if Clod thought we'd disperse, he was wrong. Whether he wanted to hear it or not, I meant to tell him my theory of the flame test. Rogalla and Bruce might still think it advisable to sniff around, but it was a solid theory from a textile expert, and they should listen to it and sleep better because of it. Doggone it.

I stopped where I could still mostly hear and pretty well see what went on in Belinda's shop. I saw Clod and Belinda move toward the trunk, for instance, but they blocked my view so I couldn't see her open it. But we all heard the single, soft word she spit when she looked inside. In fact, it rhymed with spit. A frenzied tossing of things out of the trunk followed, then silence, and then a view of Belinda's back and bent head when Clod stepped aside.

I ran back in and poked Clod on the arm so he'd look at me. I didn't need more than one word, either. *"What?"*

"The tablecloth appears to have been moved or misplaced," Clod said. "With all the excitement and upset over the vandalism, it isn't too surprising. Stress does funny things. We'll take a look around in here. I'm sure we'll find it."

I refrained from poking him again. "Belinda, would you like help?"

"We will take a look around," Clod repeated.

"Fine." I looked for Joe, so we could leave in unanimous dudgeon. He'd wandered off, so I had to make the most of my own dudgeon.

Joe waved from across the gallery when he saw me. He and Martha stood in her doorway. She'd put on a peacoat. It seemed obvious she wanted to be on her way and was doing us a favor by sticking round.

"I thought you might want to hear this," Joe said when I reached them.

"The back door's been unlocked off and on all week," Martha said.

"Oh for—did you know that?" I asked Joe.

He shrugged. "I probably could've guessed, but I keep odd hours and use my key."

"So instead of knocking on the front door, I could have gone around back and waltzed right in anytime I wanted?"

"Of course," Martha said. "People were still bringing things in and had other people helping. And everybody's excited to see what's been done with the place. It was hard to keep them from taking an early look around, and we've all been happy to show them. I seem to remember *you* looking around earlier this week."

Why did I suddenly feel guilty? Oh, right, because Martha had singled me out for her cutting sarcasm after Nervie and Belinda fussed at each other that day.

"Sierra arranged for live music tomorrow, too," Martha said, "so the musicians were in and out with equipment and checking out the space and the acoustics in the gallery."

"But doesn't it seem unbelievably random or lucky that an excited stranger rummaged in Belinda's trunk at the back of her shop, found the tablecloth, cut it, and burned a bit of it? And then either the same person or *another* one found the scraps, which didn't look like anything at all anymore, and thought, 'Gosh, I can't possibly live without *these*,' and spirited them away right under Belinda's nose? Oh."

Joe and Martha were staring at me.

"You must have loped away before Belinda discovered the scraps were missing," I said. "Well, that's the latest wrinkle in all this."

"We didn't hear a peep from over there," Joe said.

"And Belinda rarely just peeps," said Martha.

"She might be in shock at this point, and who could blame her? Cole thinks the stress got to her, and she doesn't remember moving them. He and Rogalla are going to knock themselves out being helpful and find them for her. I bet they don't find them, and I bet even more that this whole thing is an inside job and the unlocked door has nothing to do with it."

"The unlocked door complicates things, though," Joe said.

"Belinda leaving her shop tonight complicates them, too," Martha added.

"Oh, *Belinda*." I felt like banging my forehead against the wall. Banging Belinda's forehead against the wall would have felt better, though only in the short term; in the end I would have felt obliged to join Clod at anger management. "Why did she go and do that?"

"Why shouldn't she?" Martha asked. "None of us are required to be here, and most of us won't be keeping regular hours. They aren't that kind of shops."

"I know. I'm just whining on behalf of a tablecloth that can't whine for itself anymore. Where did she go? How long was she gone?"

"She went looking for anyone who would listen to her tale of woe. It's been like a B-grade drama around here with *B*-linda *b*-moaning and *b*-wailing." Martha yawned, then, and told Joe she'd see him in the morning. "And I assume you'll show up at some point, too?" she asked me.

"I wouldn't miss it. It'll be great."

"We'll hope for the best, anyway, with strong coffee in the morning and whiskey when it's over." She covered another yawn and went down the stairs.

After Martha left, I said, "I wonder if I should've told her Cole wants to talk to everyone."

"He can catch her tomorrow," Joe said. "She's exhausted, but you can tell she's keyed up, too. She isn't usually that snarky. It's this thing with Belinda. You know, she might not last long at the Vault."

"I wouldn't blame her. Poor Belinda."

"I meant Martha. I'd be sorry to see her go."

Joe was nice like that. The jury still seemed to be out on whether Martha and I were going to like each other, but I'd even heard Joe say he was sorry to see Clod go a time or two. Speaking of whom, he spotted us and marched across the gallery.

"Thought you two might have gone by now," he said, his voice hitching upward along with his belt.

"Find anything?" Joe asked.

"No, no, she was right." He looked aggravated and sucked a tooth to prove it. "The tablecloth's gone."

It hadn't taken much time for him and Rogalla to search Belinda's shop and come to that conclusion. It took infinitely less time for me to show I could be snarkier than Martha.

"The tablecloth was already *gone*," I said. "Someone reduced it to a box of scraps. And now *that's* disappeared out of Belinda's trunk and out of her shop, and the question is how. *How*?" That might have come out more like *howl*.

"Rogalla and I have done what we could in the amount of time we've had since Ms. Moyer discovered the disappearance. We made a thorough search of the shop." The starch in Clod's voice would have made Jell-O stand at attention.

"A small shop inside a much larger space," I said, never having been a fan of Jell-O. "And Rogalla's a volunteer fireman. He's an accountant. Why don't you call in backup? Where are Deputy Munroe and Deputy Dye?"

"Other priorities, other cases," Clod said. "Including a murder." It was clear he'd rather be working on that case.

There was no snark from me on that point. Gar's

murder put a mere tablecloth into perspective. But I still wanted to be sure Clod treated Belinda's case seriously, too. "The scraps definitely aren't in Belinda's shop. They might still be in the building, though."

"We can't know that without tearing the whole place apart."

"And the tablecloth is already torn apart, so what's the use? Is that it?"

"Sierra will have a heart attack if they tear the place apart tonight," Joe said. At a look from me, he added, "Or she could suck it up and run up and down the stairs a few times."

"What about Bruce?" I said. "He's supposed to be sniffing around for more signs of attempted arson. So maybe he can sniff out the singed scraps while he's at it. Or if someone grabbed them and ran, he can point which way they went."

"Huh," Clod said, with familiar Dunbar understatement. "Okay, yeah. I like that." An interesting light grew in his eye as he nodded. It was a light his anger management guru might consider problematic. When he went to tell Rogalla it was a go for Bruce to start sniffing, his regulation deputy boots had an unusual bounce to them.

"Is it okay if we tag along?" I called after him.

"Yes. Yes, it is."

"We'll start him out on a circuit of the space here on the second floor," Rogalla was saying as Joe and I joined them. "Though I want you to understand this is less than scientific. Bruce has a good nose, but he's primarily an earth dog, programmed for rodents and diving down burrows. That's why he gets so excited when he sees a possum."

Clod raised his hand. "Possums aren't rodents."

"I know that," Rogalla said. "Bruce knows it, too. But they look like ungainly and overgrown rats, and they make use of other animals' burrows, and unless you're willing to do a side-by-side rat and possum sniff test, I suggest you don't quibble over minor details with an expert."

"Oh, sure, sure." The interesting light in Clod's eye had spread to his smile. "No quibbling from me. We'll follow your lead."

"And yet," I muttered to Joe, "neither of them will listen to the textile expert who probably has more credentials and interest in what's going on than the dog who just flopped down to take a nap."

"I am not traipsing around after the dog," Belinda said. "And if you'd believed me in the first place, I wouldn't now have to go put my shop back together."

"I'm sorry for your trouble, Ms. Moyer," Clod said. "I'll file my report and keep you informed."

"And let me know if the dog finds anything."

"I will," Clod said.

"So now what are you going to do?" Sierra asked. "Just have the dog sniff around?" She glanced quickly toward the back stairs. "You won't need to dismantle other shops?"

"We'll be as quick as we can while still being thorough," Rogalla said. "As for dismantling—"

"There will be no dismantling, Ms. Estep," Clod said. "If you have other matters you need to attend to, by all means do so."

"Before tomorrow? Are you kidding? Find me before you leave, though, okay? I'll probably be in my office, but if not, then I'll be…around. Al has my cell."

"Okay, *Al*," Clod said. "Take it away."

Chief Inspector Bruce of Scotland Yard got back to his feet at a word from Rogalla. The two of them trotted toward Martha's enamel shop with Clod close behind.

"Are you going to watch them?" Joe asked. "Because I might—" He tipped his head toward the main stairs.

"Oh, yeah, of course. I'll bark if they find anything." But before I followed Bruce and his buddies, I dashed to the back stairs. Sierra had just reached the bottom when I leaned over the railing and called her.

"Sierra, hi, have you got a minute?"

"What? Oh, well, no, not really."

"Sorry, I just wanted to ask about something you said earlier." That I'd told myself *not* to ask about again. "When I asked if people had been coming in, you said no. But they have been. All week."

She blinked up at me. "I think you said 'wander.'"

"I might have, but that's kind of what they did."

"No. They didn't. The way you said 'wander' implied random people. *That* didn't happen."

After she'd gone through the door and couldn't hear me, I added, "That you know of." She would have been busy with arrangements for the grand opening all week. Up, down, in, out, sometimes stuck in her office—and sometimes, as Nervie had made it sound, unfindable. How much had she missed?

When I caught up with Bruce and his expert nose, it didn't appear I'd missed much. Bruce looked longingly at a rack of tooled wallets in the leatherworks shop.

"He passed on the pottery next door," Clod stage-whispered to me.

"Nothing of interest up here," Rogalla announced. "Let's head on down to level one."

"What we non-nose experts call the first floor," Clod whispered. I moved out of range so he wouldn't be tempted to narrate every other step of the way.

Bruce took a quick trip around the lobby, stopping for a sniff at the front door. The information and sales desk held no interest for him. *I* was interested to see Joe duck out of view in his shop before Clod caught sight of him. I didn't give him away by pointing and yipping. Neither did Bruce. What *did* catch Bruce's attention was something in Floyd Decker's antique shop.

In his younger days, Floyd could have played Mr. Rogers's stunt double. Now he was beyond the days of doing stunts, but he still had a passing resemblance to Fred Rogers, right down to the cardigan. Floyd's sweater had buttons, though, instead of a zipper. He had one of the larger shop spaces, twice what Belinda and the others had on the second floor, so about ten times the size of Joe's shop. Floyd was delighted to have Bruce come in and look over his antiques.

"Most of what I have is eastern Tennessee in origin," Floyd said. "I'm afraid you won't find any cabers to toss or heraldic shields, young fellow. What's he looking at?"

It wasn't obvious. Bruce was doing his minor-adjustment moves the way he had when we'd been outside looking at the mural.

"He's triangulating," Rogalla said.

I might have heard a muffled guffaw from Clod.

Then Bruce was on the move. He left Floyd's, by-passed Simon Grace's bookshop in the vault, and took us down the hall and around a corner toward the infamously unlocked back door. He stopped to sniff at two unmarked doors opposite each other, the restrooms farther along, and then continued on to the back door. He sniffed all along the bottom of the door, and then he reared back and did his jazz hands.

"Possum come a-knockin' there, Brucie?" Clod asked.

Bruce ignored him. Rogalla and I did, too. Bruce dropped back to the floor, sniffed around, and let Rogalla walk him back to the bookshop. Simon wasn't in. Bruce sniffed the space without much interest. When he'd made his way around the shop and returned to the door, his ears and nose perked up. He followed them back to Floyd's, where he did his jazz hands again.

"Does he want to shake?" Floyd asked.

Bruce wanted to turn around and head for the back door again. He repeated his sniffing and his jazz hands at the door and then back to do it again in Floyd's. When he started for the back door a third time, I stopped following and let Simon's miniature bookshop lure me into the vault. It looked as though he'd taken apart an old bookshop from a street in London, made the necessary modifications, and fitted it carefully into its new home. Why Bruce hadn't found it attractive I didn't know. And I didn't feel like I'd miss anything by peeking into one of the locked glass-fronted bookcases, because the guys with the badges weren't being subtle or quiet.

"I'm sorry I have to point this out to you, Rogalla," Clod said, "but Bruce isn't a real convincing sniffer dog. I'm not so sure he's a possum dog, either. Not unless a possum and all his kin moved in here while no one looked."

"We're still working, Dunbar. We'd appreciate it if you'd keep quiet."

"I'm just saying that according to the Chief Inspector and his jazz hands, Floyd Decker's shop is infested with possums and they're running up and down the hall to the back door every time we turn around."

I poked my head out of the vault to interrupt. "Maybe he does the hands thing for singed linen, too. Maybe he's tracking the scraps."

Clod and Rogalla looked at me. Bruce looked down the hall toward the door.

"Why don't you let him out to see where he goes?"

"That's the next step," Rogalla said.

"Yeah, right," said Clod.

The door, happily or not, was unlocked. We followed Bruce outside to an area of crumbling asphalt with a few cars. Bruce sat down and scratched his ear. He reminded me of the way Clod sometimes looked when he worked through a finer point of detection.

"The Chief Inspector has fleas, Rogalla," Clod reported.

After scratching, Bruce seemed to have made a decision. He turned around and trotted back to Floyd's and showed him his jazz hands.

"I've got it. I know what it is," Rogalla said. "You must have an old possum fur coat in here, Floyd. Gotta be."

"Well now, I don't believe I do," Floyd said. "No clothes for sale at all. But I know where I can lay my hands on one, over in Johnson City, if that's what you're after. I can't have it for you tomorrow, but sometime next week, if that'll do you."

While Rogalla explained why he didn't want the coat, I realized Clod wasn't with us anymore. When Bruce headed for the back door again, I found out why. Clod had gone to find a roll of toilet paper. He'd put a match to it, doused it, and set the smelly, smoldering, sodden mess in the middle of the hall.

"To see what Bruce does now," he said, that light in his eye burning as brightly as the toilet paper must have.

The experiment might just as easily have been to see what Rogalla would do. Bruce paid the singed toilet paper no mind whatsoever. He gave it the cold shoulder on his way to the door and again on his way back to Floyd's. Then he stood in front of Rogalla and did his jazz hands at Rogalla's shins.

"And that's the end of that," Clod said. "Maybe for your next trick, you two can take up tap dancing." He swiveled on his regulation deputy boot heels and marched off toward Sierra's office.

I marched after. I sounded like one of Bruce's fleas compared to Clod's tromping, but he heard me and glanced back. From the look on his face, I was about as welcome as a flea. I made myself more annoying by spurting ahead and barring his way.

"I thought you were taking this seriously," I said.

"What makes you think I'm not?"

"Because of all that baloney I just witnessed. Even with the perpetually unlocked back door, this has to be an inside job, and you didn't even begin to make this a thorough investigation. Did you check to see if anything else is missing? From Belinda? From any of the others? Did you ask any of them? Did you ask Joe if anything's missing from *his* shop?"

"I'm guessing he would've told me."

"Did you check on anyone's—everyone's—whereabouts? Did you get a list of everyone who's been traipsing in and out the back door all week? Did you dust for fingerprints? Bruce might not be up to sheriff's department standards for sniffing, but he's interested in *something* in Floyd's shop. Did it occur to you to find out what?"

Clod twitched one shoulder and then the other, the way a bull being pestered by flies might—bull and flies both knowing full well the twitching did no good. "Got that out of your system?" he asked when I stopped for breath. "The sputtering, anyway. I know you'll never be out of questions."

"At least you're right about that." I did my best imitation of Ardis, but she had a triple advantage over me: she'd been his third-grade teacher and his Sunday school teacher, and she matched his six feet so that she looked him straight in the eyes instead of staring up his bull-stubborn nostrils. "Are you at least taking Belinda's accusation seriously? I don't know that she has any proof, but there is definitely no love lost between them."

Clod's shoulders stopped mid-twitch. "What accusation would that be?"

"She didn't tell you?"

He waited, and I wondered if I knew what I was doing.

"I and several other people heard Belinda say she knew that Nervie Bales destroyed the tablecloth. She was anxious for you to get here so she could tell you. She wanted Sierra to turn Nervie out of the Vault after you arrested her. Did she really not tell you any of that?"

Clod played poker; I knew that, and I knew he must be pretty good. "You might like to know," he said, "that it wasn't all fun and games at that dog-and-possum show just now. I noticed, for instance, that you left us for a short time and crept into the old vault with the books."

"I didn't creep. I walked."

"You might also like to know that while you were thus occupied, I received a text message from Ms. Moyer telling me she no longer wanted me to look for the tablecloth."

"What?"

"It's her decision. It is, or was, her property. She called off the search."

EIGHT

I WENT LOOKING for Joe after things fell apart between Clod and Rogalla. He sat tying flies on a crate conveniently placed in a corner of his shop, where the eye of the casual brotherly passerby might miss him. Mine didn't. I made him scoot over and sat next to him. "Did you hear any of what went on out there?"

"Hard not to," Joe said. "I'm impressed. I thought I might need my earbuds, but they kept things reasonably civil."

"Until Cole started calling Rogalla 'Possum.'"

"And then that little bit of détente they'd forged because you tried to tell them something useful about flame tests went right out the window."

"But neither one of them threw the other out the window after it, so no harm done."

Joe smiled his sweet smile and shook his head. "Cole's anger management is working better than I thought it would."

"We'll see. They went off to give their reports to Sierra."

"Give her a headache, more likely."

We heard Floyd call goodnight to someone.

"Floyd's really stoked for tomorrow," Joe said. "He's a careful one with his words. Keeping them safe like his antiques, maybe, so he can take them out and look at them years from now. But the last couple of days he's been downright extravagant. He must have strung two of three dozen together three or four times."

I knew someone else who got chatty like that from time to time. I scooted a little closer. "I hope the opening turns out even better than everyone hopes."

"It's going to be fine. We'll make sure it is."

"Do you have much more to do tonight? What about supper?"

"I'm about wrapped up, here, but I told Cole I'd take care of that engine tonight."

Rats. Joe Dunbar—nice guy and good brother.

"You can come along and help, if you want."

"Gee, that's so tempting," I said. "I'll pass, though, thanks."

EXCEPT FOR THE electronic sheep greeting me with its *baa*, the Cat was quiet when I let myself in the back door a little while later. Debbie would be closing out the cash register; the TGIF meeting long over, Ardis, Ernestine, and John would have gone home. Thea had returned to the library and Mel to her kitchen—with the rest of the scones. I checked.

"Weren't they delicious?" Debbie said when I asked if she'd had one. She'd liked them so much she'd had two. "Ardis said to tell you she'll meet you here tomorrow, and you can go over to the grand opening together. Text her if that won't work."

"Thanks. How was business this afternoon?"

She'd had time to change the mannequin's clothes, trading its cape and fedora for a quilted tunic in the style of an artist's smock and a hand-felted beret embroidered to look like a palette. Geneva wasn't sitting on the mannequin's shoulder. I didn't see her on the fan or in the display window, either.

"It was a bit slow," Debbie said. "It'll pick up tomorrow with all the people in town."

"I'm sure it will. I'll come back here after I've had my fun at the opening so you and Abby can go over."

"Sounds good. Ardis told me about the tablecloth. I'm really sorry. Why would anyone do a thing like that?"

I shook my head. "Have you seen Argyle?"

"Not since he said hello when I came in."

"He's probably in the study." Geneva, too. "I'll go on up. You can lock up, and I'll let myself out later."

"Sounds good."

I checked the kitchen first, and then went up the back stairs. The study, up two flights, in the attic, was the only room in the Weaver's Cat that Granny had set aside as her own private space. Granddaddy had made it perfect. He'd built cupboards and shelves into the eaves, made a window seat in the dormer, and carried a heavy oak teacher's desk up there for her. They'd been very much in love. When he'd made her a secret cupboard in one of the walls, he'd painted the inside her favorite indigo blue and lettered across the edge of the middle shelf, *My dearest, darling Ivy.*

Now the study was mine. Granny's books about looms, plants, dyes, and weaving, and her meticulous notebooks with her own dye recipes and weaving samples, patterns, and plans were mine. And her journals, the ones she'd hidden in the secret cupboard, were mine, too. When she died, she left a letter that led me to the cupboard, a cleverly hidden space I'd known nothing about, despite all the time I'd spent in the study as a child. Granny's letter also opened my eyes to a part of her life I hadn't known anything about. Hearing it from anyone else, I wouldn't have—couldn't have—believed what she told me.

I'm a bit of what some people might call a witch, she'd written. *I prefer to think of the situation more in terms of having a talent. I have a talent which allows me to help my neighbors out of certain pickles from time to time. It's a marvelous gift, Dearie, and I hope you know I don't use the word marvelous lightly... I inherited it from my grandmother. You have inherited it from me.*

And I did. I honestly did. Wrapping my mind around the "situation" and the "talent" was a work in progress. But, for instance, I'd followed a recipe called *Juniper for Long-Lasting Friendships* in one of Granny's journals and made a lovely grayish-green dye. I'd dyed a skein of cotton rug warp with it and then braided the bracelet for Ardis. I didn't need such a bracelet. Granny hadn't mentioned anything in her letter or journals about "feeling" emotions from textiles or seeing ghosts; those seemed to be "bonus" talents all my own.

Granny's secret cupboard wasn't just mine anymore, though. Geneva had claimed it as her "room," graciously adding she didn't mind sharing it with Granny's journals. The cupboard's dimensions were close to those of a wooden coffin, something we'd both noted. She'd never said so, and it seemed indelicate to ask, but I had to wonder if that was part of the cupboard's attraction.

There were times I wished I had the study all to myself, but sharing it with a ghost who'd been moaning less frequently and a cat that not only tolerated me but sat in my lap and purred wasn't so bad.

I found the two of them curled up in the window seat.

Geneva sat upright when I came in. Argyle blinked his eyes and went back to sleep.

"You look as though you've been to a funeral," Geneva said. "Not the fun kind."

"Is there a fun kind?"

"The ones where you dance on your victims' graves. I've never done that, but I imagine there are spirits of all sorts involved. Spirits for drinking, high spirits. Ghostly spirits, too. Fun, one would assume."

"I'm not so sure." I sat down at the desk, put my feet on it, folded my hands, and rested my chin on them.

"Detective pose!" Geneva shouted. "Tell me about our case."

"Well—"

"Wait! Let me join you in the appropriate mood and posture." She brought her hand down slowly in front of her face as though wiping away her look of joy. Except that when her hand reached her chin, she still grinned. Then she went to the door and leaned against the frame. "Now, ask me why I'm leaning insolently in the doorway."

"Why—"

"Because I'm your muscle. Even though you won't equip me with a six-shooter, or even a tiny, cute, pearl-handled revolver, I'm your loyal hired gun. Look, even Argyle's spirits have perked up."

Argyle continued to snooze in the window seat.

"Are we solving another murder?" Geneva asked.

"Well, there is the murder of Garland Brown, but—"

"I knew it! And his murder is tied up with the destruction of the tablecloth. Didn't you say someone tore the tablecloth to shreds?"

"Cut."

"Cut, torn, the method of destruction doesn't matter. The *result* is the important detail, because we can use the shreds to tie up Garland Brown's murderer. Gag her, too."

"That's—"

"Genius. I know." Geneva, excited, could rarely be still, and she hadn't been able to stay in the doorway. She did her version of pacing—zipping back and forth across the room. I closed my eyes.

"Wait." I opened my eyes again. "Why did you say 'gag *her*'?" I took my feet from the desk and sat up.

"Didn't I tell you?" Geneva zipped over and skidded across the desk so we were again nose to nose. I shivered again. "I know you're Clod-strophobic as well as ghost-strophobic," she said, "but you should call the deputy. After he hears what I have to say, he will be able to tie up both crimes with one neat bow. Call him immediately and tell him that I have indisputable evidence in those despicable crimes, and he should drop everything else and arrest Nervie Bales for murder and defamation of embroidery."

"You—"

"Yes, I have proof."

"Geneva—"

"You aren't making the call. Call him!"

"Stop!" Even Argyle woke up and looked at me. "Sorry. Geneva, stop interrupting me and stop interrupting yourself. This is important—"

"I know!"

"Hush."

She put her hands over her mouth.

"Sit down and listen to me."

She settled, cross-legged, on the desk.

"You can take your hands down. Now tell me, calmly, how you know Nervie destroyed the tablecloth."

"And killed Garland Brown."

"Calmly. Tell me about Nervie and the tablecloth first." I hoped she'd forget about the dubious connection she'd made between the vandalism and the murder. "Nervie taught her class here this afternoon."

"But she left."

"Do you know when she left?"

"Before her students."

"Before the end of class or after class but before all the students left the shop?"

"Is this a trick question?"

"No."

"Because I didn't tick them off a class roster as they left the building." But she was beginning to sound ticked off.

Asking Geneva when something happened was always tricky. The way she explained it, when you've been hanging around for more than a hundred years, without a calendar or a pocket watch—without a pocket, for that matter—the finer points of "yesterday," "today," and "five years ago" get blurry. Time became a fluid concept. Less like a river, though, and more like one of Joe's shadowed fishing creeks—winding its way down a mountain, taking an unexpected tumble, disappearing into impenetrable rhododendrons, reappearing, slipping around a corner into the slow-moving eddy of an oxbow.

"I know you weren't keeping track of the class roster, Geneva. I'm just trying to figure out the timing."

"There's nothing to figure out. I told you she left."

"I know, and I'm glad you told me. I can call someone in the class to verify."

"Because you don't believe me."

"I do believe you, Geneva, but this is important information. We have to get it right, okay? So, you saw her leave."

"I saw her car leave."

"You recognized her car?"

"Why wouldn't I?"

"I didn't think you spent much time looking at cars."

"That's another difference between a ghost and a living woman. I have all the time in the world. And in the beyond."

"Okay, I just didn't—"

"Let me make this simple for you."

"Please do."

"The tablecloth was brown, right?"

"Brown linen. That was fairly common during the Arts and Crafts movement. Why are you waving your hands?"

"So that I don't interrupt you by screaming. We're keeping this simple and un-lecturey. The tablecloth was brown. What kind of car does Nervie drive?" Geneva paused. I could have interrupted her pause by screaming, but I didn't. "Nervie drives a *brown* car. Who was killed? Garland *Brown*. We have solved several cases before now, and you did your fair share of detecting, so I'm surprised that you didn't make those simple connections yourself."

"Geneva, I—"

"Stop!" She started billowing—never a good sign. "Time—human time—is of the essence. Why aren't you calling Deputy Dunbar? Why aren't we going after the villain ourselves?"

"We need more information first."

"Brown, brown, brown. It's the trifecta of browns."

"Is that a joke? You know we need to be logical about this, right?" But those were the wrong questions, because logic to a billowing Geneva was slipperier than time. Maybe it was a ghost glitch. It was definitely unnerving. She circled the room, around and around, like a pulsing eddy of frustrations. Argyle slunk under the desk. My knuckles turned white on the arms of the chair, but I didn't slide out of it to join him.

"Brown, brown, brown!" Geneva yelled. "Three strikes, and let's get Nervie outta there."

"But not yet." She kept circling, and I couldn't tell if she heard me. I kept talking anyway, trying to re-ground her. "You know how careful we need to be, in order to be fair to suspects and for our own safety, right? We have to be sure of our facts before we make accusations. It's a big responsibility."

"You think I'm making things up."

"I hope you know I don't. We have to ask questions when we investigate, though. We have to check statements, and we have to consider the impartiality of witnesses."

Her circuits of the room grew smaller and tighter until she circled and billowed directly in front of me. "We also have to trust our partners," she said. "If we don't, then there's nothing else to talk about."

She was as good as her billowing, logic-impaired word. She refused to say anything else, and she disappeared into the secret cupboard. Argyle refused to come out from under the desk.

I SLUNK HOME in the twilight. Lights were on as I passed the Vault, and I thought about stopping in to see how things were shaping up—nothing snoopier than that. I made myself walk past. Then I called Joe, and his *hey* did more good than a glass of bourbon or any amount of snooping.

"How's the engine?" I asked. "How's Cole?"

"They'll do." Just as his *hey* had conveyed more than an offhand hello, his lean *they'll do* had more going on than simple job satisfaction or family commentary. "Are you still at the Cat?"

"On my way home. Just passing the Vault."

I listened as he gave directions to Clod about where to hit something with a hammer. When the banging started, his drawl warmed my ear again. "Quick word, before he hits his thumb. He doesn't think the car gang killed Gar."

"Wow. That's interesting. Why not?"

"I haven't pressed." Again, more was going on with his words.

"And he's right there. What can you tell me?"

"He's worried."

"About what?"

"I haven't figured that out yet."

"You, know, it felt a little better knowing they had suspects and the suspects lived other places. Does he have a new suspect? Is his view shared by anyone else?"

"There's more pounding and swearing going on here than talking."

"Now I feel bad I crabbed at him for not taking the tablecloth seriously. He must be feeling a lot of pressure on this. But I wish—" I bit that off, because I wished that I could billow like Geneva to get my points across, to make people see things my way. How frustrated she must have been for so many years, to never be heard. And she still only had me and Ardis. I clamped my lips and looked up at the darkening sky. Clouds were drawing in around the moon.

"I know, I know." Joe's words tried to pat my back and console me—for what he could only guess, but that didn't stop him. And it turned out his guess came close. After a few quiet seconds, he said, "He *is* taking the tablecloth seriously. He'll be at the opening tomorrow. Rogalla, too, probably just to needle Cole."

Oh joy. "Okay, a couple of questions and then I'll let you get back to having fun with hammers and engines. Do you think there's any chance the scraps are still in the building?"

"No idea."

"Me, neither. So, what would you say to the two of us doing our own bit of looking around? Later on. Much later on. After everyone's gone."

"No."

"You're no fun."

"You know very well I can be lots of fun when we're alone."

"Why, yes, I do."

"We wouldn't be alone at the Vault, though. Sierra's in the apartment up top."

"I forgot that."

"And Cole says Rogalla and Bruce are spending the night on a cot in the gallery as a favor to Sierra. Guard duty so nothing else happens before the big day."

How irritating. I put a good face on it, though. "Well, I guess it can't hurt."

"That's not exactly what Cole said, but it'll do."

We disconnected, and I walked the rest of the way home wondering about a question I hadn't asked Joe.

I ate limp leftover salad for supper. For entertainment I finished another baby hat. I would have raised my arms in triumph, but I pictured Thea and Mel finishing three more, each, and tossing them on their piles of a dozen. My lone itty-bitty thing was variegated blue; it matched my mood.

Emails from my former colleagues had straggled in over the past few days, answering my question about stolen or newly discovered Arts and Crafts textiles. Another old friend answered that evening, making it unanimous—none of them had heard any such reports or rumors, but if I had or did, they would love it if I passed them along.

Before I went to bed, I circled back around to thinking about the question I hadn't asked Joe because I'd dismissed it as ludicrous. After a few false starts, I phrased it as simply as I could, and I sent it in a text to him and the rest of the posse.

Were Nervie and Gar ever a thing?

NINE

"DID YOU EAT something rancid last night? Because I mean, really. Nervie and Garland?" Ardis eyed me critically in the kitchen at the Cat the next morning. "What on earth gave you a ludicrous idea like that?"

I could have told her it wasn't so much something on earth as some*one* in limbo who'd put the idea in my head. I hadn't seen Geneva yet this morning, bit in case she drifted down now, I didn't want to hurt her feelings. Having a friend who could move absolutely silently had its disadvantages.

"You might be losing your touch, hon," Ardis went on. "This business over the tablecloth might have curdled your clear thinking."

"Check your messages again."

"What? Oh." Ardis fumbled for her phone. "Battling with Daddy every morning curdles any semblance I've ever had of being organized."

To hear her, anyone would think Ardis had lived the model of an orderly personal life before the worries of her father's fragility and fading memory set in. Everyone who knew her, though, knew the meticulous attention she gave to his care matched the care she took in anything she did for someone else—and was far beyond any organization she'd ever imposed on herself. Her daddy was in the same capable and loving hands the Cat had been for years.

I'd begun to regret the text about Nervie and Gar as soon as I'd hit Send the night before. I'd talked myself into letting it go, though. It was what it was, and maybe it would spark thoughts and questions that were a little less out there. That theory had settled in comfortably until about four in the morning. Then I'd groped for my phone and sent another text asking the others to ignore the first. Mel, up early to bake, had just answered the first. Whether she thought the text was a joke or *I* was wasn't clear from her all-caps LOLOLOLOLOL.

"Well then," Ardis said, after she put away her phone. "But *were* you serious?"

"I'm not sure. Do you mind if I run up and ask Geneva if she wants to come with us?"

"I'll be in front saying hey to the girls."

The girls were Debbie, our shepherdess, and Abby, our formerly Goth high school student. Abby had started working weekends for us after she fell under the spell of a spindle whorl. She turned out to be a natural at spinning and completely besotted with all things fiber. Recently, she'd been studying the ordinances about keeping multiple rabbits (angora), a goat (mohair), or a pair of sheep in town. She'd already talked her parents into turning part of their large backyard into a plot for growing flax. They'd said no to an alpaca.

Geneva sat in the window seat again. Argyle purred in a ball of fur next to her. Every so often I sat there with them, cozy with Argyle in my lap. If the three of us sat side by side it got a little cramped. Geneva didn't disappear or turn her back on me when I walked in, so I hoped she'd forgotten our upset or forgiven me.

"Good morning, you two." I bent to kiss Argyle between the ears.

"At least it isn't raining," Geneva said.

"It's kind of nice out. How are you guys this morning?"

Argyle purred. Geneva said, "I only saw one piece of litter in the street."

"Good to know." Those comments were more upbeat than I'd expected, and not nearly as dismal as some of her other greetings. "Ardis and I are going to the grand opening at the Vault. Why don't you come with us? It's in the old bank building. Maybe you banked there."

When we met, Geneva hadn't even remembered her name. A hundred and forty years in the oblivion of that cottage would probably do that to anyone. Details fluttered back to her, from time to time, but they were spotty, and sometimes she confused reality with the television shows she'd watched.

"I doubt I had so much money that I needed more than my pocket or a crock to keep it in," she said. She paused, cocked her head. "Will there be lots to look at? Pretty things?"

"Lots of pretty things, and live music, too."

"I wonder if the angels who play harps in heaven call their music live."

"I think they call it celestial music."

"So they don't hurt anyone's feelings. They must be very polite. Tell me about the pretty things."

"Rare books and old books, turned wood, antiques, there's a photographer with beautiful pictures of the mountains, pastels, enamel jewelry."

"I don't know."

"Pottery—oh, there's such a pretty blue bowl. Tooled leather, old tools and scrap metal turned into yard art. The woman who makes them is a welder."

"Will she use her welding torch? I'll consider it if she uses her torch. I wouldn't even have to stand back or wear a mask. I call that a win for being cold but not in my grave."

Geneva's love for dangerous tools and any kind of weapon made me glad she had no ability to move objects. A win for everyone.

"She has her tools there, but she won't be using them," I said. "It's a safety thing. She does her welding in her workshop and brings the artwork in. The yard art is fun. She makes smaller pieces, too."

"Smaller pieces for someone who has only a very small plot of ground. And a headstone. I can't quite picture the fun you describe if she isn't using the blowtorch. But the linens are pretty?"

"The linens. Yes! And Joe's watercolors are pretty. Some of his flies are, too."

"Flies aren't pretty. Their saving grace is that they're partial to dead things."

"These flies are fishing lures, made with feathers and fur and different kinds of yarn and fiber. Come with us, Geneva. We're leaving in a few minutes. We'll get there early and help make the opening gate a big success. Say yes."

"Will there be lots of people?"

"Probably."

She drew her shoulders up and shivered. "The very idea of rubbing elbows with so many living and breathing strangers gives me the heebie-jeebies."

"Strangers come in here all day long."

"But they don't try to sit on my ceiling fan with me or come up to my room. It's settled. I'll stay here to keep an eye on the weekend help."

"I'm sure if Debbie and Abby knew you were doing that, they'd appreciate it."

"And you can bring me a present."

"SHE'S NOT COMING?" Ardis asked as we went down the Cat's front steps.

"She didn't like the idea of a crowd. That's okay. I'd probably worry about losing her if she came along."

"Wouldn't she find her way back on her own? She is an adult."

"An adult with kind of a major difference. You know what she's like. It's okay if she's happier staying home."

"Of course it is. If she likes the comfort of four walls and a roof—oh." Ardis grabbed my arm. "That describes a box. Coffins are boxes, hon. Is this an insight into ghost psychology? Do restless spirits yearn for the closure they were denied upon their deaths?"

"Could be."

"So many ideas to ponder. Ghost psychology. What an interesting field of study that would be."

"It would, but you want to be careful being effusive about it while you're walking down Main Street on a Saturday morning. Hey, Rachel. Nice to see you."

Rachel from the new bank waved back. "Hey, Kath. Hey, Ardis."

"Walking down any street, any time, and any day of the week," Ardis said quietly to me. "You and I are in a very peculiar situation, and to think you were doing this on your own since April. No wonder you sometimes looked distracted."

"It's been interesting. Think what would happen, though, if she came with us and we lost track of her or wanted to get her attention. Or how hard it could be if she asked a ton of questions and then got upset when we couldn't answer her."

"At least with toddlers you have some chance of hanging on to their hands," Ardis said. "Or you can get one of those harnesses with a leash. I wonder if I could use one with Daddy? Taking him out in the chair is fine, but on his spryer days he likes to walk and he might have a sprint still left in him. But let's get back to talking about something else so I don't slip again. Tell me what put that harebrained idea about Nervie and Gar in your head."

"Geneva," I said.

"Lord love a duck."

"And that was only the tail end of everything that went on yesterday. Taken altogether, the afternoon wasn't much short of quackers."

I gave her a rundown on the tablecloth shreds, Clod, Rogalla, and Bruce, and then told her Geneva's "trifecta of browns" theory. Ardis looked suitably appalled—briefly. Then, in true Ardis form, she zeroed in on what we could do and should do and dismissed the rest.

"I'll check with the embroidery students, find out what time Nervie left," she said. "It's possible she ducked out early."

I quacked what sounded to me like a pretty realistic quack. Ardis turned her grade-school-teacher glare on me, stopping several yards short of the Vault's front door.

"No more joking around, missy," she said, her voice low and serious. "Something's going on in there. Mr. Rogalla might think his dog is a possum expert, and the dog may well be, or that could just be so much twaddle. But I'd be willing to bet Coleridge smelled a rat. And if he plans to hunt it down, then we'll see if we can't catch it first, even if we ruffle a few feathers to do it."

"Even if we have to wing it?"

"Even if we have to duck and run afterward."

THE VAULT, WITHOUT NEWSPRINT covering its windows, looked suddenly wide awake that morning. The doors had opened at ten. We arrived about a quarter past, and while we'd stood on the sidewalk making our plans, ten or twelve people went in ahead of us. Each time the door opened, strains of a bluegrass trio playing "Sweet Georgia Brown" slipped out to tap their toes on the worn limestone steps. We climbed those steps behind a young couple with a baby in a kangaroo carrier and went inside.

"Kath! Good morning!" Sierra, looking professionally happy, stood at the door, doling out greetings and exclamation points to people as they came in. "Good morning!" she said to Ardis. "Hello! Welcome to the Vault!" She swished her hand at a couple of tiny bugs. Ardis, taking the hint, closed the door.

"Sierra, I'd like you to meet my good friend and business partner at the Weaver's Cat, Ardis Buchanan. Ardis, this is Sierra Estep. Sierra's the director of the Vault."

"So good to meet you," Ardis said. She made a show of gazing around the old bank lobby. "The place looks fabulous. How much of this is your doing, Sierra?"

"You're so sweet! I'm the new girl, though. They just hired me to run the place."

"And I'm sure you'll fit the bill," Ardis said.

"Don't forget to sign the guest book," Sierra said. "You might win a door prize!"

The door opened behind us. I grabbed Ardis by the arm and pulled her away. "Before you say another peep."

We signed the guest book and each helped ourselves to one of Sierra's business cards.

"Now, where to first?" Ardis asked.

"Joe's."

Joe hadn't given in under pressure from Ardis to tell her anything about his shop while he planned and put it together. I hadn't told her anything, either, and even though it was the smallest possible space that could still be called a shop, keeping the details secret from her was no minuscule feat. With the trio playing "Brown-Eyed Girl" like angels in the gallery above, I took her to Joe's and watched her heart melt a little as she looked it over.

His shop was in the original teller's cage. That included the area behind the barred window, although it measured only three feet by five. It might just be big enough for two or three people to maneuver around each other, provided they were small-to average-sized people. Joe had put the shop together with a carpenter's skill, an artist's eye, and the sense of whimsy of a veteran observer of human nature. His wares were his watercolors and hand-tied trout and salmon flies. Salmon didn't live in our mountains, and probably never had, but the flies they couldn't resist were as beautiful as Martha's enamel jewelry. Joe's shop was beautiful, too, and the whole thing tickled him. He'd named it Brown's in honor of Gar Brown. Gar would have loved the tribute; he'd started his career in that teller's cage.

Calling the shop Brown's worked beyond honoring Gar's name, too. Joe specialized in pictures of brown trout and the various types of flies called browns. He also had watercolors of garfish and what appeared to be the random addition of sketches and paintings of food. They weren't random at all; they were Joe's renditions of Gar's favorite sandwich, the Hot Brown.

The watercolors Joe had painted at the Sams Gap overlook earlier in the week were on display, as were a couple of pen-and-ink sketches of Gar he'd done for the Vault's promotional material. The sketches caught a look in Gar's eyes that made me think he was about to laugh or launch into a fish story. For some reason, that look reminded me of the squirrels on the ruined tablecloth. Appropriately, they'd been brown squirrels.

"This suits you right down to the ground, Ten," Ardis said.

Joe, wearing dark brown corduroys and a lighter brown flannel shirt, said, "Thanks."

"And I don't know how any fish in its right mind could refuse your flies." She marveled over gaudy full-dress salmon flies the size of shortbread petticoat tails and peered closely at the more delicate trout flies, some no bigger than brown lentils. "They look tasty enough that I might bite them myself. What's your favorite?"

"This little feller was Gar's favorite." Joe held up a fly so small it could have been a crumb of toast. "It's a March brown, but Gar called it a sycamore. He'd say, 'You have to hide behind a sycamore tree when you put it on your line or the fish'll crawl right up your leg to get at it.'"

"The mind boggles. But which is *your* favorite?"

"That depends."

"Spoken like a true and impartial Dunbar," Ardis said.

"If it's partiality you're looking for, then I'll go with rat-faced McDougals and Scotch poachers."

"Wonderful. Show me a rat-faced McDougal."

Joe showed her a row of garbanzo-sized flies bristling with more hair than their neighbors. Ardis carefully plucked one from the display and held it in front of her nose, turning to get it in the best light, then turning again when we heard a harrumphed *hey* to Joe.

"I think I see why it's called rat-faced," Ardis said, looking past the fly. "Hello, Coleridge. I hardly recognize you in your mufti."

"Ms. Buchanan. Ms. Rutledge." Clod had dressed for a day off, but neither his jeans nor his T-shirt, nor his posture or surveilling eyes, were believably off-duty. He cast those eyes over the teller's cage, then they moved on to the sign and settled there. "Nice tribute, Joe," he said with a fly-sized nod.

Joe returned the nod. He took the fly from Ardis and went to answer questions from a customer looking through the teller's grill. Clod should have been impressed by Joe's work, and I chose to believe he was, but from his too-quick perusal and then his turned back, I'd be hard-pressed to explain why I believed that.

"A word, Coleridge." Ardis stepped away from Joe's shop, inviting Clod over with a crook of her finger.

Dozens of happy people chattered around us, and the trio launched into an energetic "Bad, Bad Leroy Brown." A sigh played around the starch in Clod's face, but I didn't hear it over the crowd and the music. We both answered Ardis's beckon.

"Do you have anything to report, Coleridge?" Ardis asked. "Either regarding Garland or the trouble here yesterday—or about the extra security laid on last night? Did Mr. Rogalla report any incidents?" She liked to pretend he regularly consulted and confided in her.

She called it harmless fun, like play-wrestling for a bone with a bloodhound. I worried it was more like tickling a copperhead's chin. But sometimes Clod surprised us by throwing us a scrap.

"He had nothing unexpected to report," he said. "He and Bruce spent an uncomfortable night. Rogalla, anyway. I have no information about how the dog slept."

"Very good. What about Gar, Cole?" She was serious now. "Is there anything new?"

"I wish I could tell you there is, Ms. Buchanan. If you'll excuse me, I need to see a man about his dog." He took off at a trot toward Floyd Decker's. Rogalla and Bruce were just disappearing into the antique shop.

"Lack of progress isn't new. I'll grant him that," Ardis said. "But winding up back at square one because you've crossed the prime suspects off your list is. We know he smells a rat. Surely he has that rat or others in his sights. Do you think he's playing his own game?"

"He could be."

"Then we'll have to step up ours. Suggestions?"

"We need to know who was in the building yesterday, who knew about the tablecloth, who has that kind of grudge against Belinda, where the tablecloth was destroyed, how, and where the shreds are now. And with the car gang off the table, we need to know if there's any possible connection between Gar's death and the Vault."

"That's what you should have put in your note last night, not that poppycock about Nervie and Gar. Get those questions down and send them to the posse."

"Mel's catering the refreshments, and Ernestine, Thea, and John said they'll be here."

"Add this to your text—our goal is the apprehension of, or any piece of information leading *to* the apprehension of, Gar's killer or the person who destroyed your tablecloth. Eyes and ears open, Kath. I think it's time to split up."

"I just saw Thea go into the vault."

Ardis looked blank.

"The bank's vault. It's a bookshop. You know Simon Grace?"

"It's his? Good. I'll rendezvous there with Thea and bring her up to speed. *And* make sure she doesn't spend all her yarn money on books."

"Shall we touch base back at Joe's in thirty minutes to compare notes?"

"Brown's. Get the name right, hon, and make it an hour. You know me once I get to talking. And make it wherever Mel is catering. We'll be thirsty by then. Put that in the text, too. Sound good? Good. Eyes and ears, Kath. Keep them open. And if we're lucky—"

"Lucky ducks?"

"If we get it right, maybe we can apprehend both sets of villains in one fowl swoop."

Geneva complained, from time to time, about Ardis being too ardent. The obvious retort was that it takes one to know one, but I tried to be the grown-up in my friendship with the ghost who was a hundred and sixty plus change.

I watched ardent Ardis go into Simon's bookshop. Then I tiptoed after Clod.

TEN

CLOD, ROGALLA, AND BRUCE appeared to be shopping for a rolltop desk. They watched as Floyd unlocked a clever door set into the side of the desk. I kept one eye on them and the other on where I went so I didn't bump into or knock over something I couldn't afford. The small, gray-glazed crock sitting too near my elbow, for instance. I ts round-shouldered shape appealed to me and its single, loosely brushed cobalt blue flower reminded me of Granny's eyes. According to its label, the crock was made near Blue Plum and almost as old as Geneva. Floyd's price asked for three times her age. I backed away and hoped the little boys who'd just come in with their dads were well-behaved.

Bruce lost interest in the desk and turned around to sniff at the legs of a small table. It looked like a bedside table, except for the square slab of marble set into the top. It had a hinged lid, too. The lid stood open. When shut, it would cover the marble. Huh.

Bruce thought *huh* about something, too, and stared back toward the desk. He did his jazz hands again. Then he plopped down and tugged on the leash, wanting to head out the door. But then he stopped tugging, appeared to do a double take, and stared at something above the little table, his ears perked. But only for a second; then he turned and sniffed at a plate of cookies one of the boys had brought in. The boy, who couldn't be older than four, dropped the plate and started to cry.

"Here, Bruce," Rogalla said. "Come away."

"Your dance partner's a distraction, Rogalla," Clod said. "Take him home and teach him the Possum Trot."

The children's fathers made no move to help. One of them watched as Rogalla pulled Bruce away from the broken cookies and Clod tried to calm the boy. The other dad, oblivious, stood in the doorway with his back to anything going on in the antique shop. Rogalla said something to him on his way out and got no response. I looked around for the second child. He'd sat down in a small rocker and gained enough momentum to start rocking across the floor toward a table. A table with a display of treenware, tartanware, and fragile red-glazed pottery. Putting myself in the mad rocker's path, I waved to catch the dad's attention.

"Ain't mine," he said. He nudged his buddy, and without a word between them, they were gone.

Floyd, looking alarmed, extricated himself from discussing a corner cupboard with another customer. But, except for Clod trying to play peek-a-boo to get the other child to stop crying, no other adults paid any kind of parental attention to the children. Taking the chance my actions might start the second little guy crying, I put my foot on one of the chair's rockers, bringing it to a halt. The boy looked up at me, his eyes as alarmed as Floyd's.

"Hey, great rocking," I said. "Yippee!" And I gave him a round of applause.

The child thought about that for a second. Then he yelled, "Yay!" and clapped, too.

Now what?

"I think I hear the mom calling," a woman near the door said.

"Not panicking nearly enough, though," another woman said. She turned and roared over her shoulder, "Here! They're in here." She looked back at us and said, "Provided their names are Ace and Axel."

The mother arrived towing a younger, third boy. Her smiling reunion with the first two sounded like a normal occurrence. Clod tried to have a word about keeping the children with her. She seemed to think he'd complimented their speed and agility. I hoped she never took up needlework and brought the boys to run loose in the Cat.

I waved to Floyd. He mouthed a thank-you, and I went to find a quieter place to compose the text to the members of TGIF. Of course, no one wanted a quiet grand opening, but maybe I could find a more peaceful corner.

Clod caught up to me before I figured out where to go. "Which way did they go?" he asked.

"Who?"

"The guys you're looking for."

"I'm not—wait. Have you ever actually said that before?"

"I took an oath. Use all law enforcement clichés once a month. You can't tell me you weren't onto that dude with the beard and his buddy in Floyd's. No way they're antique buffs."

One of the guys had a beard? Way to keep your eyes and ears open, Kath. "Maybe their wives or girlfriends are here shopping."

"Girlfriends, maybe. No rings." Clod wiggled the fingers of his left hand but scanned the crowd as he talked and didn't look at me. "You got a good look at them, though?"

Because he wasn't looking at me, he didn't see my vacillating head bob.

"Do me a favor," he said, "and let me know if you see them again."

"May I ask why?"

"Do you want the polite answer or the expeditious one?"

"Expeditious is fine."

"You're nosy."

"And?" I already knew that, so the *and* probably sounded only slightly belligerent.

"I want to know who that dude and his buddy are."

"Out of all the other people here? Why?"

"I'm nosy, too." Then he did look at me. "It's not just them, but I don't know them. It's how I do my work. Unusual catches my eye. Besides, the dude reminds me of one of Joe's rat-faced McDougals."

"What do you want to know about them?"

"I'm not asking you to find out anything about them. Just if you see them, let me know. You know what? Forget it." He started to walk away.

"Wait." I pointed at myself. "Nosy, remember? You can't ask that and then not answer questions."

"Yeah, I can."

"Well, you can't ask without expecting me to ask back."

His shrug must have meant *okay*.

"Okay, first. If 'nosy' is the expeditious answer, what's the polite one?" I waited. He avoided my eye. "Ha! You didn't have a polite one."

"Put it this way; you're a magnet for talk."

"What's that supposed to mean?"

"You collect information," he said. "You futz around, sticking your nose where it doesn't belong and you end up knowing all this…stuff. It's like it sticks to you. Like iron filings."

"What a lovely image. And so much more polite than a piddly little 'nosy.' You could have tempered that—accurately—by adding that I'm good at solving problems. Sometimes before you do."

"Sometimes creating others along the way."

"Since when?"

He rubbed his nose. *Taught you a lesson, too, didn't I?* I thought, but didn't say aloud. I felt that I'd gotten over the experience. And I kept assuming Clod would, too. You couldn't even tell his nose had been broken, for goodness sake. I pressed my luck. "One more *nosy* question, then. Do you think Gar's death is somehow tied to the Vault?"

He didn't answer and didn't look back.

I'd wasted enough time. I leaned against the wall outside Floyd's, composed the text to the posse, and sent it. Thea was the only one, besides Mel, who'd sent a response to my original Nervie-Gar text. Thea, true to her roots as a librarian and fashionista, quoted Marilyn Monroe: "It's better to be ridiculous than boring." My life since moving to Blue Plum had hardly been boring. So, where to start being ridiculous?

I glanced across at the bookshop. Joe and Belinda weren't the only ones who'd saved surprises to unveil for the grand opening. Simon had waited to hang his sign—Simon Says Books. He'd chosen one in the style of a British pub sign, with a painting of a rosy-cheeked publican offering a stack of books on his open palm.

That sign would be more inviting than a tankard of ale for a bookaholic, and that's why I found Thea still there.

"Hey."

"Shhh," Thea said. "We're in a cathedral. Do you see what he has?" Standing in front of one of Simon's glass-fronted bookcases, she pointed to one of the books. "*Murder Yet to Come* by Isabel Briggs Myers, the woman famous for the personality test. This is her first piece of fiction, and it won the Detective Murder Mystery contest in 1929. Published in 1930. First edition. I can hardly breathe."

"You keep circling back to that one book." Simon came over with a key in his hand. "I think it wants to come out and let you pet it."

Thea backed away. "Absolutely not."

"Really, it's all right. Do you want to see it?"

"Just admiring. Thanks."

"But now you've hurt its feelings." Simon looked as though she'd hurt his feelings, too.

"Blame it on my budget. It hurts *my* feelings all the time. Here, this won't make up for it, but it'll show we can at least be friends." Thea went over to a display of used paperbacks and picked out two. "Do I pay here or on the way out?"

"On the way out, and I hope you'll come back. Especially if you manage to give your budget the slip."

"Will do. How'd you rate the vault?"

"I've been telling people they let me have it because it's where they kept the bank's books. Get it?"

"Did they?" I asked. "Keep the books here, I mean."

"I doubt it, but it sounds good."

"The shop looks good, too," Thea said.

Simon laughed. "Thanks. Ardis recognized it right

off. I did the set for *84 Charing Cross Road* when the repertory theater did it a couple of summers ago. I loved that set. This is more substantial, of course."

"The locked cases are smart," I said.

Simon made a quick, unhappy face. "It isn't the best business plan to have stuff locked away, but I can't have my most valuable stock walking off, especially after—" He glanced around before continuing. The space was cozy, but other customers weren't jostling us for room. "You were here yesterday. You know what happened to Belinda."

"Yup. I'd love to know *how* it happened, though."

"No kidding. But it's not like there weren't a million people in and out of here yesterday. So if a few paperbacks walked out the door? It happens."

"Did you lose some yesterday?" Thea asked.

"None of my treasures. Ten bucks, tops."

"Did you tell Deputy Dunbar?" I asked.

"Oh yeah. And Sierra. But it's not like I'll get them back."

"Sometimes there's hope," Thea said. "If any of your high-end beauties ever walk out the door, list them on the Stolen Books Database. It would be worth a shot, anyway."

"No point, for most of what I have. Thanks, though." Simon nodded toward the other customers. "I should get back to business."

We left Simon Says, and Thea asked, "A little jaded, do you think?"

"About the theft? Yeah, but realistic."

Thea went to pay for her books, and I decided to go see Belinda. Maybe she'd cheered up with the happy crowd. That was my altruistic motive. Really I wanted to see what she'd put in the place of honor. Did I dare hope she'd produced something more delightful than the ruined tablecloth?

Mel's refreshment table stood near Martha's shop in the gallery. She had plenty of takers for whatever she was serving, and a crowd of hip-swayers and toe-tappers listened to the bluegrass trio. When the women in front of me swayed in opposite directions, I saw that one of the musicians was the soon-to-be father of the next generation of Spiveys, Aaron Carlin. Almost any time I saw Aaron, he was doing something I'd never seen him do before. There was the rattlesnake incident, when he'd handled them as though they were as cuddly as kittens. I'd seen his old-time medicine and curiosity show and heard him accompany Angie's sweet voice on guitar. Now I could add seeing him sitting on an upturned five-gallon bucket and playing a washboard to the list. His guitar and a banjo lay beside him.

The swaying women re-synced, blocking my view before I had a chance to wave at Aaron, so I slipped around the back of the crowd to Belinda's shop. She'd hung her sign, too, the curlicues in the name not much easier to read even though I didn't have to tip my head sideways. Graceful and feminine, the sign suited Belinda. Or suited how I imagined Belinda saw herself.

A man greeted me when I went into Belle's, Belinda nowhere to be seen. And hanging in the place of honor...a perfectly nice tablecloth. Probably 1940s, this one was a square of white linen embroidered with baskets of flowers in each corner. A good, if typical, example from that era of needlework. Just disappointing in a way that my face couldn't disguise.

"Not your cup of tea?" the man asked.

I tried to smile my way out of it. "Sorry, I had my mind on something else. Is Belinda all right?"

"Why wouldn't she be?"

"No particular reason. I didn't see her and wondered." *Wondered what bug flew up your nose. Sheesh.* "I heard there's some silk embroidery."

He showed me to the gorgeous piece with the strawberries and climbing roses, unnecessary because, like a beacon, the silks called to me. I basked in their glow for a few minutes, but my heart didn't feel it. With a sigh for what had been, I left the silk embroidery, Belinda's disappointing plan B, and her snappish help behind. I put in a few toe taps in the gallery, then stuck my head in the pastel artist's shop. She did interesting things with light that involved a lot of magenta and coral, but she had too many people in the shop to stop and answer my nosy questions.

Nervie's shop overflowed, too. Good for her, I guessed. She looked happier than I'd ever seen her, anyway. Or happier than I'd ever bothered to notice. On that self-recriminating note, I headed for the potter's shop. Maybe the blue glazed bowl I'd seen the evening before could sweeten a soured mood.

But the disappointments kept coming. Not only had someone else gotten to the bowl before me, but Shirley and Mercy were there. They wore matching mint green sweatshirts with "Proud Grandma" embroidered on them, and I decided I didn't care which twin was which.

"You stopped in Nervie's?" one asked.

"And Belinda's?" the other asked.

"Nervie's tricky," the first said. "She prods and picks at others to distract."

"She's done that much already," the other said. "Picking on Belinda. Dropping a word here."

"Poking a hole there."

Pots and kettles, I almost said.

"It's no wonder Belinda's not front and center."

I'd turned to make my getaway but turned back at that. Should I ask them if they knew anything about the tablecloth? But I didn't like the idea of feeding them information. Especially if they hadn't known it existed in the first place.

"Did you miss Angie singing?" one of them asked.

"I did," I said. "Oh, I'm sorry. Will she be back?"

"She didn't sing," the first one said. "We just wondered if you missed her."

"She had an appointment," the other one said.

"We offered to sing in her place," the first one said. "Aaron said maybe another time."

"They only signed a contract for instrumentals," said the other.

I wondered if Aaron would come to regret that postponement. I'd never heard Shirley or Mercy sing, and I knew I shouldn't prejudge, but somehow I didn't think either of them had Angie's voice.

"I'VE BEEN ENJOYING myself immensely," Ardis said over a cup of coffee when we met at the refreshment table. We'd both arrived a few minutes earlier than the appointed time. Thea had sent a text saying she'd find Ernestine and get her up the stairs. John could be expected on the dot. Joe, probably not.

"Did you find anything you couldn't live without?" I asked.

"No, I treated it as a study of neophyte merchants

versus seasoned pros. Those with a certain amount of retail experience—Floyd and Joe, for instance—kept with the program. They stayed in their shops, greeted their customers, carried on appropriate conversations. Some of the others are as excited by the opening as the customers, and just as flighty. They showed their amateur status by wandering. I found Nervie leafing through pastel prints across the hall and shooed her back where she belonged."

"Belinda wasn't in her shop when I stopped by."

"And the inappropriate comments some of the merchants made," Ardis said. "Carping here, snarking there, and a bit of TMI in several places."

"I didn't hear any of that."

"That's because of your rosy disposition; it filters out the negative vibes."

"Not really."

"Don't burst my bubble, hon." Ardis loved her illusions. "Some of the merchants weren't happy about customers bringing refreshments into their shops, either."

"People do tend to be slobs. You know how we hate it when kids come in with lollipops."

"Lollipops and yarn." Ardis shuddered. "I need more coffee."

In addition to coffee, Mel offered a selection of cookies, mini-muffins, and fresh fruit kebobs with a honey yogurt dip. She was in her element serving her good food to people happy to get free snacks. Her hair spikes looked ecstatic, too, and ready to do a jig. I didn't tell her the lack of pear-and-ginger scones disappointed me. How could I complain with a mocha chip muffin in my mouth? I turned my back on the table so I wouldn't embarrass myself by taking yet another. Ardis didn't worry about such things.

"Don't look now," I said as she thanked Mel for a lemon poppy seed muffin, "but Shirley and Mercy are almost within range. Stationary for the moment, but that could change with the jab of an elbow."

The twins stood shoulder to shoulder gazing at the trio. I gave in, snatched another muffin (in case of emergency), and moved to a clear space a few feet off the end of the table. It was close enough to our designated meeting place, and near the stairs. I half expected Ardis to disappear down the stairs, but she came and stood beside me.

"Look your fate squarely in the eyes," she said, facing the twins. "It's the only way to go through life with dignity."

"Thanks. I'll remember that." And maybe I'd remind her of it the next time the twins showed up at the Cat and she tried to disappear.

"I wonder how Aaron likes playing while they stare like that," she said. "He's holding his own. Doesn't appear to be rattled. It must be the music that calms him. Not too long ago you could get a rise out of him by sneaking up behind him and whispering *Spivey* in his ear."

"I hope you never did that."

"Me? Oh no, hon, no. I would never. Good heavens, though. Don't they look like a couple of Greek Fates standing there?"

"As though they hold something in the balance."

"Weighing their next move—and Aaron's life."

"But they're missing the third Fate," I said. "I know

who it should be, too. She could hover between them. In fact, sometimes she does."

"She'd be perfect," Ardis said.

On the dot, John arrived, looking shipshape as ever. His white beard and mustache were trimmed with precision, his trousers creased, and his Greek fisherman's hat tucked under his arm. John Yarn Berry—Yarn being his mother's maiden name—was average in looks and height, but his eyes snapped, and he had a way of walking that made it look as though he might kick up his heels and dance like Gene Kelly any minute. I'd never seen him salute anyone, or anyone salute him, but I could picture Clod doing it by reflex. Clod would certainly never refer to bearded John Berry as a rat-faced McDougal.

Ernestine puffed up the stairs on Thea's arm. They stopped for a moment at the top to let Ernestine catch her breath, Ernestine turning her thick lenses toward the music and smiling as though it were sunshine. When they joined us, John emitted a single word almost too soft to hear but as crisp as his trouser crease.

"My apologies for the Anglo-Saxon," he said. "We're about to be boarded."

Shirley and Mercy were on the move, headed for the refreshments. But at a jab from Mercy, they changed course and came straight for us. I locked my arm with Ardis's to remind her to stand on her dignity and look these Fates squarely in the eyes. Thea maneuvered Ernestine to take evasive action, and I thought I might lose Ardis, whose arm strength perhaps surpassed her dignity. Then John stopped them with a whisper of common sense.

"Hold steady. If we scatter, they'll know we met here with a purpose. Pretend we didn't."

"Hello, John. That is you, isn't it?" Ernestine asked.

"Yes," John whispered urgently. "I was just telling everyone— Oh, I see what you're doing." He switched to normal volume. "Nice to see you out and about, Ernestine. Thea, always a pleasure. Ah, Ms. Spivey and Ms. Spivey, how good to…uh…that is, the embroidery on your sweatshirts is admirable."

Shirley and Mercy beamed. Perhaps too brightly to be sincere? But their wattage turned out to be for another reason altogether.

"We just had a call," bubbled one twin.

"From Angie," bubbled the other.

"We'll need blue yarn, too!" they said together. "She's having twins!" Their cheeks grew pink enough to look unhealthy above the mint green sweatshirts.

"Congratulations," I said. "That's wonderful."

While the others offered their congratulations, Ardis whispered to me, "This puts things in perspective. I only need strength to deal with the twins occasionally. But Angie and Aaron's twins, bless their hearts, will need strength every day of their lives."

"You folks look as though you're having a meeting of some sort," one of the twins said.

"We do, don't we?" I said. "We came for the opening, and Mel's muffins lured us up here. Can I bring you something, Ernestine? John? Thea?"

"Why thank you," Ernestine said. "I was just bopping through, but why not?" She loved playing a role.

John waved me off. "I was on my way out when I saw you. The music's good, though, isn't it? I might stick around for a few more minutes."

"Great. Anything for you?" I asked the twins.

"We'll come with you," they said.

Great.

The others didn't come with us. Just as well; the talk would have been so small as to be tiny and torturous, or too full of repertory-grade baloney.

"Ladies, help yourselves." Mel smiled with all her teeth. Teeth and hair spikes together would have frightened lesser beings than the twins.

One twin put several fruit kebobs on a plate. The other added muffins. I did the same for Ernestine, Thea, and John. If John really didn't want it, Ardis wouldn't be shy.

"The dip looks interesting," the twin holding the plate said. "I wonder if it's as good as ours?"

"Would you like the recipe?" Mel asked.

"Are you willing to share?" the other twin asked.

"Sure," Mel said. "Just…" She hesitated.

"Just what?" the twin asked.

"Just not the antidote."

The Spiveys removed themselves. Not completely; they stayed where they could keep an eye on us.

"The better to give you the evil eye," Thea told Mel. She'd come over to help me carry plates and cups. "While you folks exchanged recipes over here, we discussed our goal over there. None of us has anything worth reporting. The bottom line is we bottomed out; we shopped more than we sleuthed."

"The hallmark of amateurs at a gala event," Mel said.

I glanced at the twins. They looked rooted. One had her eye on us at the table. The other watched Ardis, Ernestine, and John. "The merchants don't have time for questions, anyway," I said. "Too bad, because they're all here today. We'll have to come up with another way to get our answers."

"And you can't stand here, taking up space in front of my muffins, kebobs, and *fabulous dip* while you come up with your alternate plan, Red." Mel projected *fabulous dip* toward the twins.

I might not have seen anyone give John a salute, but Mel always deserved one, and I gave her one now. She never misinterpreted my salutes as sarcasm, either.

On our way back to join the others, a plate in each hand, I saw the rat-faced McDougal and his buddy slinking past and down the stairs.

ELEVEN

SLINKING? REALLY? OR had I let Clod's interest in the guys intrude on my objectivity? Regardless, I was missing a chance to find out who they were.

"Thea. Quick." Still holding plates, I pointed as best I could without sending fruit kebobs and muffins down the stairs after the men. "Did you see those two guys? Do you know who they are?"

"See *them*? Are you kidding? Did you see *that*? I got dip on my *shoe*. It's *suede*. Doggone it, now I'll have to go back and ask Mel what she puts in it so I can get it out without making things worse."

"Ardis, John, did you see those two who just walked past?"

"Sorry, hon. Who?"

"If you describe them, I might be able to help you," Ernestine said, peering in the wrong direction.

"Would you like me to go after them?" John asked quietly.

"I don't know—"

"If you're talking about the two who just went down the stairs, we've seen one of them before," a twin said behind me.

Thank goodness for steady nerves. I handed the endangered plates to John and Ernestine and turned to the twins. "I just wondered who they are. I haven't seen them around before. But you have?" I sounded as wooden as a kebob stick.

The twin looks on the twins' faces said, *Mmm-hmm*.

"We couldn't help overhearing," the right-hand twin said.

The twin on the left stroked an imaginary beard on her chin. "We saw that one sitting in a truck on the side of a road."

"Not just *a* road." Mercy's elbow identified her. "Angie and Aaron's road. The day of their housewarming."

"Just sitting there," Shirley said.

"Not just sitting," Mercy said. "Sitting and watching."

"Watching what?" I asked, trying to tell myself the hair on the back of my neck wasn't rising.

"The house next door to Angie's."

The twins were positive they remembered the rat-faced McDougal, and I believed them. There were a lot of things I'd question about the twins, but their eyes were sharp. They didn't know who he was, though, and it didn't sound as though they considered watching a house while sitting in a truck on the side of a road odd behavior. But of course they didn't. In Spivey World, one occasionally—or often—did things other people thought odd.

"Where are Angie and Aaron living now?" I asked.

"They're renting out in the county between here and Shady Spring," Mercy said.

"Closer to here, though," Shirley added.

I didn't want to alert their sharp eyes any more than I already had with my own odd behavior, so I didn't ask if they remembered the make of the rat-faced McDougal's truck, or if they'd happened to write down his tag number. I was grateful when John went downstairs with me, but of course we didn't see the guys again. I didn't see Clod, either.

"What is it about those two?" John asked.

I told him what I knew—not much. "I wouldn't have thought anything about them, except Cole pointed them out and asked me to let him know if I saw them again."

"So they're already on Cole's radar," John said. "That's probably as far as we can go with them, for now. Yes?"

"Hm? Oh, yes. It is."

"You're all right?"

"Yes, thanks. I thought I saw someone I knew. Thanks for coming with me, John. Even without any idea of what we were going after or getting into."

"At my age, I never know when it's my last chance to be a superhero, so I take every one I get," he said. "Now I'm going back to reclaim my muffin as a just reward. See you later."

"See you."

And now to go see if I could find...there outside Floyd's shop. A flicker of fruit flies? I'd seen something like that in the shop, too. So had Bruce. *Geneva?* But I didn't see even the smallest hint of her filmy shape. Sometimes, when she hovered around people, I could see that they caught a flicker of movement. Then they'd blink or bat at something in the air. Had Geneva come with us after all?

I saw the flicker again, moving, heading toward the back door. Like Bruce the night before, I followed.

Following fruit flies past gaggles of shoppers, even gaggles of only two or three, was not easy. I took a quick look around, didn't see anyone I knew, and called, "Geneva?" But if she'd come to the opening, after all, why hadn't she let me know? She didn't answer or flicker into view.

Around the corner in the hallway, beyond the shops, I lost sight of the fruit flies.

"Geneva?"

I saw a bit of a flicker outside one of the unmarked doors Bruce had sniffed. Then, from behind the door, I heard a faint, *"Oh."*

"Geneva?" I tried the door. Locked. "Geneva?"

And then there were the fruit flies again. They flickered their way toward the back door. They came back toward me. I followed them back to Floyd's. And I lost them. I stood outside Floyd's and understood exactly how Bruce felt when he'd stopped to scratch his ear.

I met Ardis coming down the stairs with Ernestine. Ernestine held the railing with one hand and Ardis's arm with the other.

"Thank you, Ardis. I can take it from here," Ernestine said. "Thea's picking me up at the front door. Isn't the sun nice and bright coming in those big windows?"

We watched her make her way to the door. She was more capable than we sometimes gave her credit for. She didn't drive anymore, but until the past spring she'd worked as a receptionist and secretary for a local lawyer.

"Where's the restroom?" Ardis asked.

"I'll join you."

I took her to the back hallway, wondering if I should tell her about Geneva. It was quieter around the corner, quiet enough to hear the soft, sad voice singing behind the unmarked door.

"What am I hearing?" Ardis asked.

There were people coming down the hall behind us.

Ardis put her ear to the door. "It's hypnotizing. Who do you think—"

"Shh, Ardis." I smiled and waved at the women passing us. Then I yanked on Ardis's sleeve. It startled her, but when she looked at me, I whispered, "No one else can hear it." That startled her more, until she realized what I meant.

"Hon." She looked at the door. "I've never—" She nodded at a man looking for the men's room. "What's she doing in there? I've never heard anything like it in my life."

I had. I'd heard Geneva sing the peculiar dirgelike lullaby when she felt most depressed, or to someone else she thought was dying. I whispered that to Ardis, between people passing to and from the restroom.

"She shouldn't be alone," Ardis said. "She needs us."

"The door's locked."

Ardis tried anyway.

A young woman towing two small children came down the hall, the children singing about wheels on a bus going round and round. Their piping voices and joyful tune clanged and clattered against the lullaby they couldn't hear.

"Try calling her," Ardis said. "I'll let you know when someone's coming."

I called, trying to project my voice—softly, which made no sense. I knocked and tried putting my lips to the crack between the door and the jamb. She didn't hear me, or heard and didn't answer.

"Wait," I whispered to Ardis. "We don't need to whisper."

"Why not?" she whispered back.

"Because we're just talking about a friend."

She bounced the heel of her hand off her forehead. "It takes some getting used to, doesn't it?" she said in her normal voice.

"It does, and I wish *Geneva* would let us know what's going on. I get worried when she doesn't answer. I thought *Geneva* was here."

Geneva didn't answer. Her singing didn't falter.

"This isn't good," I said, whispering again. "We probably shouldn't have touched the doorknob."

"Wipe it?"

I shook my head. Maybe Geneva's song was getting to me. I felt like I might cry.

"It's all right, hon," Ardis said. "I know what to do. I'll be right back."

I took out my phone and leaned against the door feigning interest in it. I looked up when I heard Joe's soft *hey*. If I ever heard Geneva's lullaby in his sweet, deep voice it would break my heart.

"Ardis said she'd watch the shop," he said. "Do I want to know why she says you need to get in here?"

I shook my head a very little bit, afraid what sound might come out if I shook it any harder. I was also that little bit afraid to know why Ardis thought Joe could get me in there. But we needed to get in. "You can open it?"

"Not if you're standing in front of it. It's a storeroom. I've got keys. We all do."

Did I know that? Blame it on being rattled.

He nodded for me to move aside.

"But don't touch it," I said. "Don't touch the door or the knob if you can help it."

"It's kind of fussy. It helps to pull up on the knob while you turn the key."

"I'll do it. Ardis and I already touched it."

Joe handed me the keys. He was right about the fussy lock. I was rattled and it rattled, but with a bit of jiggling, and after applying John's crisp Anglo-Saxon, the key slid into place and I opened the door into a narrow, deep, dark closet.

Geneva crouched there, on the floor, rocking and singing, next to Belinda. Belinda lay on the floor, face-down, silent and unmoving, a pair of scissors sticking out of her back.

TWELVE

MY FIRST THOUGHT should have been to check for a pulse.
Or to tell Joe to call 911. To scream? No, that wouldn't help
anyone at all. All I wanted to do was the impossible—
hug a ghost who mourned for a soul she'd never known.

Geneva looked around when the light from the hall
spilled into the narrow space. She didn't stop rocking
and singing, and she continued as I knelt and reached for
the side of Belinda's neck. No pulse. Skin cool but not
cold. Had I seen anyone near the door or leaving the area
when I followed the fruit flies? I couldn't remember.

I held out my hand to Geneva and asked quietly, "Did
you see anyone?"

"Don't touch anything else," Joe said. He blocked
some of the light while also blocking the view of anyone passing. "But to answer your question, no, I didn't
see anyone. Or, I saw plenty of people, but no one who
looked like they'd… I called 911. I'd better call Sierra,
too. You should come out, Kath. We'll close the door.
Keep folks from…"

It was so easy to trail off. Easy to lose the thread.
Don't touch anything, Joe had said. But I had to. For
Belinda's sake, if it would help find who did this to
her. I brushed my fingertips across the fabric of her
blouse, afraid of what I would feel. *A whisper. Like a
secret. Like something hidden away in a box in a corner.* I had no clue at all how that could help. I looked at

Geneva, one of *my* secrets, and whispered, "Come out with me," and she did.

Sierra arrived before we'd pulled the door shut.

"That was fast," Joe said.

Geneva shivered beside me.

"I was on the back stairs when you called," Sierra said. "You might be surprised what I *don't* consider an emergency on a day like this. So what is it?"

I let Joe tell her. She didn't seem to believe him at first. That made sense, really, because who would think... Those trailing threads again. I looked at Geneva. She huddled next to me against the wall, but she was beginning to come around. I waited until she looked at me. Then I used some of Argyle's universal cat sign language—I gave her the slow blink of comfort and connection.

Sierra insisted on seeing for herself, first putting her head around the door, and then, keeping a hand on the doorframe, stepping inside. She spent more time looking than I'd wanted to, maybe letting her eyes get used to the dark, maybe taking that long to process the tragedy. When she finally backed away from the door, the cherry red of her hair stood out more dramatically against her pale cheeks. Like me, she didn't scream, but she did stammer.

"We should, we can't just, we, um, can we, can we work *around* this?"

"Work around how?" Joe asked. He sounded slightly strained, as though he'd had to keep a less strained *what the hell* from slipping out.

"I mean, look, we close the door. We lock it. That preserves the, the scene, and we wait until we close tonight—no. *No.*" She worried that away with small shakes of her head, wrapping her arms around herself. "No. Wrong idea. Wrongwrongwrong. But the opening, can we at least, is there some way we can salvage it?"

"Let's see what the deputies tell us," Joe said.

"Close off this area?" Sierra asked. "With a screen or something?"

"The restrooms and emergency exit are back here," I said. "Talk to the deputies."

"But the door," Sierra said.

"Don't touch the—" I didn't bother to finish that.

Sierra didn't listen, anyway. She grabbed the door-knob and pulled the door the last few inches shut. It probably didn't matter. If there had been any useful prints, my hand and Ardis's had probably already made them hopeless.

Rogalla was the first official to respond. He looked from Joe to Sierra. "Where?"

"It isn't a fire," Sierra said.

Joe nodded to the door.

Sierra hadn't moved from in front of it and didn't then. "Shouldn't we wait for the real—"

"I'm real enough," Rogalla said.

"You're wearing running shorts."

"He's an EMT," I said. "He's trained. Come on over here. We should think about closing—"

"We can't," Sierra said. "We can't close."

"Come on over here and let me finish." I took a few steps back, and she followed. So did Geneva. I saw Rogalla slip into the storage room. "I meant the hallway. Like you said, Sierra, we should close it off, at least for now. You don't want little kids coming along here and seeing this. There are all kinds of problems with people walking by."

Joe had already moved to the corner in the hall. I couldn't hear his words, but presumably he was turning people back. Then I heard two burps of radio static, and as Rogalla backed out of the storage room and closed the door, Clod arrived. On Clod's heels another radio burped static, this one attached to Deputy Shorty Munroe. Clod's jeans and T-shirt looked happier now that they were doing something official. Shorty's uniform and eyes looked equally tired. Shorty seemed to share Clod's opinion of Rogalla—tolerant in professional matters and like members of opposing teams in everything else. For the time being, they cooperated. Clod and Rogalla went into the storage room. Shorty stood with us.

"You probably want us to get out of your way," Sierra said.

"No ma'am," Shorty said. "For now, we'd like you to stay right here." He must have had a first name other than Shorty, but I'd never heard it. The nickname hadn't taken any imagination; he wasn't much taller than me, and he looked more like my idea of an accountant than Rogalla did. I always expected to see a pencil behind his ear. He wore wire-rimmed glasses that looked as though he'd picked them up in Floyd's antique shop or borrowed them from Ebenezer Scrooge's overworked clerk. Where Clod's eyes always looked alert but pained, Shorty's, though tired, looked ready to laugh. His voice was pure Willie Nelson.

Clod looked up and down the hallway when he and Rogalla came out of the storage room. He called to Joe, still at the bend in the hallway. "You all right there?"

Joe nodded.

"Has anyone cleared the restrooms?" Clod asked.

"I'll go," Sierra said.

"Shorty will. More than one stall in each?"

Sierra held up three fingers.

Shorty took off down the hall.

"I'm sure, now, you really would like us to get out of your way," Sierra said.

"Not just yet," Clod said. "Who found the body?"

Geneva looked at me and raised her hand. I raised mine, too. "Solemn solidarity," she whispered. It was good to have her acting more normally again.

"Cat got your tongue, Ms. Rutledge?" Clod asked.

"What? No. I opened the door."

"Why?" Sierra asked. "How?"

"We'll get to that, Ms. Estep, but thank you," Clod said. "Did you go in, Ms. Rutledge?"

"Yes."

"We'll need to talk to you. Did anyone else besides you and Rogalla touch the door or go inside?"

While I hesitated, waiting for Sierra to say she had, Shorty emerged from the men's room, knocked on the women's, and then went in. Sierra crossed her arms and looked on the verge of a pout, but she didn't say anything.

"Did Joe?" Clod prompted.

"He was with me," I said. "But I'm the one who opened the door and went in. As far as I know, Ardis, Rogalla, Sierra, and I are the only ones." I hoped the way I slipped Sierra's name into that short list sounded natural and not like finger pointing.

Geneva squashed that hope by repeatedly pointing both index fingers at Sierra, as though directing traffic straight at her.

Clod flattened it further. "Any reason you didn't offer that information, Ms. Estep?"

"Because it was obvious." Sierra barely kept the derisive *duh* in her voice in check. "Of course I went in. I'm the director. When Joe told me what happened, I was obliged to verify that report. I had a legitimate reason to go in. A legal reason, even. I'm responsible for the building and what happens—"

Shorty came out of the women's room, and Clod cut Sierra off with a terse, "Thank you."

"I'm not finished."

"Thank you, Ms. Estep," Clod said. "We'll take all of that into consideration. We'll want to speak with you further, and we will try to cause as little disruption as possible."

Instead of rejoining us, Shorty stationed himself at the back door. He and Clod exchanged nods that must have meant something to them. Then Shorty replanted his feet and hooked his thumbs in his belt—probably meant to show he couldn't be budged. Considering his general pencil-pusher vibe, it was kind of adorable, but I would never say so to anyone who might repeat it to him.

"Out of respect for the deceased, please do not pass along any information before an official statement is made," Clod said. "That includes phone calls and text messages."

"You can't confiscate our phones, can you?" Sierra asked.

"We'll trust your good sense," Clod said. "A statement will be released as soon as possible. Now, if you'll please wait here, I'll be back momentarily."

Rogalla started after him but stopped at a look from Clod.

"What are they going to do?" Sierra asked.

"Procedure," Rogalla said. "Protocol. Logistics."

"I meant specifically. And what are they talking about?"

"I'm not a lip reader," Rogalla said.

"I always want to know what they're talking about at a time like this, too," I said, trying to sound reassuring, like an old hand. *An old murder hand.* A chill ran down my spine. "For now, though, we wait. That's the way this works."

"But I'm the director," Sierra said. "I should be part of that conversation."

"You will be soon enough," I said.

"What's *that* supposed to mean?" Sierra asked.

"Just that—"

"That I just heard my cue." Geneva said, and she darted down the hall to make the deputy duo a weird trio.

"Just what?" Sierra demanded.

"They're trying to decide the best way to handle this!" Geneva shouted over Clod's shoulder. "They have a building full of potential witnesses. Should they shut everything down now? Let everyone go? Make everyone stay? Big decision! Maybe take some heat? Ramifications! What's a lawman to do?"

She sounded like a newsie trying to sell papers by reading out the headlines. I was sorely tempted to show off my "lip reading" skills by repeating her, but a nanosecond's thought convinced me there were too many ways that could backfire. "I just meant that situations like this can get confusing really fast," I told Sierra.

"They're wondering if the murderer is still in the building!" Geneva yelled at the top of her lungs. "Deputy Munroe says that he hopes so. He wants to solve this thing fast and tie the perp up with a bow. That rhymes.

I should take up shouted-word poetry. Is that a thing? Now Deputy Dunbar is complaining. He says any trail the perp left is being trampled. He's probably talking about *her*." She pointed at Sierra. "We should call her the treacherous trampler."

Clod probably meant everyone in the building, not just Sierra. She paced back and forth, looking neurotic and a lot younger and less polished than she had when she'd greeted Ardis and me at the front door earlier. Clod and Shorty were blocking her access to the back stairs, but at this point even the Empire State Building might not have enough stairs to relieve the stress from this wretched ending to her promising grand opening.

Geneva suddenly whooped. "Deputy Dunbar just said they have a building full of meddlers, too. He looked straight at you when he said that. Such a card, our Deputy Dunbar."

My next sore temptation was to shout, *Thanks a lot, Clod!* I refrained, although he might have wondered why I gave him a nasty look when he returned from talking with Shorty.

"You need me to stick around?" Rogalla asked.

"You're dismissed," Clod said. "We have it covered and it's pretty obvious we don't need an expert in CPR at this point. Or possums."

They stared at each other, as though each dared the other to put 'em up. They'd actually come to blows a month or so earlier, hence Clod's anger management sessions. Clod looked away first, and Rogalla made a tough-guy exit past Joe. He had the good grace not to sneer, and Clod gave him the grace of a thirty-second head start so it didn't look as though he was following him. Then Clod went over to have a word with Joe. Geneva and I didn't give Clod the grace of even two seconds; we followed right behind.

"Closing?" Joe asked.

"Have to," Clod said.

That's when I realized Sierra hadn't come with us. I glanced back and saw her fiddling with her phone. If I were Clod, would I tell her to put it away? If I were Geneva, would I go read texts over Sierra's shoulder? I was glad I didn't have to make either decision.

"Has anyone spoken to Russell?" Joe asked.

"Who?" I asked.

Clod gave me an *ahem* sort of look. "Who's Russell?"

"Belinda's husband," Joe said. "Ex. He's in Belle's. Her shop."

"You didn't think to tell me that sooner?" Clod asked.

"Did you want me to interrupt your discussion with Shorty? Maybe I should have gotten in between you and Rogalla?"

"Smart-ass."

"When he said 'as little disruption possible,' I believed him," Sierra said an hour later.

It felt like two or three. At Clod's request, more deputies had descended on the Vault to respectfully take names and contact information from visitors and merchants before shooing them out the door. Ardis, Joe, Sierra, and I had been asked to stay. Geneva stayed, too, although she wasn't hanging around in the gallery with us or the deputy standing solidly in front of Belinda's shop.

"I pictured little to *no* disruption," Sierra said as she passed us, and then the deputy, on another lap around the gallery. "*Minimal* disruption. I call this *catastrophic* disruption."

"*She* certainly keeps disrupting any chance we have of quiet or calm while we're waiting," Ardis said under her breath.

"She's just worried and blowing off steam," I said. "Maybe scared, too. Any idea where Geneva is?"

"Lord love a dead duck," Ardis whispered. She glanced around, not very subtly, and then shrugged.

"Whispering isn't cool," Sierra called from across the gallery. "It makes the people who know that you're whispering paranoid."

"Sorry, hon," Ardis said. "I'm an angst mutterer. Give me something to be anxious about and I'll jump at the least little peep and then mutter 'til the ducks come home to roost, which isn't something ducks do, so there's my problem in an eggshell. I tell you what, though, let me do the worrying and the muttering for all of us. I'm a certified expert. Or maybe certifiable. But that way you can sit down and try to relax."

"Not unless I can sit in my office," Sierra said on her way past again. "And it won't be to relax. I can't relax in the middle of a nightmare. They had the whole building to choose from, and they couldn't talk to Dusty or Rusty or whoever he is somewhere else?"

"It's Russell," I said.

"But why my office? And where'd he come from, anyway? And why don't they haul him off to *their* office?"

"I think you're right," Ardis whispered to me. Then she called to a scowling Sierra as she marched past the enamel shop, "I'm just telling Kath she's right. If walking in circles helps you blow off steam, then march on, hon, march on." In a quick aside to me she whispered, "How many laps has she done? I'm not sure it's working."

I wasn't sure, either. I felt sorry for Sierra and her ruined event, but she had to know her office provided more privacy than the open plan of the shops and gallery. Ardis, Joe, and I sat in the chairs intended for people who'd wanted to take a load off while they enjoyed the music in the gallery. The musicians had packed up and left, along with Mel and the refreshments. Early in our wait, Shorty and the other deputy had been in and out of Belinda's shop. Then Shorty disappeared down the back stairs and we continued to wait.

Ardis sat bolt upright, making her folding chair look even less comfortable than it was. I tried to look calm, but sitting on the edge of my chair probably gave me away. Joe accomplished both sitting and relaxing beautifully, his legs stretched out and his hands knitted behind his head. He might have been thinking about fishing, a go-to topic for him, but I chose to believe the furrows between his eyebrows meant he was asking himself some of the same questions that kept me from relaxing. Not all of my questions, though. He didn't have Geneva to worry about.

She hadn't floated off with Clod when he'd asked Russell to accompany him to Sierra's office. She'd stayed quietly near me, growing hazier as we waited, even though she'd enjoyed eavesdropping on Clod and Shorty earlier. Her quiet could mean she was thinking things over. As she said, thoughts of death and dying came naturally to her. But she was a mercurial soul, infatuated with the make-believe world of TV detectives, and she had trouble turning off her excitement over real-life deputies. She might have been floating in a melancholy funk somewhere nearby, but if I were given a guess, I'd say Clod had a nosy ghost hanging over his shoulder while he interviewed Russell.

While I enjoyed that image and finally began to relax, Ardis nudged my shoulder. "Look sharp and don't laugh. Stubborn cop, short cop, and ghost cop just walked in."

THIRTEEN

GENEVA THOUGHT THE appearance of any law officer
would be improved with a swagger. If Clod and Shorty
had seen her, they could have learned how to do it from
the swagger master. Even without her guidance, Clod's
official deputy posture and blank face gave nothing
away. And although Shorty's uniform might look as if
it wanted to yawn, his posture was no less crisp and no
more communicative than Clod's.

Geneva's swagger didn't give anything away, either,
and neither did her yell. "All rise!"

I started to get up. Ardis stopped me with a hand on
my shoulder. "We'll be respectful, but we don't want
it going to Cole's head. Or hers. Do you think they've
solved it that fast? She looks triumphant."

"She looks like her hero," I whispered back. "Bar-
ney Fife."

Joe couldn't have heard Ardis from where he sat, but
he took the same casual approach to Clod's entrance.
He re-crossed his ankles but otherwise didn't interrupt his languid ruminations by so much as glancing
at his brother.

When Sierra saw the deputies, she cut her current
gallery circuit short and marched over to meet them.
"Well?" she said, stopping in front of Clod. "Did the
ex-husband do it?"

Before answering, Clod dismissed the deputy who'd

been standing at the entrance of Belinda's shop, and then he turned back to Sierra. "The sheriff will release an official statement later today."

"But Belinda's ex did do it, didn't he?" Sierra asked. "I mean, I'm sorry, I truly am. I'm beyond horrified. I can't even tell you how… I've never been involved in something like this. But I have to be practical. I don't want to sound callous, but if you've arrested him, can we reopen? This afternoon?"

"As I said, the official statement will come out later today."

"That doesn't tell me what I need to know." Sierra looked as though she wanted to stomp her foot. I felt her pain. I often wanted to stomp a foot when Clod was being officious. Usually his.

"Here's the way it works," Clod said. "You tell us what we need to know and then we'll give you what information we can. If it helps, it's been my experience that a situation like this won't hurt your business. It might even help. Ms. Buchanan and Ms. Rutledge will probably back me up on that."

Clod, Shorty, and Geneva looked at us. Sierra didn't. Ardis and I nodded anyway.

"I wouldn't worry too much," Shorty said with his Willie Nelson twang. "Looked like you had a good turnout this morning. Folks'll be back."

"Is that your *professional* opinion?" Sierra asked.

Shorty didn't appear to take offense, but Geneva huffed a bit.

"What about tomorrow?" Sierra demanded.

"We'll know when the official statement comes out later today." Clod, still playing cool cop, sounded just as calm repeating that for the third time. Geneva gave him a thumbs-up. Sierra might have swallowed some-thing rude.

Shorty took on the role of placatory cop. "Would you be more comfortable ssitting down, Ms. Estep?"

"No."

"Fine, we have a few questions, then," Clod said.

"The Arts Council Board will have a few, too," Sierra snapped. She immediately put both hands to her mouth and looked at the floor. "Excuse me," she said in a smaller voice. "I'm sorry. I'm rattled."

"We understand," Clod said.

"Thank you."

Ardis used her honeysuckle to cut through the last shreds of Sierra's bravado. "Sierra, honey, come sit next to me and we'll get through this together." She patted the chair on the other side of her. Sierra came and sat on the chair's edge, and Ardis patted her knee.

"Thank you," Sierra said again.

"Be sure to thank Ms. Rutledge, too," Clod said. He followed that remark with an odd, guttural noise.

"Gesundheit," Geneva said, and pretended to wipe something from her sleeve.

Everyone else looked blank.

"I mean," Clod said, "you should thank her, because if she'd gone nosing around in storage closets earlier, then you wouldn't have had even as much business as you did. You would have had to close earlier."

"Zing!" Geneva shouted.

"Zing, *indeed*," Ardis said, sitting up straighter and skewering Clod with an affronted glare.

That actually made me laugh, and between Ardis's seeming non sequitur and my reaction, Clod lost some of his starch. He scratched a spot below his right ear.

His resemblance to Rogalla's Bruce, puzzling over the presence or absence of possums, really was uncanny.

Ardis muttered a soft *oops*. Then she went on the offensive. "We don't have time for tasteless jokes, Coleridge. I believe I can speak for Kath, Ten, and Gen—and Sierra—when I say that we're happy to help with your investigation into this terrible crime in whatever way we can."

"Thank you, Ms. Buchanan."

"So sit down and ask your questions."

"Yes, ma'am."

Clod and Shorty pulled chairs around to sit facing us. Now that it was getting serious, Joe pulled in his legs, put his elbows on his knees, and rested his chin on the tips of his fingers. Shorty stifled a yawn.

"Before we get into the specifics of the incident this morning," Clod said, "I'd like some background information to flesh out the details of the report."

Sierra tipped her head, trying to bring his request into focus. "Like…"

"What you know about how this enterprise got started. The impetus. The people involved. The people interested in its success. That kind of thing."

Now Shorty tipped his head at Clod, and Joe's eyes shifted from phantom fish at his toes to his brother's face. *That kind of thing?* What did Clod mean by that? What was *he* fishing for?

"Everyone I've met is interested in the Vault's success," Sierra said. "And I think you know that Garland Brown was a huge supporter. He and the Arts Council recognized, early on, that there's been a revitalization of the arts community in Blue Plum and the surrounding area. Now, with the Vault, we're in the forefront. The details of the renovations—"

Sierra continued, but the easily bored ghost caught my attention when she propped her elbow on Shorty's shoulder. "Lecturey," Geneva said through a yawn.

It did sound like a practiced spiel, like something Sierra had delivered in one form or another while making the rounds of Blue Plum civic clubs. When she stopped for breath, Shorty, who didn't seem to be on the same page as Clod (and might be as easily bored as Geneva), uttered something odd: "Arrrr."

Sierra cut herself off and stared at Shorty. "Excuse me? Are you mocking me?"

"No, no," Shorty said, turning pink. "Sorry. I'm in the middle of a never-ending remodeling project for my folks. Renovate, repurpose, revitalize, rejuvenate— those *R*s you're talking about haunt my nightmares. But you're right; this place has the *R*s covered."

"Revenant," Geneva said. "Regurgitate."

"Ridiculous," Ardis muttered beside me.

"Let's move on," Clod said. "Who took the reins, so to speak, after Mr. Brown's death?"

"No one person that I can think of," Sierra said. "The project was virtually complete when he…died. The members were devastated, of course, but plans for the opening were in place, and it was more a question of dotting *i*s and crossing *t*s."

"Joe? Ms. Buchanan? Ms. Rutledge?" Clod asked. "Any insight on that?"

Rutledge. Arrrr. Russell.

"Ms. Rutledge?"

"Oh, sorry. But why would Russell kill Belinda? If

they were on such good terms that he was helping her in the shop, then I don't get that."

"Thank you, Ms. Rutledge," Clod said. "We'll take your opinion into consideration."

"And please be sure to wipe your feet," Geneva said. "He's dripped sarcasm all over the floor."

"She has a point, Coleridge," Ardis said. "Kath does, I mean." She sat forward and looked at me and Joe. "Are either of you members of the Arts Council?" We shook our heads. "Are you familiar with the accused?" We shook our heads, again.

"I don't know him, either," Sierra said.

"That clears that up, then." Ardis sat back, crossed her arms, and looked at Clod as though she planned to revoke his parole. "We can add little or nothing to help you flesh out your report."

"Some of us have no flesh at all," Geneva said.

Clod, who tended to watch his manners with his elders, thanked Ardis with less sarcasm than he'd thanked me. "Even so," he said, "Ms. Estep, will you please give us a rundown on how this place operates? Is each shop independent?"

"Are they even shops?" Shorty asked. "Most of them aren't any bigger than the booths out at the flea market. Joe's isn't even as big as the closet where you all found the body."

"Call Joe's a shoppette, then," Ardis said. "You don't mind that, do you, Joe?"

"Suits me."

"Ms. Estep?" Clod said. "How the Vault operates. A general idea, if you don't mind."

Sierra launched into another recitation. Geneva groaned, then lay on her back, floated up to the ceiling, and pretended to snore. I felt like joining her. Instead I wondered what Clod was gleaning from this. Was he absorbing the information, or were he and Shorty looking for something else? Were Ardis, Joe, and I being used as extras in a scene they'd engineered?

"Excuse me, Ms. Estep," Ardis interrupted. "The Arts Council obviously hired the right person for this job. I applaud your grasp of details and your energy. If you don't mind, though, I have another suggestion for Deputy Dunbar."

"What would that be, Ms. Buchanan?" Clod asked.

"If you have more pertinent questions that might wrap this up faster, why don't we get to them? You're busy, we're busy, and I have a sitter I'll need to rescue from Daddy sooner or later."

Clod's excellent poker face didn't tell me how he felt about Ardis's interruption. But why did he break eye contact with her? Was it a cloddish lapse in manners? Easy enough to believe. Or did he not trust his poker face to her expert scrutiny?

"Are storage rooms and the back door normally kept locked, Ms. Estep?" Clod asked.

"Yes."

"Yesterday, when Ms. Moyer reported the vandalism to her tablecloth, Al Rogalla and I went out the back door. It wasn't locked. But I understand your merchants were still moving things in."

"And you can always get *out*," Sierra said. "But it's locked from the outside. It takes a key to get back in."

"We also came back in," Clod said.

"It should have been locked," Sierra said.

"Was it locked properly today?"

"The last time I checked, yes."

"When would that have been?"

During the second or two it took Sierra to answer that question, Geneva floated back down beside Clod and stuck her thumbs in an imaginary belt. A glance at Joe showed a narrowing of his left eye. Ardis leaned very slightly forward, although she might have been reacting to Geneva more than to Sierra's minuscule hesitation.

Or did I imagine all of that? And imagined that Clod and Shorty were looking for significance in insignificant words and actions?

"I didn't go around checking all the doors before we opened this morning," Sierra said. "I did before I went up to my apartment last night. It was locked then. I've told the merchants not to leave it unlocked."

"She did," Joe said.

"Who has keys?" Shorty asked.

"All the merchants," Sierra said.

"Board members?" Clod asked.

"Not all," Sierra said.

"Did Garland Brown?" Clod asked.

"I'm sorry; I should know that, but I don't."

"We'll need a list of the merchants and their contact information."

"Your deputies went around collecting that information before closing us down, didn't they?"

"It will be better to have an official list," Clod said. "Board members, too, whether or not you know if they have keys."

"But when did this happen?" Sierra asked. "She was in her shop."

"You saw her there?" Shorty asked.

It didn't surprise me that Sierra sounded defensive by

then. Geneva surprised me, though, by maintaining her focus and standing beside Clod. She had great respect for the fictional cops in '50s and '60s television shows, but she often showed less respect for him. If possible, she now looked more stuffed and starched than he did.

"We had a sort of pep rally before we opened," Sierra said. "I thought it would be fun. Get us in the spirit and get us going for the day."

"What time was that?" Shorty asked. "And where?"

"Here in the gallery. Nine-thirty."

"Ms. Moyer attended?" Clod asked.

"Of course. I brought donuts. Everyone shows up for donuts, right?"

"Was Ms. Moyer's ex-husband at the rally?" Clod asked.

"I—there were some people I didn't know. People here to assist the merchants. The musicians. The caterer." Sierra looked at Joe. "Did you see her ex?"

"Sorry," Joe said. "I missed it."

"Where were you?" Clod asked.

"In the shoppette. Had a few more browns to tie."

"Isn't that always the way?" Shorty said. "You can always use another fly."

"That's been my experience," Joe said. "I heard the cheering, though. It sounded nice and peppy."

"Well, I'm sure Belinda was there," Sierra said. "She was hard enough to miss. And the ex must have been there, too, unless *he* had one more thing to tie. But you still haven't said when it happened. Or how."

"We'll be able to answer those questions better when the official statement is released later today," Clod said.

Geneva's staunch pose slipped then. She shook her head, pinching the bridge of her nose. I couldn't tell if she meant it as a comment on Sierra's repeated question or Clod's repeated lack of information.

"Ms. Rutledge," Clod said, "a few questions for you."

"Excuse me, may I go now?" Sierra asked.

"Not just yet."

She'd already started to get up and dropped back into the chair with the grace of a sullen teen. If Geneva's hollow eyes could skewer, they would have skewered Sierra.

Sierra wrapped her arms around herself and crossed her legs. Closing herself off?

"Ms. Rutledge?"

Had Clod actually asked me a question? I glanced at him. Talk about skewering. "Sorry. Would you mind repeating that?"

"I haven't asked anything yet."

"Good. Then I haven't missed anything. What *would* you like to ask?"

"When you found Ms. Moyer this morning was the storage room door locked or unlocked?"

"Locked."

"Locked," Sierra echoed. "See? Properly locked, like I said." Her arms didn't unlock themselves, though.

"I asked Joe to open the closet for Kath," Ardis said. "And as we've already established, merchants have keys."

"Thank you, Ms. Buchanan. Ms. Rutledge, are you in any way a part of this business?"

"This—"

But Geneva got in ahead of me. "Absolutely *not!*" She reared back and looked at Clod. "She did *not* murder that woman!"

A jolt of adrenaline like a lightning bolt woke up every last cell in my body. Was *that* what he meant?

"Did you really just ask—what do you mean by 'this business'? Are you asking if I'm involved in this murder? Because the answer is absolutely *not!*"

Clod didn't close his eyes and massage his forehead, but I could hear it in his voice. "No, Ms. Rutledge." He swirled a finger around the gallery. "I only meant *this* business. Are you part of the Blue Plum Vault? Are you expanding your business horizons?"

"False alarm," Geneva called. "False alarm. It's okay, folks. Huge relief. My bad. But *are* we expanding our business?"

I *did* close my eyes and massage my forehead. "No, we aren't expanding."

"We have quite enough excitement in our lives as it is," Ardis said. "And quite often *too* much."

"There's no need to be insulting," Geneva said. "I was only asking."

Then Clod asked the question I'd been dreading, the one I knew he or Shorty would have to ask. I'd been trying to think of a reasonable answer to it from the moment I'd opened the door and found Belinda. Answering the question I *thought* he'd asked—did I have anything to do with her death—had been easy, if horrifying. This question, though...

"Why did you need to get into the storeroom this morning?"

Because I heard a ghost mourning.

Ardis started to say something. Clod put up a hand. "I want to hear from Ms. Rutledge."

Because I knew I'd find a body.

"Does it matter why?" Joe asked.

"*I* think it might," Sierra said.

"Ms. Rutledge?" Clod prompted.

"A dustpan," Geneva said. "Tell the flatfoot you were looking for a dustpan."

"She was looking for a dustpan," Ardis blurted.

"Popular item," Clod said. "Ms. Moyer had one in her hand."

"I wonder if that was another oops on my part," Geneva said.

"One more quick question, Ms. Rutledge," Clod said. "About the scissors in Ms. Moyer's back. They're labeled 'Weaver's Cat.' Any idea why?"

My shoulders rose. If I'd been a cat, and on my feet, I would have danced away from Clod's question with my back arched.

"*Our* scissors?" Ardis and Geneva asked.

"You didn't notice?" Clod looked only at me.

I shook my head. *How? Who?*

He kept looking at me but didn't say anything else—so of course I did.

"You know very well why I didn't notice. There were more important details to notice. Like whether or not she was breathing. Whether or not there was any hope. And there were more important things to do than notice a small label on a murder weapon that I really, really didn't want to look at."

Ardis or Joe might have tried to say something. I didn't let them.

"So now I have a quick question for you, Deputy. How long *has* she been dead? You must have some idea. And did those scissors really kill her? Because that would have to be an awfully lucky jab. In the upper back like that? With all the bones that could have stopped the blades? Belinda was a big woman—and the blades on those scissors aren't very long."

"That was at least two questions," Geneva said.

"More long-winded than quick," said Shorty.

"How do you know how long or short the blades are?" Clod asked.

"If they're from the Weaver's Cat, as you claim, then I have some knowledge of blade length."

Geneva hovered between Clod and Shorty, making them look like a weird trio again. She was enjoying herself, and she leaned a smug elbow on Clod's shoulder.

"We'll all know more when the official statement is released," Clod said. He didn't know Geneva was there, but from the way he rolled his shoulder and then rubbed it, he felt the chill of her presence. He stood up, leaving her hanging in the air. She rubbed her elbow and stuck her tongue out at him.

"Good for you," I said. I meant that for Geneva, but I was happy to let Clod interpret it any way he liked. He chose to turn his back on me. Good for him.

So what was going on? What trail was Clod chasing? Were his questions and this strange après crime conference only to do with Belinda's death, or was he casting a wider net?

And what about Belinda's wonderful tablecloth? Did she die because of *it*? I had no reason to believe that, but more than ever, I wanted to know the history, the story, the *secrets* of the poor shredded thing. And that showed how callous I was. Did I really feel more hurt and sorrow over the tablecloth than I did Belinda? I closed my eyes and tried to see one of the cloth's peaceful, playful squirrels.

"You've been dismissed," Geneva said in my ear, making me jump. "You're sitting there, taking a nap, and your menfolk are standing over there yukking it up over some manly pursuit."

Joe, Clod, and Shorty were only standing five or six feet away. I wanted to tell her they were quietly talking, not yukking, and that they weren't *my* menfolk, but I didn't want to miss any more of what they were saying than I already had. And I wanted to know why Joe and Clod were both rubbing the backs of their necks. Shorty seemed to be immune to that ailment; he stood with his hands in his pockets, his fists ruining the lines of his already droopy uniform. Sierra and Ardis were lost in their phones.

"I didn't get much of a look," Joe said. "They weren't interested in flies or watercolors, so they didn't interest me."

"Who are they talking about?" Geneva asked.

I put a finger to my lips to hush her. It didn't work; she wasn't looking at me.

"Do you see how your beau mimics his brother? When that happens on television, it often indicates an attempt to prove sincerity."

I tried quietly shushing her. That didn't work, either.

"Some sort of hilarity usually follows," she said, "but the brothers don't look like they're about to break into guffaws or start capering."

"He didn't hike much these days," Joe said. "I doubt he'd be out there hiking by himself."

"*Now* who are they talking about?" Geneva asked. "Why do they keep leaving out vital details?"

"Or that he couldn't find a better or more comfortable place for a roll in the hay if that theory's right—" Shorty cut off the rest of that and squinted at me. I'd just tried getting Geneva's attention again. It might have looked as though I'd been practicing semaphore. I slapped my hands together, catching an imaginary mosquito for good measure. The clap shook Ardis away from her screen.

"Men," she said. She put away her phone and got to her feet. So did Sierra. "Elderly men in particular," Ardis added. "Daddy's got it into his head he has a date with Mama at the roadhouse tonight. Dancing. And you three"—she pointed at the men—"can quit your grinning. Your senile days are coming, and you'll be lucky if you have someone as tolerant as I am to put up with all your natural-born foolishness. The way you switch gears from somber to snickering isn't decent."

"If you need me to take Hank off your hands this evening, I'll be happy to," Joe said.

"You're kind, Ten, but I can wrangle the old devil."

"Switching back," Clod said, "did you happen to notice a couple of men this morning, one with a beard, Ms. Buchanan?"

"That's so generic a description as to be useless," Ardis said. "Kath? Are you going back to the shop? I want you to call me if you hear anything or if you need anything. Or if anyone bothers you further about dustpans or scissors. I might have to bring Daddy along, but you call me."

"Don't you worry, young 'un," Geneva said, flapping around her. "I'll make sure she gets back safe and sound through the mean and wild streets of this den of iniquitous Blue Plums and pandering buffoons. Danger won't know who it's messing with if it tries waltzing past me."

"Thank you. Thanks, Ardis, I appreciate it."

I did sincerely appreciate the offers, but I also wanted

to bat them both out of the way. I'd forgotten about the rat-faced McDougal, and I'd forgotten to tell Clod what the Spiveys said about seeing him, too. "Deputy Dunbar, I saw—"

"*I* saw them," Sierra interrupted.

We all looked at her, Geneva stopping mid-flap and looking like a large, lacy bat.

"You described them better to Joe," Sierra said. "I'm sure I saw them, though, doing just what you said. Walking around, not really shopping. Do you know who they were? Why do you want to know?"

"Curiosity more than anything," Clod said. That was pretty much what he'd told me, too, but now it sounded more like a brush-off—as smooth and uninformative as his poker face.

Sierra must have felt the brush-off, too. "You're sure?" she said. "Because you know what they say about curiosity, and I'd hate to think you arrested the wrong man for this murder."

"Thank you for the info, Ms. Estep," Shorty said. "That you happened to notice them, out of all the folks here, proves you've got a good eye. You're asking good questions, too. Never stop asking questions. My daddy taught me that, and that feller Einstein backed him up. Best thing to do, now, is let us handle things. We'll keep you posted."

"Sure," Sierra said, not sounding as sure as she had the moment before. But Shorty's name dropping might have thrown her. His friendly twang made it sound as though Einstein might be a good old boy living down the road apiece. "I've got a few more questions, then. When you say you'll keep me posted, do you mean you'll call and let me know when we can reopen? Because, otherwise, how will I know where and when to find the official statement you keep talking about?"

"We won't leave you in the dark, Ms. Estep," Clod said. "We'll be in touch."

"Thank you. When?"

"If I knew, I'd tell you."

"*Now* may I go?"

I waited until Sierra was gone before asking if she'd be staying in her apartment upstairs. "Isn't the building a crime scene?"

"Her apartment isn't," Shorty said. "She can come and go by the outside stairway 'til we give the all clear."

"Until the official statement is released?" I didn't try very hard to sound super impressed. Or even slightly whelmed.

"You started to say something, Ms. Rutledge," Clod said. "Just before Ms. Estep said she saw the men I pointed out to you."

"Oh! Right." I told him about seeing the men again and then what the Spiveys had told me about seeing one of them watching the house next door to Angie's. But as soon as the name Spivey left my lips, I knew I'd made a mistake.

"Huh," Clod said when I finished. Talk about a lack of whelm.

"Huh, what? Huh, and that's it?"

"I'll look into it," he said.

Two could play the huh game. I *huh*ed right back at him and narrowed my eyes for good measure. Maybe he would look into it. Or maybe he'd treat the Spiveys with the same disdain I so often did.

FOURTEEN

JOE HAD BEEN promising to clean Ardis's gutters for several weeks, but somehow had never found the time. "And now you have a whole unexpected afternoon free," she said as we left the Vault through the back door. "How convenient!"

Joe laughed and gave in. And that was why he and Ardis—why he and almost everyone—got along so well. Easygoing Joe. After he helped her into his truck, he and I got along well for a few warm seconds. Then I assured him his brother's questions didn't worry me.

"What about the scissors?" Joe asked.

"*That* freaks me out. But anyone could've picked them up at the Cat and brought them here. The killer used them, but that doesn't mean the killer came in the shop. Or tried to frame someone from the shop."

"Your logic's good and steady," Joe said. "Hold your hand out."

I did. "See? Nary a quiver."

He kissed my steady hand and then hopped into the truck. He knew better than to fuss and get all protective. Ardis could get away with it, though. She lowered her window, and I assured her, again, that I would call if I needed her. When they drove off, I realized I didn't see Geneva. No glints, nothing at all like a shimmer of water vapor. No fruit flies.

"Geneva?"

She didn't answer. Had she actually come out the back door with us? I tried the door. Locked. Sierra and Clod would be happy about that. Had she gotten into Joe's pickup with Ardis? That seemed unlikely. I called Ardis, anyway. Caller ID gave her a jump on jumping to conclusions.

"Hon, do you need me? What's happened? Should I tell Ten to turn around? Stop the truck—"

"No, no, no, Ardis, it's okay. I just wondered if Geneva's in the truck with you?"

She must have put her hand over the phone, because I heard a muffled, "Nothing to worry about, Ten." Then she spoke into the phone again. "Not that I can tell. Did we leave, um, *it* inside?"

"Hang on. I think—" Something flickered near the back door. Flickered and disappeared, and then Geneva was beside me. "She's here. It's okay. Talk to you later, Ardis." I disconnected but kept the phone to my ear so I could "talk" to Geneva. "Hi, are you okay?"

Geneva wavered beside me, preoccupied, pensive, and watery. No flickers or glints now.

"I'm heading back to the shop," I said. "Coming?"

She didn't answer, but when I started walking, she came along like an odd, localized patch of fog on an otherwise sunny day. By the time we'd gone a block, she'd started humming.

"That's a nice tune," I said into the phone. "What is it?"

"Something I'd forgotten. My mama used to sing it when she made biscuits."

"I don't think I've heard it before."

"Why would you? Mama never taught you to make biscuits, did she?"

"No, and that's too bad, because I'm pretty hopeless at biscuits."

"I used to help Mama make them. Did you see how well I helped the deputies?"

"You were very helpful."

"I'm also helpful because I keep my eyes open. I'm constantly noticing what goes on around me."

"Oh, hey, did *you* see those bearded guys at the Vault?"

"I heard so much and so little about them, I almost think, and certainly wish, that I had seen them. But if I said I did, then that would be a lie and *un*helpful. Just like Sierra Nevada's story. Did you see how well she pretended that she knew what she was talking about when she talked about them?"

"How do you know she pretended?"

"The same way I know your burglar beau wasn't entirely truthful when he said he *didn't* notice them. The mimic trick I pointed out to you—they mimicked Deputy Dunbar's posture while they lied to him."

"Sierra didn't notice them, but Joe did?"

"I believe so, even though I don't have a degree in body language. Why would Sierra Sonoma lie about noticing those men?" Geneva asked.

"I don't know."

"That isn't a helpful answer."

"No, but it's why we ask questions."

"Like Einstein."

"Sure."

"I didn't know he and Deputy Monroe were friends."

"Neither did I. So I wonder if Deputy Dunbar *also* thought Sierra was lying? And if he *didn't*, I wonder if he'd believe me if I told him?"

"During my television heyday, I watched a documentary about Deputy Monroe's buddy and probability. I would say that the probability of Deputy Dunbar believing you, if he hasn't already thought of it himself, is something like this." She made a circle with her arms. "A big, fat zero."

"You're probably right." I put my phone away and listened to Geneva hum her mother's song the rest of the way back to the shop. When I opened the Cat's front door, she stopped in the middle of the sweetest part of the tune.

"Do you know what I just remembered?" she said as the camel bells on the door jingled our arrival. "You promised to bring me a present. How sad that you forgot."

Debbie waved from where she was helping a customer at the pattern display.

"I'm glad to be home, though," Geneva said. "And aren't you glad the deputies didn't go all huff-and-puff and blow-your-law-and-order-down when they found our scissors at the dead center of the crime scene? I'm glad I won't have to visit you in the hoosegow. And I'm especially glad that I got such a good look at the murderer."

"What?"

Debbie and her customer startled and turned. I pretended to have a phone at my ear, waved, and quickly whipped around. Geneva whipped around, too.

"What is it?" she asked. "What happened? Who are you talking to?"

"You," I said, keeping my voice low. "I'm talking to you. Calmly, though, okay?"

"Calmly."

"Did you just say you saw the—" *Murderer* was too terrible a word to let loose into the colors and soft wool surrounding us. "Did you really see the person who did it?"

"Yes."

"And you didn't think to say that sooner?"

"Sooner," Geneva mused. "It's such a relative term."

There was no point in arguing.

Debbie's customer brushed past me. I smiled and nodded and waited until the door closed behind her before continuing. "I want to hear all about this," I said quietly into the phone. "It's extremely important. Let me check in with Debbie, and then I'll go up to the study."

"Shall I meet you there?" Geneva asked.

"Yes, please."

"Sooner or later?"

"About as long as it takes for Argyle to eat his breakfast."

"Cat time. Purrrrrfect." She floated up to the ceiling and disappeared.

When I turned back around toward Debbie, she looked suddenly busy shaking out and then folding a length of fabric. She'd witnessed other odd snippets of conversation since I'd been at the Cat, but she never asked, never commented. Maybe because she'd worked with and been so fond of Granny. In her letter to me, Granny had said she'd never discussed her "talent" with anyone…. *not at the Weaver's Cat or anywhere else. There are inklings and "quiet understandings," shall we say, at the shop, in town, and around out in the county, but I'm quite good at leaving them unacknowledged and going about my business.* I'd become fairly good at it, too.

"Sorry about that squawk," I said. "Have you heard about the opening?"

"Ernestine and John stopped in. They didn't have any details other than someone passed away. Ernestine said you'd know more." Debbie only had to look at my face before deciding for herself. "You do, and it isn't good."

Abby, our tame teenager, came down the stairs and into the front room with an effusively thankful customer.

"She helped me conquer my fear of French knots," the woman said. "Why did I think they were so mysterious?" She piled a rainbow of worsted embroidery yarn on the counter. "And add one of your T-shirts, will you?"

Abby delighted in designing fiber-related T-shirts, and we delighted in selling them for her. Her latest model showed an embroidery hoop, with work in progress, and the saying, "There are worsted ways to spend your days."

My day felt kind of worsted so far. I told Debbie I needed a little time to process what had happened at the Vault and that I'd be down later to tell them what I knew. She was a gentle soul, and I didn't like leaving her hanging like that, but she was also a young widow and a farmer, and she knew how to be realistic. She nodded and went to ring up the next customer.

I went down the hall to the kitchen. As I climbed the back stairs to the study, I thought about the concepts of time, mortality, and home. Kind of a lot to cover in three flights, but they weren't new thoughts, and when I reached the top, they'd plied themselves into a single strand. Geneva—time-challenged and not-quite-mortal—was right. It was good to be home where the comfortable smells of wool, cotton, and coffee mingled with the familiarity of worn floorboards, high ceilings, and friendly voices. Home softened the real world.

I'd expected to find Geneva brimming with excitement or self-importance when I got to the study. At the very least, I thought she'd be hovering in the middle of the room, vibrating with her information. But she crouched in the window seat with her knees drawn up to her chin. If I could take a picture of her, it would make a good illustration for "hopeless." An awful thought occurred to me. I scooped Argyle from the cushion beside her and sat cross-legged next to her. Argyle went back to sleep curled in my lap.

"Geneva, were you there in the storage room? Did you see it happen?"

"Do I look like someone who's recently seen a murder take place?"

It was hard to tell. Even as close as we sat, she didn't look like much more than an animate wisp of fog. "But you saw the murderer and you can identify him?"

"Or her."

"You couldn't tell if it was a man or woman?"

"But I can describe her," she said. "Or him."

"Is it someone you've seen before?"

"Oh, yes."

"Here in the Cat?"

The shop was the logical place. She was a homebody. Or, as she liked to say, a home-disembody. That morning, though, she'd gone to the Vault, either tagging along with Ardis and me, or on her own. And there were the "fruit flies" that morning—and the day before when a "possum" distracted Bruce. Argyle saw Geneva and liked her, but she'd told me that mice and beetles ran away. She hadn't answered my last question, so I asked the next carefully.

"The weather's been beautiful lately. Have you been getting out and about a little bit?"

If she'd ever been good at avoiding questions or lying, that art had faded over the decades of her solitude. She didn't look at me. She wavered where no breeze crept in.

"It's okay, you know, if you have. There's nothing wrong with getting out and seeing things, Geneva. Did you come to the Vault with me and Ardis this morning?"

"And a few times on my own."

"Good for you, Geneva. I think that's great."

"Three or four. Maybe half a dozen."

"What do you do there?"

"I watched the man unpack his antiques."

Bingo. Bruce showing his jazz hands in Floyd's.

"And I try to remember," she said.

"Has going there helped?" I asked. She wavered again, and I decided not to press her. Besides, there were more important questions. "Geneva, do you think I know the person you saw this morning?"

"You might. You seem to know any number of sketchy people."

"Is it someone you've seen before?"

"Yesterday."

"Where?"

"Also at the Vault."

"Good! There were fewer people there yesterday. We should have a better chance of identifying him."

"Or her."

"Do you remember where you saw her at the Vault? If it was morning or afternoon?"

She shook her head.

"Did your person talk to anyone?"

"A murderer is not my person."

"No, sorry. That was poorly worded. Did you see him working with anyone? Helping anyone?"

"I didn't know yesterday how important she would be today."

"That's okay. That's perfectly understandable." Also frustrating. "But you recognized her today. Can you describe her?"

"Or him? Of course."

"Good." If surprising. *Of course* and Geneva's memory rarely went together. "What was he wearing? How long was his hair?"

"And what's the shape of her ears? Or his nose? They're important features. Do you remember what I said a moment ago? That you know many sketchy people?"

"Yes. Why?"

"This is like being in an episode of *Dragnet*." She shifted around to sit cross-legged, facing me. "You're more like Bill Gannon, so I'll play Sergeant Joe Friday. That's because Bill Gannon is warmer and fuzzier, without literally being fuzzy like the men Detective Dunbar is so interested in. Bill Gannon is also not as bright, but don't take offense at that. We each do what we can in life."

"Thank you."

"And in death. So here is what we will do—we will sketch the villain. Grab a piece of paper and a pencil. I'll describe. You draw."

"Bill Gannon wasn't much of a sketch artist, was he? I know I'm not."

"Pencil! Paper! Chop-chop!"

It was worth a try. Maybe the exercise would bring some of the details she thought she'd forgotten bubbling to the surface. I transferred Argyle back to the window cushion and went to sit at the desk. But after half a dozen attempts, and as many wadded-up pieces of paper (and three times as many rude noises from Geneva), she announced that drawing was something I couldn't do.

"Go get Ardis," she said.

"She isn't here." And if she were, *she'd* know better than to try.

While Geneva billowed her frustrations, I doodled a tiny squirrel in the corner of a paper I hadn't wadded. Granny had drawn pictures of her cats in the letters she sent me. I gave my squirrel an acorn.

"At least you can draw a recognizable squirrel," Geneva said. "I would surround it with forget-me-nots, though."

I tried to doodle a wreath of flowers around the squirrel.

"Those look no more like forget-me-nots than the ugly mugs you drew looked like the villain."

"I did warn you."

"Your faces are as hopeless as your biscuits."

"Faces are hard to draw at the best of times." And no way was trying to follow her descriptions of the killer's ears, nose, lips, forehead, hair, and chin the best of times. The clearest part of her description, and the only part I was sure of, worried me.

"Thin, like so many of the men who came home from the war," she'd said. She meant the Civil War.

"*Thin* doesn't describe Russell Moyer at all." So what could I, or should I, do with that information? Geneva wasn't a witness who could be questioned in any traditional way. Most sane people wouldn't believe she existed. "Why couldn't you tell if it was a man or a woman?" I asked.

"Trousers. They throw me every time. I didn't get where I am today by wearing trousers."

"Too bad. You'd love them. Did you listen in when the deputies questioned Russell?"

"Who?"

"The guy they talked to in Sierra's office. The guy I just said *thin* doesn't describe."

"I can't say that I did."

"Why not? Where were you?"

"Alternatively, I can't say that I didn't. I might have peeked in."

"Did you hear them caution him? Do you know if they actually arrested him?"

She shrugged.

To avoid fussing at her, I checked the time and my messages. Nothing about the vaunted official statement yet.

"Now that we're discussing trousers," Geneva said, "we should also talk about hats. If I were to wear trousers, I would also like a fedora. One like the mannequin's, only dark gray to match the rest of me. They would give me an air of authority when we interview people in our effort to track down the perp."

"I'm not going to wear a fedora."

"I don't blame you. On you it would look silly. But you do need to practice asking questions."

"That's not a bad idea. It can get tricky. I have to be careful not to ask leading questions."

"Or annoying ones, because you do that."

"But as you pointed out, the other day when you compared me to Deputy Dunbar, sometimes annoying gets results."

"But you also ask vexatious questions. And distressing ones."

"Thanks. I'll work on that."

"There's more."

"I'm sure there is, but why don't I start there?"

"And you can work your way up to eliminating obnoxious and repellent questions."

I swallowed several obnoxious and repellent words. "How about a question that might require some thought?"

"I'm good at those. What is it?"

"How do you know the person you saw was the murderer?"

"I saw her go in the storage closet, and then come out. Then I went in, and when I did, I found Belinda."

"How do you know she didn't just go in and find Belinda like you did?"

"When you find a dead body, do you look like you've done nothing more than take a stroll?"

"I can't believe I'm saying this, but not usually, no."

"That's how I know. She didn't look like someone who just found a dead body."

"But did she look like someone who'd just killed a woman?"

"Do the successful murderers, walking among us, look any different than you or I?"

"Again, I can't believe I'm saying it, but not the ones I've known."

"Makes you think, doesn't it?" Geneva asked.

"Makes me shiver. You've been saying *she*. Are you clearer on that? Do you think it was a woman?"

"There are several things that befuddle me about the villain. That's one of them."

"What are the others?"

She wavered back and forth. "Befuddlement doesn't clear up for the asking."

"That's okay. If things clear up, will you tell me?"

"You will be the first to know."

"Good. Geneva, why did *you* go into the storage closet?"

"I was…curious."

That could mean she really had been curious. It could also mean she'd forgotten why she went in and curiosity made a handy excuse. But during my short, intense indoctrination into the habits of ghosts—this ghost, anyway—I'd learned she was a lot like Argyle, especially when it came to curiosity.

"You should be happy," she said. "I solved the case."

"But we'll have a hard time proving it. We don't know who it is, and you didn't actually see it happen. Did you hear anything?"

"You mean like a gasp? A scream cut off by death?" My hopes rose.

She shook her head. "My ears are exceptionally good. For instance, I heard when the guitarist broke a string. That caught my attention, and I missed any sounds coming from the storage room. It would have helped if I had paid more attention. It also would have helped if I had not waited before going in. Also if I had X-ray vision. But I'm not Superwoman. I'm not even a normal woman. Or an effective ghost woman. You think you feel useless as an old person?"

"I don't feel useless, Geneva, and I'm only thirty-nine."

"And I'm forever twenty-two. Trust me. You're old. Try being an unseen, unheard ghost who can't do so much as pick up a pencil, turn the page of a book, or tickle a cat under his bored chin. If you don't believe me about feeling old and useless, go ask Ardis's ancient daddy. I shall now remove myself to my coffin-like room and contemplate my useless eternity that you so kindly reminded me of."

I wondered if I had the world's most unreliable witness on my hands.

FIFTEEN

ARGYLE CAME DOWN to the kitchen with me and asked politely for a snack. I gave him a couple of crunchy things that were supposed to be good for his teeth. He ate them, and then rubbed his chin against my ankle, thanking me for looking after his dental hygiene, I assumed.

"But how's your *mental* hygiene, old boy? Are you bored? Or just yellow cat mellow?"

He listened and blinked at me. That he didn't glance at the top of the refrigerator or make cat eyes toward the dish drainer, both places Geneva liked to sit, convinced me she hadn't followed us downstairs.

"Do *you* ever feel like getting out and about?" I asked him. "Our friend does. And she has been. Much more than I realized. Did you know that?" I picked him up, and he purred as we rubbed foreheads. "Yup, that's what I'm beginning to think, too. If I can project my thoughts onto you, so can she."

I set him on the floor, and while he tidied his fur, I got a drink of water at the sink. Then I called Ardis to fill her in. She listened without comment, and I pictured the cogs and wheels in her head readjusting as she thought over this new information.

"Unreliable." She let out a long breath. "That takes care of why she didn't tell us sooner. Boredom can explain her trips to the Vault. Curiosity, too. And when you mix boredom and curiosity together you've got a powerful combination. I saw that over and over in the classroom. Kiddos operating on that combo caused plenty of trouble. But if I could tap into the boredom and curiosity, I'd often find the best imaginations. I'm telling you this, because I want you to think, hon. Geneva loves cop shows and Westerns. She's excitable and likes being part of the action. So, did she really see this person, or is she fabricating?"

"Her description makes me believe she saw someone. Look, we know there's nothing wrong with her imagination. If she invented this person, she'd know the number of freckles on his or her nose and there'd be a scar—she loves scars. And she would know if it was a man or a woman."

"You know her better than I do, hon."

"She saw someone. It might not be the killer, but it's someone who saw the body and didn't report it."

"All right then. What's our next step?"

"Find out who it is."

"It'll be difficult with that description," she said. "Risky, too, if anyone knows who we're talking about—including the killer. Killers aren't so keen on being identified. Why not get the professionals to handle it? Call it in to Crime Stoppers."

"And say what? My friend saw a thin person wearing pants leave the murder scene shortly before that snoopy woman found the body?"

"They must get all kinds of cockamamie tips. If that's all we have, then that's all we can give them. At least they'll know there's someone else out there they need to find and talk to."

"It's a long shot."

"Since when do we let long shots stop us?" Ardis

asked. "Let's not invite bad karma by talking about shots, though. And let me make the call. I've never called a tip line before."

"Are you sure?"

"I'll say I'm calling for a friend with laryngitis. They won't believe it, but that doesn't matter. And they say it's completely anonymous, but I think I'll disguise my voice, just in case. Give me the description, again. I'll write it down."

"Medium height, thin as a vet from the War Between the States, ears flat to the head, narrow nose and chin, small mouth."

"Hair?"

"She didn't know."

"Hoo boy."

"Yeah. Try drawing that. With her hanging over your shoulder."

"But she saw this person at the Vault yesterday, too? Coleridge needs to know that. They need to get a list of everyone who was in and out of there yesterday."

"We should get one, too."

"And do what with it, hon? Remembering risk. Whoopsie there, Daddy. Got to go. Honest to—"

She disconnected, leaving me to wonder what risky thing her daddy was up to and how we could follow up on Geneva's information without being too risky ourselves. No further inspiration struck. I stared out the window at the back wall of the business across the service alley. The brick wall stared back—old bricks with imperfections and character, but still a blank wall. Like my mind. I tried exhaling one of Ardis's long breaths. It didn't help.

When I turned around from the sink, a man appeared

in the hall doorway. Appeared? Or had he been standing there? It was the rat-faced McDougal. I probably stared.

"Didn't mean to startle you." He pointed at the back door. "On my way out."

"Sure. Thanks for coming in."

He said nothing else. The electronic sheep at the back door only said *baa*. And then he was gone. I walked— wanted to run—to the front room.

"You saw that guy?" Abby asked. "Did he leave?"

I nodded, and she pretended to collapse in a fit of giggles on the counter. "Biggest fish-out-of-water mo- ment I have ever witnessed," she gasped. "I don't know what that poor guy was looking for, but it wasn't knit- ting needles and embroidery hoops."

I went out on the front porch and looked up and down the street. Debbie, who hadn't laughed, followed me.

"Did he take something?" she asked.

I didn't see him or the second rat-face. "Did he say anything when he came in?"

"I was helping another customer. Abby talked to him." Debbie followed me back inside.

"Are there other customers here?" I asked.

"It's been busy off and on," Abby said. "There are a couple of women knitting upstairs."

"Did that guy come in with anyone?"

"No. Why?" Debbie asked. "What's going on?"

"I don't know. Maybe nothing." Hard to tell if they believed me. I listened for footsteps or voices approach- ing but didn't hear any. "It's just that he and another guy were at the Vault this morning. Deputy Dunbar pointed them out and asked me to let him know if I saw them again. No particular reason, except he didn't know them. Abby, did the guy just come in, look around, and leave?"

"Pretty much," Abby said.

"Pretty much?" I asked. "Is that a yes or a no?"

Abby didn't look or sound ruffled, so maybe I hadn't really snapped at her. "He said no when I asked if I could help him find anything," she said. "Then he walked through the rooms down here, went upstairs, walked around up there, came back down, asked if we had a back door, and left."

"I wonder what he thought of the electronic sheep?" I said. "He kind of surprised me, and I missed the look on his face when it said *baa*."

"Kind of surprised you? Is that a did or a didn't?" Abby asked, still unruffled and looking innocent—until she made a fish-kissing face at me.

"I love you, too, Abby. He and his buddy walked around the Vault the same way this morning. And fish out of water is exactly how Deputy Dunbar felt about them."

"Walked around looking for what?" Debbie asked.

"Or looking for who," Abby said.

"Who. It definitely could've been who," I said. "But why here?"

"Call Deputy Dunbar," Debbie said.

The camel bells at the front door jingled, and Abby went to greet the women who'd come in. I stepped into the office behind the counter and called the non-emergency number at the sheriff's department. Debbie came and stood sideways in the door, one ear on me, the other alert for customers in need. The sheriff's dispatcher put me through to Clod's voicemail. Irritating, but not unexpected. I left a short message summarizing the rat-faced McDougal's visit to the shop and hung up. As soon as I did, I remembered the official statement and called back. The dispatcher told me they were still waiting to release it.

"Waiting for what?" I asked.

"Do you think they tell me?"

"Yeah, I think they— She hung up on me. Of all the nerve."

"It's okay," Debbie said. "Nervie told us."

"Nervie? What did she tell you? And when?"

The camel bells jingled again, and Debbie waved and called hello to the people who'd come in. "That it was Belinda Moyer and it wasn't natural causes," she said when she turned back to me. "Why are you so surprised? You know official statements don't keep tongues from wagging."

Surprise was only part of it. "When was Nervie wagging?"

"She came in while you were upstairs."

"Is she still here?"

"Mm, not sure." Debbie pointed over her shoulder. "Customers."

The trouble with investigating a crime—or even just being actively nosy—while running a business was the amount of time customers took away from it. Such an odd problem to have. Debbie had things under control, though, so I took a quick tour of the rooms downstairs. I didn't find Nervie, but I met Abby coming down the front stairs. I crooked a finger at her, and we let a couple of women with knitting bags pass us.

"Is Nervie upstairs?" I asked.

"You missed her."

"Was she here when that guy came in?"

"Is that who he wanted? He didn't say. She'd already left, anyway."

CUSTOMERS FLOWED IN, many of them finding something else to do after making the trip to Blue Plum for the canceled opening. I stayed to help out, happy for the distraction from what I *should* be doing, namely puzzling out what to do with Geneva's information. Argyle contributed his expertise by supervising the display in the front window between naps. Geneva didn't float in to curl around the ceiling fan.

Joe called late in the afternoon. I told him about the McDougal in the shop and the message I'd left for Clod. He was quiet for a minute, then said, "Good."

"Gutters clean?" I asked.

"They are. I'm not. I'm going home to grab a shower. Mel asked Aaron's group to play at the café this evening. Might be fun."

It might be. Crashing early and ignoring the ruthless world sounded good, too.

"Ardis and Hank are going," Joe said. "She's going to let the old coot do a two-step."

"Sold. That will definitely be fun."

Ardis called soon after. "The call to Crime Stoppers was a piece of cake."

"I hadn't realized how relieved I'd feel knowing they've got that information," I said.

"A burden lifted? I've been thinking about that, hon. The tip was anonymous. Let's keep it that way for now."

"You don't want to tell the posse?"

"The information, such as it is, is in good hands," Ardis said. "The posse has other questions to sift through. We can't call that little gathering near the refreshment table this morning a meeting. I contacted Thea, Ernestine, and John. They're meeting us at Mel's."

"Won't it be too noisy and too public?"

"Perfect cover," Ardis said. "If nothing else, all eyes will be on Daddy."

MEL, OFFICIALLY off for the day, reserved two tables for the eight of us. She further reserved the seat next to herself for Hank. "I plan to keep him busy," she said. "I haven't been dancing in years."

"Daddy hasn't been dancing since before you were born," Ardis said. "He gave it up after Mama died. It's only since he started talking to her that he's been itching to kick up his heels again."

"I'll try not to step on his toes *or* his heels," Mel said. "You'll dance with me, won't you, Hank?"

"You give the word," Hank said. "I like a woman with her hair on fire."

"Where's Aaron?" Joe asked.

"Stepped out back with Angie," Mel said.

The café had a back door for customers just as we did at the Cat. Joe and I found Angie and Aaron on the small porch there, and we congratulated them on the impending twins with hugs and backslaps.

"You're out there in the country now, aren't you?" Joe asked.

"Watauga Branch," Aaron said. "Mile beyond the bridge."

"I took a big bass under that bridge a few years back," Joe said.

"It's our compromise location," Angie said. "I'm all-town and Aaron's all-mountain, and out there it's some of both. It's peaceful."

Aaron said, "Heh," crossed his arms, and looked at his feet.

"Well, except for the Riley and Taylor show." Seeing Joe's raised eyebrows, Angie added, "Aaron's cousin Taylor and her boyfriend. Trust me, you don't want to know more than that."

"Your mom and Shirley mentioned something about it," I said.

"What'd they say?" Angie asked.

"Not much. No details."

"Good. We're trying to keep it that way." She leaned her shoulder against Aaron's chest, and he put his arms around her. "You know what Mom and Aunt Shirley are like, though."

"Actually, they said something about the day you had a housewarming," I said. "About a guy sitting in a pickup truck on the side of the road, watching the house next door."

"What house next door?" Angie asked. "There's houses a half mile down in either direction, but no house next door."

"Might be they saw one of Riley's uncles," Aaron said. "Waiting, though, not watching. Riley lost his license for a time, and they'd take him to work."

"Did you see either of the uncles at the opening this morning?" I asked. "Does one of them have a beard?"

"He does," Aaron said. "I didn't see him, though. Too busy playing."

"Do Shirley and Mercy know either of them?" Joe asked.

"Don't know why they would," Aaron said. "We only met them after Taylor and Riley hooked up."

"Another episode in the Riley and Taylor show," Angie said. "That's a couple more names we won't give the kids."

We left them giggling over other names they wouldn't give the new twins. While we ordered at the counter, Thea and Ernestine arrived. Thea parked Ernestine at our table and came to stand in line behind us. John walked in as we sat down with our drinks.

"Are you still lusting after that book you saw this morning?" I asked Thea when she joined us.

"Shh," she said. She looked around, as though checking for who might be near enough to hear. "I don't think he knows the value of some of his old paperbacks. The two I bought? Out-of-print romance. Not impossible to find, but worth more than he's charging. That's why I didn't want to see the delectable Briggs Myers."

"An old mystery," I told Joe and Ernestine. Then, to Thea, "If he's pricing low, why not look at it?"

"Because once I had that book in my hands, I wouldn't be able to stop myself. I'd buy it. And either he knows how much it's worth, and I'd spend more than I can afford, or he'd doesn't know and I'd feel guilty for cheating him."

"The bibliophile's dilemma," Joe said. "Martha just came in. Be right back."

"Who's Martha?" Thea asked. She was territorial, on my behalf, as far as Joe was concerned.

"It's all right," I said. "She's the enamelist at the Vault."

"The bibliophile's dilemma would be a good title for a book," said Ernestine.

"Not for the book I'm writing," Thea said. "We've had so much practice solving crimes, it'll be a walk in the park. I'm calling it *Dog-Eared to Death*."

"Are you really?" Ernestine asked.

"I wish."

"You could do it, though," I said. "What's stopping you?"

"Time and typing."

"They wait for no woman," Ernestine said. "Don't wish you had. It's a hard place to be."

"What are you wishing, Ernestine?" Ardis asked from the next table.

"It's useless, but I wish I'd had more coffee this morning, so that I'd spent more time going back and forth to the restroom. I might have seen something. Or stopped it."

"None of that," Mel said.

Joe and John reached the tables at the same time. John took the empty seat at Mel's table.

"How's Martha?" I asked when Joe sat down.

"Shocked, like everyone else. Do you remember I wondered if she'd stay on with her shop? She says after this morning, she owes it to the Arts Council. To support the Vault and Sierra."

"Good for her," John said.

"Did she notice Belinda wasn't in her shop this morning?" Ernestine asked.

"I doubt any of us had time to notice anything outside our own shops," Joe said.

"But what do we know about her movements?" Ernestine asked.

"I thought we were working on what happened to the tablecloth," John said from the other table.

"We might not be able to separate the two," said Ardis.

"Didn't they arrest the ex?" Thea asked.

I leaned over to Mel. "This isn't going to work."

"No kidding. Good thing I keep plan B in my apron pocket."

Plan B called for enjoying our food and the music, leaving Mel's in ones and twos, and regrouping at the Cat.

"I'll stay here with Hank," Mel said. "If he gets rascally, I'll rascal right back."

Plan B performed as smoothly as Aaron's trio. Thea and Ernestine finished eating first and left with Ardis's keys. John followed some minutes later, as Hank held a hand out to ask Mel for a dance. Before Ardis made her move, Simon the bookseller came to say hello, and Ardis invited him to sit.

"For a minute," he said. "I'm meeting someone. She isn't here yet. Terrible what happened this morning…"

"Shocking," Ardis said.

"Did you know the ex was in the picture?" he asked. "I didn't until I heard them fighting this morning."

"Fighting?"

"Sniping more than fighting," Simon said. "That's what I told the deputies. Tight lips and nasty looks. As a theater director, you'd have loved it, Ardis. A perfect example of how to get across the idea of an argument without raised voices or physical contact."

"Interesting. Are you still traveling so much for Embree?" Ardis asked, referring to the area community college.

"That's what makes being department director bearable," he said.

"Well, if you have enough time between that and your books, the next time we do *Who's Afraid of Virginia Woolf,* make sure you try out."

"Really? Thanks."

"Sad they fought on their last morning," I said. "I hope it wasn't over something trivial."

"I shouldn't have said fighting. That's where subtlety comes in. That's what I would explore in *Virginia Woolf*. This sounded like dialogue they'd gone over before, maybe for years. The 'fight' was there in the tone, the shading. Anyway," he said, getting up, "I'll let you be, and we'll hope for better days ahead."

Ardis watched him go, then said, "We'll hope for better clues ahead, too. Subtlety's fine, but I'm a big fan of a poke in the eye or a pie in the face. They'd make it easier to figure out what happened today, too."

"I didn't know you were thinking of doing *Virginia Woolf* again," Joe said. "Gar played George last time."

"I'll make sure we *don't* do it again. Simon is a director's nightmare. He always wants to rewrite the script."

"Then why did you tell him to try out?" I asked.

"Because it made him feel good about himself. Everyone needs a little bit of that. Like those two dancing fools." She waved at Mel and Hank; then she did an energetic two-step of her own past Aaron's trio, and slipped out the back door.

"She's right," I said.

Joe slipped his arm around my shoulders. "About feeling good?"

"About subtlety, which you've mastered. But wouldn't it be nice to have clues even the Three Stooges couldn't miss?"

"Right on cue," Joe said. "Look who're about to poke each other in the eyes."

Clod and Rogalla were both headed for the order counter. Rogalla got there first and stood with his back as squarely to Clod as humanly possible.

"Did they come in together?" I asked.

"Maybe they're following each other. Which one's Moe, and which one's Larry?"

"And where's Curly?"

"Pooch parking?" Joe said.

Mel had a spot out front, with an awning for shade, where dogs could enjoy a bowl of water while their people went inside.

After ordering, Rogalla found a table farther from the music. When Clod stepped away from the counter, he took his time scanning the room, and then headed for us.

"Did you get my voicemail about that guy in the shop?" I asked when he sat down.

"Nice way to say hello. Yeah, I got your message. And I'd say that I didn't figure either of those boys as yarn-shop types, but one of you two might stab me with a knitting needle."

"That's insensitive, under the circumstances," I said.

"It gets the point across. Oh, and just so you know, I caught up with the buddy of the rat-faced McDougal. They were in the area scouting locations for their organization's next annual meeting. Looking over the venue, as he said. Making sure the spousal members of the organization will have plenty of opportunities for entertainment and shopping."

"What organization?" I asked.

"Tennessee Herpetological Society. And yes, I checked. Their next annual meeting is being held in Johnson City, near enough to make Blue Plum a day trip."

"Huh."

"Disappointed?" Clod asked.

"Wondering if you got their names and checked to see if they're actually members."

Joe, Mr. Subtle Intervention, stepped in before I went too far. "Any official word yet?"

"The Vault can open tomorrow," Clod said. "We're officially looking for a person or persons unknown."

"I *knew* it."

"Good for you, Ms. Rutledge. Is what you *knew* more than what you told us this morning?"

"Nope."

"Did you see anyone else near that door? Anyone you forgot to mention?"

Someone he'd learned about from an anonymous tip? With complete sincerity, I shook my head. Then, also with complete sincerity, I jabbed back. "You know more than you're letting on about Belinda. About *all* of what's happened. But you're looking for something else. A connection? Is that what you're fishing for?"

"Sorry?"

"Your questions this morning; they weren't just about what happened to Belinda. You're fishing for something else."

"Fishing," Clod said. "Good point."

"Huh?"

He ignored me and turned to Joe. "Fishing makes sense."

"Fishing always makes sense," Joe said, "but what are you talking about?"

"Gar. Maybe that's what he was doing up there."

Joe shook his head. "He never fished up that high. Water's too cold."

"You ever hear of insulated waders?" Clod asked.

"Doesn't matter," Joe said. "Gar went after browns.

Browns like warmer water than what you find up there above the gap. And even the warmer water was too cold for Gar these days. He always said browns and Browns stick together. They like the bigger, lower creeks and rivers. Besides that, he didn't fish alone. Not for the past three or four years."

"Won't ever again, either," Clod said.

"Catch this guy, Cole."

"Catch both guys," I said. "Or is there only one?"

SIXTEEN

"COLE ACTUALLY SAID the same person might have killed Gar *and* Belinda?" Ardis looked from me to Joe. She'd met us at the door to the TGIF workroom.

"He said he doesn't know if we're looking for one person or two," I said.

"Same difference. Do you believe him?"

"No question," Joe said.

"I was only surprised he answered," I said. "Not *by* his answer."

"Well, come on in and sit down," Ardis said. "We got that vibe from him this morning when he corralled us there in the gallery."

We didn't often use the TGIF workroom in the evenings. Before Joe and I arrived, the others had moved extra floor lamps over to the circle of chairs, making it cozier and easier to see stitches. They were all knitting. Even Joe, as soon as he sat down next to John. *Where had his knitting and needles sprung from?*

"Sorry," I said. "I seem to have left mine at home."

Ardis handed me a dry-erase marker and pointed at the whiteboard they'd brought from the other end of the long room. "You know your place. The board is yours."

"Where do we start?" Thea asked.

"With this." I tossed the marker up in the air, caught it, and drew two lines from the top to the bottom of the board, trisecting it.

"Showoff," Thea said.

Along the top of the left section of the board, I wrote *Connections?* Then I made a list:

Belinda
Russell
Nervie
· *tablecloth*
Vault
Gar
gang

John narrated for Ernestine as I wrote. "A long list," she said at the end of it.

"Covering bases," I said. To be thorough, and because I couldn't help blaming them for setting our part of all this in motion, I added *Spiveys*. And then I felt something I couldn't quite believe—a pang of remorse because maybe I was being unfair to them. A pang so small it was more of a ping, but still there. I erased *Spiveys*.

"We're covering bases," Ardis said. "Put them back."

As I rewrote *Spiveys*, memories tickled: Mercy, positive she saw the rat-faced McDougal watching the house down the road from Angie and Aaron's... Clod blowing off that information...the McDougal in the Weaver's Cat, looking for something or someone, and in no way acting like a guy scouting a venue for a group of spouses.

"What are you thinking?" Ardis asked.

"About covering bases." I added *rat-faced McDougals* below *Spiveys*. "These are the guys John and I tried to follow this morning at the Vault." I recapped my tickling memories, then told them Aaron's version of the McDougal sitting in his truck.

"And Cole says they're members of the Tennessee Herpetological Society," Joe said.

"Presumably Aaron and Cole know their names, then," Ernestine said, "but rat-faced McDougal can be our code name for them."

"And seeing them on the list makes me feel better," I said, "just like seeing Spivey."

In the middle section of the board, I wrote *Timeline* and below that three words:

Gar
tablecloth
Belinda

"Headings and lists only on this side," I said. Then I flipped the board to the other side. "There probably isn't enough room for all the questions those three events have generated. If we fill the board, I'll take a picture of it, erase, and start again. Did you all hear what we told Ardis? That Cole isn't sure if we're looking for two killers or one?"

"Is that because they're completely flummoxed," Ernestine asked, "or only partially flummoxed?"

"Partially," Joe said, "but I don't know the percentage of fact to flummox. Cole doesn't think the smash-and-grab gang killed Gar. He's working on why Gar was up there at the trailhead."

"Theories?" John asked.

"Hiking, fishing, flirting," Joe said. "The first two Gar wouldn't have done alone. The third most people *don't* do alone, but I don't think Gar was likely to do it at all. Personal opinion, but he was an old friend."

"We don't know what Belinda was doing in that storage closet, either," Ardis said.

"But we're sure Russell's in the clear?" Ernestine asked.

"Why should he be?" Thea said. "Just because the deputies didn't arrest him?"

"You're right. What a silly question," Ernestine said. "How's this one? Did Gar know Belinda and Russell?"

"That's a great question, Ernestine," I said. "I'm writing it and the question about Russell being in the clear on the board." I did and then flipped it back to the first side. "We need to look at the connections between these people. That's what the deputies will be doing."

"According to Rogalla, Sheriff Haynes has a pet name for the gang," Joe said. "The Saggy Bottom Boys."

"Do you want me to add that?" I asked.

"No," Joe said. "Add Rogalla to the list."

"Your reasoning?" John asked.

"He keeps turning up," I said. "Turning up for good reasons. *But.*" I wrote *Rogalla* at the bottom of the list.

"But we're covering bases," Ardis said, "so fair enough. Here's a connection involving arguing. Simon Grace heard Belinda and Russell arguing this morning. And Kath heard Nervie and Belinda arguing."

"There was no love lost between Nervie and Belinda," I said. "Did I tell you Nervie came in the shop today and told Debbie about the murder?"

"Word was bound to get out before the official statement," Thea said. *"But."*

"But we're being suspicious on all fronts," Ernestine said. "I'm afraid I don't have any connections to add. I'd like to know more about the gang, though. Do they have colors and graffiti signs?" Her needles clicked faster.

"Nothing so identifiable," Joe said. "I think 'gang' is being used loosely. Cole says they aren't even sure it's more than one person."

"Ah." Ernestine nodded, and her needles slowed.

"Here's a connection that rankles," I said.

"Don't you love the nasal quality of that Illinois accent when she uses words like 'rankles' when she's rankled?" Thea said to Joe.

"I surely do."

"Thanks, guys." I gave *thanks* an extra twist of Illinois nasal. "There's something going on between the twins and Nervie. It might be one way. I've never heard Nervie mention the twins. But Shirley and Mercy are out for Nervie's reputation. They're accusing her of selling other designer's patterns as her own."

"To her face?" John asked. "Are the Spiveys that open and above board?" He paused. Then, ever the naval officer and a gentleman, he asked, "Was that question unnecessarily harsh?"

"No." That answer came from at least three mouths.

"Nervie accused Belinda of selling fakes and stolen goods," I continued. "She told me the shredded tablecloth was stolen."

"Did you ask her why she says so or how she knows?" John asked.

"No. Somehow I didn't want—"

"You didn't want to encourage her?" Ernestine asked. "It's that way with the grandchildren, sometimes. Better to let certain remarks pass without comment. Is that how you felt?"

"Like that or like I didn't want to get mixed up in anything."

"You didn't succeed," Thea said. "Make a section below *Timeline* and call it *Sources*. We need to keep track of where and from whom we've heard things. And we need to consider whether or not we can trust them."

I added the new section. "I like this, Thea. How about, for now, I list names of people we've heard things from. Then, as you hear other things, text me. I'll keep a database." In the new *Sources* section, I wrote:

Spiveys
Nervie
Belinda
Simon
Rogalla

"What's Simon director of," I asked, "and why isn't that enough to make him feel good about himself?"

"Outreach and Distance Learning," Ardis said. "It might be a case of being the wrong size fish for his particular pond."

"What's your assessment of the tablecloth?" John asked. "Is it collateral damage? Or was Belinda killed because of it?"

Rather than answer, I flipped the board and scribbled those questions.

"What if she stumbled onto something that led her to Gar's killer?" Ardis asked. "If we're looking for connections, the Vault is the hub for all these connections. Gar and Belinda might not have met, but they're connected through the Vault. Is the likelihood of her discovering something about his death any more far-fetched than someone killing her over a tablecloth?"

"Less far-fetched, if you put it that way," I said.

"Don't sound so glum," Thea said.

"I can't help it. And don't judge me; I want to know who killed the tablecloth almost as much as who killed Belinda. *She* said Nervie did it."

"Could she have?" Ernestine asked.

"I don't know. Maybe." I felt as sulky as Geneva. *She* thought Nervie shredded the cloth, too. Ms. Unreliable Witness, who also said she saw Nervie drive away from the Cat. "Nervie taught her class here Friday afternoon. She *could* have left early. She knew Belinda kept the tablecloth in a trunk; we both saw Belinda get it out."

"Was the trunk locked?" Ardis asked.

"I don't know. Belinda kept her back to us when she opened it. She looked over her shoulder at us, like maybe she'd catch us sneaking up on her, but she didn't make a secret out of where she kept it."

"Trunk locks are worthless," Joe said.

"What if Belinda lied about the time frame for the vandalism?" Thea asked. "Maybe Nervie did it earlier, avoiding the time crunch with her class."

"Or did Belinda do it herself?" Ernestine asked. "When my youngest went through his divorce, *his* youngest acted out that way. It's hard to believe you can be quiet using a hammer, but he quietly and methodically smashed every one of his favorite toys. Therapy helped him out of that dark place. Hiding the hammer helped, too."

"From Belinda's reactions when she showed us the shreds, I'd say no, she didn't do it," Joe said. "What do you think, Kath?"

"She seemed genuinely devastated."

Ernestine nodded. "Heartbroken. My grandson, too. He also blamed the destruction on the dog."

"A different direction," John said. "Backtracking, actually. In her text the other night, Kath asked about history between Nervie and Gar."

"Except she was more specific and less euphemistic and got laughed at," Thea said. "But if we drag your mind out of the gutter, Kath, and use 'history,' it's a good question."

"Nervie certainly knew who Gar was," Ardis said. "Because of the Vault, but also because her husband worked at the bank. It's less certain Gar knew Nervie, but hard to believe he didn't."

"I didn't know her husband worked there." I added *bank* to the *Connections* list.

"Peter," Ardis said. "He died in a hunting accident out in Wyoming. Ten, maybe fifteen years ago."

"There was a nasty rumor at the time," Ernestine said, "that it wasn't a hunting trip. Not for Peter, anyway."

"Don't be coy with the details," Thea said. "This is an investigation, and three out of the six people in this room didn't live here ten years ago."

"Go on, Ardis," Ernestine said. "You and Ivy heard the rumor and did something about it."

"I'll only repeat it with the understanding that we're picking our way through the muck and mud of hearsay." Ardis looked at each of us, and we nodded. "According to the story, Nervie is the one who said he died in a hunting accident. But, also according to the story, she followed Peter out there because she found out he was having an affair with a woman in the bank's regional office in Nashville. She confronted him. He said he was leaving her. Instead, she killed him and made it look like an accident."

"And people spread that around?" Thea asked. "Why would someone start a rumor like that? *Who* would? Even Shirley and Mercy have their standards."

"Nasty," Ernestine said. That might have covered the rumor and the twins.

"Was there a funeral?" I asked.

"Yes, but not here," Ardis said, "and this part is true, because I heard it from Nervie. She buried him back wherever Peter came from. Maybe the rumors came from someone's soured wishful thinking. Someone who wanted out of a bad situation and didn't have Nervie's strength. Nervie's proved she's tough as a three-week-old biscuit."

"That's not quite my image of her," I said. "And you and Granny trusted Nervie enough to let her teach classes here at the Cat."

"That was Ivy's doing," Ardis said.

"If Granny liked her, then that says something about Nervie."

"I didn't say she liked Nervie. She just didn't see the wicked in her some folks wanted to," Ardis said. "And she didn't like to hear any kind of rumor."

"What's your last section for, Kath?" Thea asked.

"Assignments. We need to know more, especially about connections. Let me know if these are all right."

Ardis—Nervie
Thea—Vault

"We need to know more what?" Thea said. "I need specifics."

"History of the project," I said. "Records of discussions for and against—"

"Meeting minutes, lease agreement, etc.," Thea said, tapping notes into her phone. "Okay. On it."

"Put me down for the gang," said Ernestine.

"Mind if I tag along with you on that, Ernestine?" Joe asked.

"Not at all. We'll be our own gang."

Ernestine—gang
Joe—gang, Gar
John—Russell, Rogalla
Mel—Belinda
Kath—tablecloth, Spiveys

"Thank you for sacrificing yourself to the twins," Ardis said. "You're a braver woman than I."

Or crazier, but I was glad no one said so.

We said our goodnights soon after that. Before leaving, I snapped pictures of the whiteboard and then erased it. That should have been an obvious precaution, but I'd learned it the hard way during an earlier investigation. Someone had once found our notes on the board and relayed them with nearly disastrous results.

It wasn't late, but it was already dark. Ardis went to corral her daddy back at Mel's. Joe walked me home.

"Do you hear that squeak?" I said as we went up my front steps.

"Ivy called it an old friend. I can fix it if you want."

"No, she had the right idea. I might want you to add a few squeaks to the hallway in the Cat. I didn't hear that rat-face coming this afternoon when I was in the kitchen. Big guy like that? It spooked me."

"Reverse carpentry," Joe said. "That might be a useful skill to advertise. You know, in case anyone wants to claim their house is haunted, but it doesn't have enough rattles and squeaks to prove it. Hey, are you okay?"

I'd started laughing, and when I tried to stop, it turned to coughing, and then hiccups. I unlocked the door, and by the time I'd dropped my purse and slipped off my shoes, Joe had brought me a glass of water from the kitchen.

We sat across from each other in Granny's blue comfy chairs. She'd never had a sofa in the little house. Prime floor space went to her looms. I could have changed that, but I liked her looms and I liked the way the back of my head nestled where hers had in the chairs. While I drank the water, Joe told me about rebuilding the stairs on a Carpenter Gothic up on Vestal Hill.

"I copied and replaced some of the scrollwork on the porch, too," he said. "This was a few years back. Russell and Belinda got a good deal on that house. He moved out when they split."

"I wondered where this was going. You did the porch work for them?"

"Before she arrived. Russell moved in first. It's a sweet little place. I guess it's his again, now."

"Do you think Cole was right to let him go today?"

"I don't know."

"Maybe John can find out if Russell gets the house. And I wonder how Russell would feel if we tried to reach out to him."

"He might appreciate the thought," Joe said.

"Depending on how many nosy questions follow the thought."

"Good point. What do you say we practice reaching out in a kinder, gentler way?"

Of course, I never had to reach out to the Spiveys.

SEVENTEEN

A YARN SHOP ON a Sunday afternoon might sound like a quiet place, especially a shop with a cat snoozing in the window and "cat" in its name. Sometimes it worked out that way and Debbie had time to change displays and I could attend to paperwork or ordering or extra cleaning. The hominess of Blue Plum attracted people on Sundays, though, and the coziness of the Weaver's Cat brought them through our doors.

That was where the twins reached out to me. More specifically, during an inopportune lull in Sunday afternoon business, they pounced.

"We need to talk," one of them said, catching me off guard in the kitchen, thanks to our squeak-less floorboards.

"We told Debbie and Abby we'd make it quick," the other said. "They're okay with it."

Their matching black slacks and gray cardigans gave them an air of seriousness I didn't associate with them. In tandem, they pulled chairs out from the kitchen table and sat—across from each other. Without Mercy's elbow, it would be harder to figure out who was who. Frustrating, but only because it gave them the edge in their game of verbal and mental keep-away. And if I decided not to play? A thin layer of stress fluttered away. I moved to the head of the table and stayed on my feet.

"We said we'd be quick," the twin to my right said.

"So we'll spell it out. Nervie slashed that tablecloth. She's the only one who would."

"Why?" I asked.

"A vendetta," the left-hand twin said.

I hesitated to ask them too many questions. They might read something into them and jump to conclusions. That was probably exactly the way Clod felt about TGIF. "What proof do you have?"

"We told you she'd be trouble," the left twin said. "We aren't psychic. We know because we keep our eyes and ears open."

"But warning me she'd be trouble isn't proof she *was* trouble."

"We have proof," the right twin said, her voice low and with a glance toward the hall.

I held up a finger and went to check, staying in the doorway for five or ten seconds to listen. They really were being serious. But even with their careful voices and firm opinions, were they any more reliable, as witnesses, than Geneva? Could I take the chance they weren't? I went back to the table. "All clear."

"She shredded the tablecloth," the left twin said. "Then she killed Belinda."

The right twin watched my face. "She doesn't believe us. Let's go."

"Wait," I said. "You *know* it takes more proof than saying so."

"That's why we came to you," Right Twin said. "You know how to find proof."

"You listen when others don't. Take a seat," Left Twin said.

"Please," said Right Twin. "We'll tell you what we know about Belinda."

I pulled a chair around to the head of the table and sat, trying to exude *this better be good* from every pore.

"Belinda liked to say she wasn't much of a joiner," Left Twin said.

"But that's what people say when they don't get asked to join," Right Twin said.

"She traveled a lot," Left Twin said. "Collecting trips around the southeast in that BMW behemoth her ex-husband bought her after the divorce."

"How do you know Russell bought it for her?" I asked.

"He's the kind who knuckles under and moans about it later," the right twin said.

"He isn't much of an ex," the left twin added.

They nodded to each other and stood up.

"That's *it*?" I didn't even try to keep the disbelief from my voice. "That's about as useful as noticing a suspicious guy in a truck watching a house and not thinking that getting the tag number would've been a normal, useful, logical, and community-spirited thing *to do*."

After the twins slammed out the back door, Geneva materialized and swirled down from the top of the refrigerator. She sat in one of the chairs the twins hadn't bothered to push back in. "Alienating informants left and right, I see."

"How much of that did you hear?"

"From 'v is for vendetta' through your bellowing 'to do.'"

"I hope I didn't really bellow. At least I let them know they shirked their duty, because even if those rat-faced McDougals are helpful uncles and members of a reptile club, they're acting like snakes in the grass."

"Your way of letting the dear twins know sounded

more like a dare, but I don't blame you. I'm also disappointed in them. They insist Nervie is the killer. But they weren't there, and she didn't do it. That's not to say she hasn't killed any number of other people and shredded scores of tablecloths that would make you weep. Have I told you that I don't like Nervie Bales?"

"Why don't you?"

"She complains."

"Aren't you complaining right now?"

"My complaints are nothing like hers. We inhabit different planes of existence, in case you've forgotten."

Without warning, she swept her arm through me. I didn't really feel anything, except cold, and yet...

"Please don't do that."

"We're in completely different situations, and we handle those situations differently, too. And I'm handling mine better."

"I'm amazed at how well you handle your situation, Geneva. Being unseen and unheard must be hard to deal with. Hard to even bear."

"Thank you for recognizing that."

"I wonder, though, if we don't all think that we're handling our own situations better than other people handle theirs, or at least better than some do? That might be part of human nature."

"But some people *do* handle their situations better. Difficult, heartbreaking, and horrifying situations. Even joyous ones."

"They do."

"And some take the easy way out and kill."

I SENT THE pictures I'd taken of the whiteboard to the posse so they'd have them for reference. I sent a longer text to Mel, letting her know what she was looking at in the pictures and giving her the gist of our discussion. Her return text asked why she and Hank hadn't been assigned to the gang. Another LOLOLOL followed. I asked John to find out what he could about the house. Ernestine sent a picture of the picnic she and Joe had Sunday afternoon at Beauty Spot on Unaka Mountain. A separate message from her apologized for failing to make contact with the gang.

"Did you expect to make contact?" I asked Joe when he dropped by that evening.

"Not a chance. I've had feelers out, and you know Cole has. Gar's death sent any lowlifes scurrying back into the cracks they crawled out of. It scared them because people are looking for them, and it scared them because it means they were out there with a killer."

"And you went out there for a picnic?"

"With my sidekick. She brought binoculars, a spyglass she borrowed from John, and deviled eggs like I've never had them." Joe was a true connoisseur of potluck and picnic fare.

"You were probably safer out there with Ernestine and your eggs. I think this devil's working closer to home."

MONDAY MORNING, I got to the Cat earlier than usual. I'd forgotten to tell Geneva about the posse meeting and wanted time to bring her up to speed before we opened. She often skipped our meetings when everyone clicked away with their knitting needles (a sound she disliked), though it surprised me that she hadn't even mentioned the meeting.

She waved to me from the kitchen window as I

approached, and I waved back. I unlocked the door, avoided tripping over Argyle as he guided my feet to his food dish, and asked Geneva if she'd noticed us in the workroom Saturday night.

"I must have been otherwise engaged," she said. At that moment, she was engaged in sitting in the kitchen sink, an odd habit if she weren't a ghost—although maybe for a ghost, too.

"Would you like to hear what we discussed?"

"How to find the perp, I would assume."

I told her about looking for connections as a way to find her "perp," and I showed her the photos of the whiteboard.

"And these are the assignments?" she asked. "Where's mine?"

I hadn't even thought about an assignment for her.

"I see what you've done, though," she said.

"You do?"

"These are all pedestrian assignments—if you'll forgive me for saying so."

"Sure."

"Each according to his or her strengths. Correct? Leaving my strength—my estimable brainpower—to come up with the plan that will catch the villain."

She followed me out to the front room, stroking her chin. She was still stroking it when Ardis arrived. Ardis wasn't stroking her chin, but her eyes were wide with a new idea.

"Russell is assigned to John, isn't he?" she asked. "We should ask him to find out if Russell plans to keep Belle's open. The rent's paid. He's retired. The pieces are priced. It wouldn't be a huge time commitment. On the other hand, if the linens are as gorgeous as you say, he might be afraid to touch them. You know how some men are."

"Didn't you get in there to see the linens on Saturday?"

"I took my time downstairs, hon. And by 'took my time,' you know I mean I talked to everyone under the sun. And then I only got as far as the refreshments upstairs."

"You'll have to go back." I described the pieces that made up the bulk of Belinda's inventory—kitchen towels, napkin sets, doilies, and small tablecloths from the '40s, '50s, and '60s, mostly in straight-stitch variations and heavy on hoopskirts, animated fruit, and cartoonish animals. Ardis had a softer spot than I did for that kind of kitschy kitchen linens.

"I probably have some of the same towels stuffed in the back of my linen closet," she said. "I should get them out and use them."

"Or see if Russell will take them in trade for the art embroidery runner. You really need to get back over there, to see it, Ardis. It's—" I clasped my hands and closed my eyes to show her how overwhelming it was. And then I slipped and told her how I'd heard about the runner.

"*Spiveys!* Kath Rutledge, you stood right here and told me you wouldn't let them get you tangled up in whatever trouble they were brewing. And then you walked straight to the Vault and right into it. You lied to me."

"No, just left the Spivey part out."

"On purpose."

"Look at you," Geneva said, blustering up to Ardis. "Look how you're behaving. I believe you enjoy having these childish fits over the twins. My goodness, and you're nearly five times older than I am."

"Three times, tops," Ardis snapped.

"Whoop-de-do."

"The point is"—Ardis turned her back on Geneva to continue berating me—"you said you weren't going to meddle in Spivey meddling when you went to the Vault."

"And I didn't. I didn't say a word about Nervie's patterns when I was there, not to anyone. Here's something interesting I just realized, though. Through all the yelling and Nervie's accusations about fakes and fraud, Belinda never retaliated. She never said anything about Nervie's patterns."

"That just proves it then," Ardis said. "Shirley and Mercy were up to no good and you'd better watch your step, or you'll end up deeper in their whoop-de-do with no one to pull you out." She walked to the door and threw another "whoop-de-do" over her shoulder. The electronic sheep at the back door said *baa*, and all was quiet.

"What have I done?" I whispered.

"Lied and cut her to the quick," Geneva said. "I understand why, though. Deception is the better part of valor where crotchety old women are concerned."

ARDIS CAME BACK half an hour later, at the beginning of a downpour, with a peace offering. "I know you can't help yourself where textiles are concerned, hon. The same way I can't help myself around Mel's bakery counter."

She handed me a bag with two of Mel's pear-and-ginger scones and went to put the kettle on. When she brought two cups to the counter, I insisted she have the second scone. Geneva floated over us, like a fog of steam and ginger.

"If only the world's miseries and mysteries could be solved with ginger scones," Geneva said with a sigh.

"It would truly be a better place," Ardis agreed. "I'd even settle for solving our own."

"Think globally, solve locally. You've inspired me to try," Geneva said. "Thank you. I'll go up to my room and listen to the dull drumbeat of the rain and watch for drips. It will be like meditation. And I'll let you know when I have an inspired plan to track down the villain. I'm sure it will leave you speechless."

"I'm sure it will," Ardis said.

But Deputy Darla Dye dropped by the Cat before Geneva or her plan materialized, and Darla's news left us speechless first: "The scissors didn't kill her."

EIGHTEEN

"CAN YOU EXPLAIN THAT?" I asked. "Because I saw them in her…" I reached behind me but couldn't bear to touch my back where I'd seen the scissors. "Yeesh, Darla."

"Are there customers?" she asked.

I shook my head at her and the solid, soaking east Tennessee rain.

She checked for customers, anyway, walking quickly through the downstairs rooms and then running up the front stairs. Darla, the newest member of the sheriff's department, gave the impression of waking up each morning surprised and delighted to put on her uniform. She carried a joy with her that eased tense situations. She also carried a torch for Clod and seemed to be making progress along those lines. We had another reason for liking her at the Cat—she was a serial knitter of scarves. I heard her footsteps as she went through the rooms overhead. When she ran back down the stairs, Geneva came with her.

"It's hard to concentrate on plans during a police raid," Geneva whispered. She settled on the counter between Ardis and me.

"The scissors were a decoy, not a weapon," Darla said. "That fact might have been missed, but the medical examiner did some meticulous measuring during the autopsy that—"

"Can you explain without those meticulous details?" Ardis asked.

"Another weapon made the fatal wound."

"Then why use the scissors?" Ardis asked.

"To throw us off," Darla said.

"To throw suspicion on *us*," Ardis said.

"Only if the killer knew the scissors came from the Cat." Darla, usually calm enough on duty that she might be knitting, started pacing.

"What about the label?" I asked. "Where did the killer get the scissors, if not from here?"

"Someone could have taken them to the Vault and left them," Darla said. Was she pacing or casing?

"What was the real weapon?" I asked.

"Unidentified." Her steps slowed as she passed the notions display that included a range of sharp objects. Definitely casing.

"Unidentified?" I echoed. "Yet here you are looking."

That earned a quick smile from Darla. "Nothing wrong with being obvious in my work. We're looking for something longer and narrower than the scissors, but not by much."

"Not a knitting needle?"

"The pathologist says no. The trouble is, there's all manner of tools in the shops at the Vault, too."

"And you wouldn't know if one was missing."

"Unless someone told us," Darla said. "Or something could've been used and returned."

"So why look here?" Ardis asked.

"Inspiration as much as anything, in case the scissors weren't just a decoy of convenience. Maybe the killer slipped up by using something familiar, and the real weapon is related. Maybe I'm all wet. But I thought

I'd take a look, and I wanted to ease your minds about the scissors, too."

Why she thought we'd be relieved about the scissors while she searched the shop for something else lethal, I didn't know. Still, I liked Darla's earnest concern better than Clod's stuffiness. Though, come to think of it, where *was* His Stuffiness?"

"How come you're telling us about this instead of Cole? Was he afraid I'd say 'told you so' about the scissors? Because I did."

"Cole? Nah."

"Aren't you working on Gar's case, Darla?" Ardis asked. "Any progress?"

"Do you know that point you get to in a complicated embroidery project, when it looks more like a rat's nest, but if you keep at it you know it'll come out all right? We're not quite at that point of knowing it'll come out right, but we hope to be there soon. Mind if I look around in the workroom? Strictly for inspiration."

I looked at Ardis. She shrugged. Darla took that as an affirmative and headed back upstairs.

"Don't worry," Geneva said. "I won't let her out of my sight."

Ardis cocked her head, listening to Darla climb the stairs. "Question," she said. "If Darla's working on Gar's case *and* she's here on Belinda's, does that illustrate the efficiency of a small department?"

"Or does it mean they've discovered a connecting tunnel between two rat nests?"

Darla came back down the stairs faster than she went up. Called away, she said, and she didn't stop to tell us what inspiration she'd picked up from the tools in the workroom. Geneva swirled down with her.

"Did she find anything?" Ardis asked.

"No. We either never had one, or ours is missing."

"Would we *know* if something is missing from the workroom?" I asked Ardis.

"It would depend on how often it's used."

"Rarely, I suspect," Geneva said.

"You know what she's looking for?" I asked.

"*And* who did it." She pulsed with excitement. "I'm surprised I didn't recognize him. It was Errol Flynn in the storage room with a rapier."

"Oh, for—we need to be serious," Ardis said.

"She is being serious."

"And I'm correct," Geneva said. "I have a wealth of information gleaned from my years in filmology. I practically have advanced degrees in history, fashion, and criminology."

We watched as Geneva lunged and parried with an imaginary rapier. I'd become so used to picking out the details of her filmy appearance that I could almost believe I saw the sword, too.

"Do we know if the victim had an exit wound?" Geneva asked. She brought her rapier upright to touch her nose, and then slipped it into a scabbard at her waist. "Now that I think about it, a rapier might go right through her. I keep hitting these dead ends. So unnecessarily appropriate. I'll return to my room and my plans."

The rain kept customers away that day, but not deputies. Clod, in his regulation raincoat, stopped in shortly before lunch. The leery eye he couldn't help giving the yarns and threads amused Ardis.

"Come in, Coleridge," she said, spreading her arms

wide. "Welcome to the comfort of crewel and the balm of bolts of fabric."

Clod ignored her and asked, as Darla had, if he'd be interrupting business.

"Sadly, no," Ardis said, "and I'm sorry they don't equip you with swim fins for days like this. What can we do for you?"

"Sheriff Haynes is appealing to the public."

I opened my mouth to say that seemed unlikely, because he didn't appeal to anyone, but Clod hadn't finished.

"It's to do with the Gar Brown case. Ahead of the appeal, we're releasing details. Please hold your questions until I'm finished.

"Hikers found Gar beside his truck. There were signs of a struggle. He died from a blow to the head. The same rock used to deliver the blow was then used to break out the driver's-side window. We know the sequence because we found blood from the head wound on the rock and on the pieces of glass that were at the point of percussion. We originally thought Gar interrupted a burglary in progress. Similar vehicle burglaries have occurred at other remote parking areas, with similar details—busted window, glove box broken into, anything of value gone. Gar's wallet was gone, as was his phone. No confrontations were reported in the other burglaries. No witnesses have come forward in any of the crimes."

"Are deputies really going door-to-door with this information?" I knew I must look as skeptical as I sounded.

"This is a special visit because of your past activities."

"I see. I wonder why that doesn't sound like a compliment?"

"But it's smart of the sheriff's department to recognize our activities," Ardis said.

"But not because we want or need your help," Clod said. "Because we do *not* want or need it. I want you to have as much information as we can give you, so that you *won't* go snooping for more. So that you leave this to *us*. So that you *don't* get in our way."

"In that case, I'll take notes so we keep it all straight." Ardis took paper from a drawer and sat down on the stool.

"This crime—" Clod started to say.

"First, is the gang officially being called the Saggy Bottom Boys?" Ardis asked.

"No."

"Good, because I think anyone, even a gang, might object to a demeaning name like that. Now wait while I catch up." Ardis wrote for longer than seemed necessary, shielding her work from Clod as though she thought he'd cheat off her paper. When I went to look over her shoulder, I saw that she'd summarized his points neatly in very few bullet points. The rest of what she'd written looked like a grocery list followed by a to-do list, and then two sentences. While I watched, she drew an arrow to the sentences and then underlined them each three times. They were, "Infuriating man," and "I have always said and always will say that Ten is the smarter and better behaved Dunbar."

"*This* crime," Clod said again with a tone of aggrieved forbearance, "matches the other crimes in all but one detail."

"The death, which you just told us about," Ardis said.

"Two, then. Two details. There is a difference between the other crime scenes and the murder scene.

That could mean the confrontation and the killing rattled the gang so they went off script. But we think, now, that the killer targeted Gar and used the gang's MO as cover."

"Do you know yet why Gar went to the trailhead?" I asked.

Clod looked at us for several seconds before answering with a frustrated "No."

"Could there be anything in the liaison idea?" I asked. "Who came up with it?"

"Shorty."

"Based on what?"

"Scene-of-crime details."

"Do we want to hear those details?" Ardis asked. "Ten doesn't believe that scenario."

"You don't either, do you, Cole? So why did Shorty?" I turned to Ardis. "You can cover your ears if you want."

"There's nothing to worry about, Ms. Buchanan," Clod said. "We found nothing of a private nature, if you catch my drift."

"I would rather not."

Clod held up his hands. "It's nothing. It's safe. Shorty's full of—excuse me. He found a couple of paperback romance novels on the front seat. They seemed out of character, and Shorty spun this explanation of them belonging to whoever Gar was there getting his jollies with."

"Coleridge."

"*I* don't think that's why he went up there. I'm telling you what the situation is. You might take this as a lesson in how not to read too much into random items found at a crime scene. Do I make myself clear?"

The rain looked more monsoon-ish than ever. Clod looked happier to risk drowning in it than stay with us.

After he sloshed out the door, Ardis said, "I think he handles himself well under duress, don't you? He should give serious consideration to running for sheriff in the next election."

"He'd probably hate the paperwork. Darla should run."

"True on both counts. *Did* he make himself clear with that information? What did we learn?"

"That Gar's killer probably used another crime to cover his tracks. And isn't it interesting that Belinda's killer used our scissors to cover *his* tracks?"

"But in all the excitement, Cole forgot to tell us what the missing detail is. Maybe I should call and ask him." She did, but her call went to voicemail.

LATE THAT SOGGY AFTERNOON, Ardis told me there was something in the kitchen I needed to see.

"Tiptoe, hon, and peek in."

I did as instructed, hearing the murmur of Joe's voice as I approached. He sat at the kitchen table, quietly reading a picture book aloud. Argyle sat on the table watching him, obviously enjoying either the sound of Joe's voice or the story. Geneva sat on top of the refrigerator, obviously enjoying it, too. I watched for a while and then went back out front without disturbing them.

"Isn't that a sweet domestic scene?" Ardis said. "He's practicing to be a guest reader for the kindergarten. Ten says they wanted Cole, but he couldn't do it."

"Joe to the rescue. Ardis, what if Joe could listen to Geneva's description and sketch her villain for her?"

Ardis touched the circlet of green braiding on her

wrist. "I've never asked you how this works. I won't ask now, either, but can you do it again?"

"I'm not sure it'll work again, but what do you think?"

"That you need to be honest with yourself. Is it that you aren't sure it'll work, or is it that you aren't sure you want it to work?"

"Is there a right and a wrong answer to those questions?"

"I'm not sure there's a right or wrong answer to *that* question."

"I should ask him first. I should probably think about it first, too. Mind if I go up to the study?"

"Take your time, hon."

Geneva found me a while later with my feet propped on Granny's desk. Granny used to say she did her best thinking like that. I closed the dye journal I'd been reading and set it on the desk next to a hank of green cotton rug warp.

"Your beau was reading, too," Geneva said. "Reading is a singular pleasure."

"It is. I especially like reading my grandmother's journals. Do you remember when I dyed this cotton?"

"You did that for Ardis."

"And you."

"Your granny had peculiar talents."

"That she did." I met her gaze. "Geneva, you know that Joe is a talented artist. What if you could describe the villain to him so he can sketch the face?"

"That could revolutionize the investigation."

"Or at least solve it. But I should ask Joe first."

"You should ask me first. We're talking about my

privacy, after all. Perhaps I don't like the idea of a gen-tleman burglar ogling my ankles."

"He isn't really the ogling type. And I am asking you."

"What if he doesn't believe I'm here? What if he thinks you're crazy? Are you willing to take that chance?"

I'd thought about those questions and a few more with my feet propped on Granny's desk. I didn't have them all sorted out, but I knew the answer to her last question. "Yes."

"Then let's go ask him."

As simple as that.

I braided nine strands of the sage green cotton to-gether, and we took it downstairs. Ardis and Argyle were in the front room closing shop for the day. Ardis dropped her keys when she saw us.

"Ten's in the basement checking for water. Did you make him a bracelet like mine? Will he want to wear a bracelet? Are you nervous, Geneva? Were you nervous before I met you?" She dropped her keys again.

"No, because I didn't think it would work. Now there is more at stake. If I had keys, I would put them in my pocket."

Ardis slipped her keys into her pocket, and then we heard Joe coming up from the basement. We stood in a row facing the hall doorway.

"Damp in one corner," Joe said. He came in looking at his hands as he wiped them with a cloth. "The rain's let up, so nothing to worry about." He tucked the cloth in a back pocket, glanced at us, and then looked again. "What's happened?"

"Nothing yet," Geneva said.

Ardis giggled and then stopped. Joe gave her a puzzled look and turned to me.

"You're always up for new experiences, right?" I asked.

"Tell him you'd like him to meet a relative of mine," Ardis said.

"He can hear you, Ardis. You're not the one—"

"With the dis-em-*bodied* voice," Geneva said.

Ardis tittered.

"Straighten up," Geneva said. "The *ghoul* of this meeting is to introduce me to the *boo*-tiful burglar beau."

Ardis sputtered.

This wasn't how I'd pictured asking Joe if he believed in ghosts. "Stop it, you two," I said. "You're going to spook him."

Ardis howled.

"Come here, Joe." I took his hand. "We have someone we'd like you to meet." I put the green braid in his hand and watched his face as Geneva floated over. He looked at the braid, at me, at Ardis, and shook his head.

"Sorry," he said. "I don't get the joke."

NINETEEN

GENEVA WAVED HER hand past Joe's face, then both arms. "He can't see me at all."

Was that a note of relief in her voice?

Notes of desperation caught in Ardis's voice as she said, "Hold on, Ten. Wait there." She scrabbled at her green bracelet, got it off, and handed it to him. "Yes?"

"Sorry, Ardis."

"Give me yours." Joe handed his braid to her. She blinked at Geneva. "As plain as the nose on your face. Well, now, that isn't true, but plain as a raindrop on that window."

Joe looked at the window, he looked at me, and he waited, patient and unflapped. A good man.

"A ghost," I said. "Joe, we have a ghost named Geneva living in the shop. She and I met in the cottage at the Homeplace when I stayed there."

"She's my great-great-aunt," Ardis said.

"I'm sure you'd be pleased to meet me," said Geneva.

"Why don't you guys give us a few minutes," I said to Ardis and Geneva. "Joe, come on to the kitchen. I'll fill you in."

Joe and I sat across from each other. He listened, his elbows on the kitchen table, his hands clasped and resting against his lips. With his thin, serious face, he looked monkish and meditative. I didn't tell him about Geneva in exhaustive detail. That could happen over the

next days and weeks, if he was interested. I did tell him
why we'd hoped the green braided cotton would work.

"If it's any consolation," he said, "I can't be hypnotized either. Cole could never make me squawk like a
chicken."

"Cole knows how to hypnotize people?"

"*He* thinks he does."

"But you don't believe him. Do you believe me about
Geneva?"

He took a moment, and I tracked the consideration
going into his answer by watching his eyes. Kind eyes.
"Put it this way," he said. "I don't believe that you and
Ardis are both delusional. One or the other? An outside chance. And I won't use the word 'crazy.' I never
believed that about Ivy, either."

"Geneva loved to draw," I said. And then *I* had to
take a moment; I hadn't expected to cry. "John found
one of her drawings, in the archives at the Homeplace,
on one of his research binges. A miniature portrait
sketch of her friend Maddie."

"If she's willing to try, she and I can still sketch her
villain," Joe said. "She can hang over my shoulder and
tell you what I'm doing wrong. Then you can tell me."

And so we did, although Geneva preferred sitting in
a chair so she didn't chill the artist. Joe's obvious talent
encouraged her. Their shared vocabulary of line, shape,
shadow, and proportion helped her focus. I repeated her
directions and corrections, and I showed him where she
pointed on the sketch or on her own face. Ardis reluc-
tantly went home to make supper for her daddy. Argyle
fell asleep in my lap.

Half an hour after she left, Ardis called for a progress report.

"We might be almost there," Joe said when I relayed the question. "What do you think, Geneva? Another half hour or so?"

Geneva nodded. I nodded for Joe and told Ardis.

"Good," Ardis said. "I won't interrupt again. Call me as soon as you have it."

We settled back into the peculiar work of watching a person emerge from paper and graphite.

"Give him a pat on the back," Geneva said after a tricky negotiation over the corners of the eyes. "He can put his pencil down."

"Do we know who he is?" Joe asked.

"Why didn't I know it was a man?" Geneva said.

He looked like any slim, middle-aged man who might walk into the shop. Not like Joe, but not so different—the tightness of the mouth, the shape of the eyebrows and cheekbones.

"Do you recognize him, Geneva?" I asked. "We're both shaking our heads," I told Joe. "I guess we didn't expect to, but it would've been handy."

"What now?" Joe asked.

"Call Ardis." I did, and she said she had the obvious answer.

"Call the posse, hon, and and see if any of us recognize him."

"A more obvious answer is turn the sketch over to the authorities," I said.

"A tricky business," she said. "How would we explain it? Where did we suddenly get it? From a witness? And if not suddenly, then why didn't we report it sooner?"

"But how do we explain it if we *don't* give it to them and it turns out to be vital?" That unleashed a torrent from Ardis. When she stopped for a breath, I got a question in. "Are you sure you aren't just rationalizing? Whoa." I took the phone from my ear, then returned it gingerly. "She has a compromise," I said to Geneva and Joe. "We go over to her place, let her see the sketch, and then turn it over to Darla. I can live with that. How about you guys?"

"Sure," Joe said.

"If only," Geneva said. "But it won't *haunt* me if you do." She left her chair and floated to the top of the refrigerator.

"Will you come with us, Geneva?" Joe asked—turning to look at the top of the refrigerator as he did.

"If he can't see me," Geneva whispered, "how does he know I'm over here now?"

"Good question." I had the braid in my pocket, so it wasn't that. "Joe? What's going on? How do you know Geneva's over there?"

"I'm a fisherman. I know how to read water. Ripples. A disturbance that means something's there or moving." He nodded at Argyle. "He can see you, right? I was looking at him. He turned his head and watched you move from the chair to the fridge. He's looking at you now. He's listening to you. Will you come with us to see Ardis?"

"I'll stay here so I don't make ripples."

"You don't need to worry about that," I said. "There aren't many fishermen as good as Joe. You aren't a fish, anyway, and if there are ripples, no one will think anything of them or know why they're there. Not in a million years."

"I don't know if that's true," she said, "and the man in the sketch is out there. We don't know who he is. He frightens me. He might find out who *we* are first. You take the sketch to Ardis. I'll work on my plan. Then Argyle and I will keep watch."

"I WENT WITH *my* obvious answer," Ardis said when we knocked on her back door. "It seemed most expedient." She handed us each a glass of iced tea, and we followed her to the kitchen. Mel, Thea, Ernestine, and John, already at the kitchen table, sipped from their own glasses. Hank laughed at something on the television in the family room.

"At times like this, we need to stick together," Ardis said.

"Were you two really going to leave us out of the loop?" Thea asked.

"We didn't want to," I said, "but we really can't identify the witness."

"Call the witness W," Mel said. "Use 'they' for the pronoun." She picked up her knitting—a bittersweet baby hat with faux spikes.

"What can you tell us about W?" John asked.

"W is sincere and honest," I said.

"That leaves out Shirley and Mercy," Ernestine said with a thump of her glass. "Oh dear, I hope I didn't hurt the table. And we shouldn't make guesses about W, should we?"

"W is scared and feels they can't go to the police," I said. "After working on the sketch with Joe, and seeing the face again, W doesn't want to leave home."

"That's actually ridiculous," Ardis said.

"I don't imagine it's easy being W," Joe said.

"You're right, Ten. I was unkind."

"Is it Nervie?" Thea asked.

"We scanned the drawing before we left the Cat," Joe said. "I'll send it to everybody, but here's the original."

The sketch went from hand to hand. Mel and Thea spent the most time with it. John didn't put down his knitting before shaking his head. Ernestine took out her magnifying glass to pore over it, and then passed it to Ardis. No one recognized Geneva's villain.

"He doesn't *look* unpleasant," Ernestine said.

"W firmly believes he's the killer," Ardis said.

"Full disclosure," I added, "W means well, one hundred percent, but—"

"But *W* isn't one hundred percent?" Mel pointed to her head.

Ardis, Joe, and I looked at each other. They deferred to me. "W has issues. The issues sometimes make W unreliable."

"It sounds like you know W fairly well," Mel said. "Will you ever tell us who W is?"

"Let's let W be," Joe said quietly.

"Good enough," Mel said. "I'd say between the three of you, W is in good hands."

"What did W see?" Ernestine asked.

"This guy went into and came out of the storage closet shortly before I found Belinda. No way he missed Belinda. I asked W if he could've seen Belinda and left because he didn't want to get involved. W said the guy didn't come out immediately, and when he did, he showed no emotion or reaction. W said the guy strolled."

"Did W hear anything?" John asked.

"They were focused on the music and didn't hear any noise from the closet."

"You know how weird this sounds, don't you?" Thea said. "How does a guy stroll into a storage closet, kill someone, and stroll out again? And what was Belinda doing in there?"

"We need to find out," Ardis said. "W is convinced this man is the killer. He might not be, but he was in the closet with the body, so he's a person of interest."

"How does this affect our investigation?" Ernestine asked. "Are Joe and I off gang patrol to hunt for this man?"

"Yes and no," I said. "Did Ardis tell you we're turning the sketch over to Darla? The deputies might find him faster than we can. We'll do that tonight."

"Good," John said. "Being seen to cooperate with the authorities is always a good move. Then we can keep working in the background."

"Looking for the connections," I said. "With luck, finding them will help identify opportunity and motive."

"And we'll all have the scan of the man with the plan," Mel said. "Do you hear how with-it we sound? I will *not* be printing the sketch and posting it on the bulletin board at the café, though. And, Ernestine, I know you're raring to mix it up with the gang, but I want you to promise you'll be careful. If you see this guy, or if you run into the Saggy Bottom Boys, you call Red. She's like a tiger in threatening situations. If you can't get her, go ahead and try Darla, Cole, or Shorty. In that order."

"Are we all sticking around for Darla?" Thea asked.

"Better you don't," Ardis said. "She'll assume you're involved, anyway, but if you're gone, you won't be in the direct line of deputy ire."

"I have a short report on the bank building, then," Thea said. "It was for sale off and on for years. The corporation that owned it finally deeded it over to the town. The town is leasing it to the Arts Council for a hundred dollars a year. I wondered if anyone was angry about that, or if anyone's still angry. It seems like someone always is in situations like this, someone feels cheated or thinks the town is playing favorites. So maybe Gar's death was a reaction to that kind of anger or resentment? I got no sense of that, so far, but I'll keep looking."

"What if that kind of baloney led to Gar's death," Mel said, "but Gar's death didn't get the killer what he wanted, so he went after Belinda?"

"But did *her* death get him what he wanted?" Ernestine asked. "If it didn't, are others in danger?"

"Kath's tablecloth was in danger," John said. "What if destroying it was act two and Belinda's death was act three?"

"The beginning of a pattern," Ernestine said. "Rip one, kill two. You can have that line for your book, Thea."

"Thanks."

"How does stealing the shreds fit in?" I asked. "That theft is minor compared to the murders, but it happened. If nothing else, it's weird."

"Call that act three, scene one," Thea said. "Simon's books are scene two."

"What about his books?" Ardis asked.

"Someone boosted a few that same afternoon," Thea said. "Have you heard of anyone else losing anything?"

We hadn't.

"Have you learned anything useful about the table-cloth, Kath?" John asked.

"Nervie says it was stolen. The Spiveys say Nervie slashed it because of a vendetta."

"So, no, nothing useful," Mel said. "Does it matter where the tablecloth came from?"

"It does, because it's part of the puzzle," John said. "If you'd like, I can summarize an article I read about archives leading from one to another and the value of the resulting accumulation of facts and artifacts to a research project. It's a wonderful theory."

"Email it to me," Thea said. "Someone in my Library Nerd Club will love it."

"Is Library Nerd Club a thing?" Mel asked.

"Sure," Thea said. "None of the members know they're in it, though."

"John, have you ever heard this?" Joe asked. "'Exploring all the little by-ways, / Sighting all the distant stars, / And I was not far from home.'"

"A sailor's song," John said. "That's the idea exactly. Wandering and wondering are fine, as long as we keep our destination in sight."

"A Pete Seeger song," Joe said to me. "I'll sing it for you sometime."

"We only made the assignments last night," I said, "but does anyone else have a report? Anything on Russell, Rogalla, or Nervie? No? Then we'll plan to meet, as usual, for Fast and Furious on Friday. If anything comes up in the meantime—anything—let us know."

"You've heard my report," Thea said. "Now here's my theory: Russell, Rogalla, and Nervie aren't W, or we wouldn't still be talking about them."

"I'm not sure that follows," Mel said, "but here's my theory. It comes from working in restaurant kitchens, but I'm sure John noticed the same thing in the navy when he faced down hurricanes. Some people need to look at the chaos around them, to keep an eye on it in order to keep it at bay, be ready to help, fix, resist, whatever. Other people need to ignore the chaos so they don't become paralyzed. Red's in that first group when it comes to investigations. It's why we look up to her. She's in the second group when it comes to knitting."

"I have a theory about people and chaos, too," Ernestine said. "We all know people who attract chaos, and some who enjoy it. But I think this killer has taken it many steps beyond that. He's looking at the chaos he created, he likes it, and he's adding to it."

"Or they," Joe said. "Thea asked how a guy strolls into a storeroom, kills someone, and strolls out again. Maybe he strolled in *expecting* to find the body, and he was making sure his partner did the job right."

"What about your rat-faced McDougals?" John asked.

"Cole's given them a pass," I said. "I'm not sure I'm willing to do that, but those guys weren't exactly subtle, and the guy in the sketch seems to have traveled under the radar."

"Maybe the McDougals provided misdirection," Ernestine said.

I told Ernestine I liked the way she thought. They all stayed to hear Ardis call Darla, and then Mel, Thea, John, and Ernestine took off. After that, it didn't take Darla long to get there. Ardis ushered her to the kitchen, as I put the four used tea glasses in the dishwasher.

"Hey, Kath. Joe."

"Hey, Darla."

"Iced tea?" Ardis asked.

"No, thanks."

Joe offered Darla a seat. She declined that, too.

"We'll get right to it, then," Ardis said. "We're acting

on behalf of a third party—someone who saw a man leaving the storeroom shortly before Kath discovered the body. We have a sketch of that man. In order to protect the witness, we hope you'll treat this like a Crime Stoppers tip with no questions asked."

I handed Darla the sketch.

"When and how did you obtain this drawing?" Darla asked.

"That's a question," I said.

"I have a whole lot more."

"Darla, hon," Ardis said, "sit down and have a glass of tea. We understand your concerns, we truly do, but we need to move forward. No resentment, no recriminations."

"No bullshit," Darla said. But she pulled out a chair and sat and took a sip of tea. "And don't think I don't know why you called me instead of Cole. You think I'll go easier on you for withholding evidence."

"We called you because we know you'll listen," I said.

"And we withheld nothing," Ardis said. "I called in a tip as soon as I heard about this man. It wasn't a great description of him. But we're dealing with a frightened witness. Believe us when we say, if W—we're calling the witness W—could stand here before you, they would. But that isn't going to happen."

"It really isn't," Joe said.

"You drew this?" Darla asked him. "It looks like your work. How, if the description wasn't great, did you end up with portrait-quality art?"

"I can't account for how W's memory works," Joe said.

"But I'm sure you've heard of leading a witness. Did

you make suggestions while you drew? Can you tell me for a fact that this image is from W's head and not a product of your own artistic license?"

"Well," Joe ran a finger along his jawline a few times as he thought about that. "If you think the image is more mine than W's, then it's useless and you can toss it, and we haven't wasted your time at all. That's my take on it."

"That's actually pretty good," Darla said. A dimple came and went. "But you're playing around—"

"You have the picture," I said, "fresh from Joe's pencil. We don't know if it's accurate, because we don't know this guy. Wait, do *you* know who this is?"

"Not a clue. Tell me what W said." She took out a notebook and pen, and while I repeated what I'd told the others, she wrote. "How tall?"

Ardis, Joe, and I looked at each other.

Darla glanced up from her notebook. "What are you, a bunch of amateurs? Did you ask what he was wearing?" Her dimples came and went again as she shook her head.

"I'll ask W and let you know," I said. "But, Darla, the picture scared W. I think it looked more like the guy than they expected it to. And W doesn't scare easily. W loves the idea of doing dangerous things."

"Really?" Joe said.

"Say something about six-shooters and horses and see what happens," I told him, then turned back to Darla. "The point is, we couldn't force W any further or faster than we did. We seriously thought about looking for this guy on our own, first, so you wouldn't waste your time on a tip from an unreliable witness."

"Now you're saying W is unreliable? Which is it?" Darla asked. "Eyewitness or unreliable witness?"

"That's the problem in a nutshell," Ardis said. "That's why we did our civic duty and turned it all over to you."

"Do you suppose that was a rookie mistake?" Ardis asked after Darla left. "She didn't ask if we kept a copy of the sketch. And that could account for why she also didn't tell us not to show it around."

"We can start first thing tomorrow morning." Joe held up his phone. "Text from Sierra. She's having a 'breakfast and renewal of spirits' meeting. Want to come?"

"Ardie?" Hank's reedy voice called from the family room. "Ardie? Did I remember to put gas in the chain saw?"

"Daddy and I will be renewing our breakfast right here," Ardis said.

"Kath?" Joe asked.

"I'm hungry already."

TWENTY

I DIDN'T THINK Sierra's renewal of spirits meeting would do much for mine. The breakfast part might fulfill its promise, but generally speaking, at seven A.M., my spirits preferred turning over and snoozing for another half hour or so. I ignored the sweet talk from my pillow and only yawned every half-block on my way to meet Joe outside the Vault. I yawned again for him.

"Special delivery from Mel's, it looks like," he said, nodding his chin toward someone coming down the street behind me.

I turned to see. "Hey, Angie. How's it going?"

For years, fairly or unfairly, people had referred to Angie as Mercy Junior. Hooking up with Aaron, though, and taking the job at Mel's seemed to be setting a new pattern for her life. "Can I hand these to you so I can get back?" She'd juggled two pastry boxes and a to-go box of coffee the few blocks from Mel's.

Joe took the coffee, and I took the boxes. "Don't let Mel run you ragged," I said.

Angie looked up and down the street. "Mel offered me time off. I asked for extra hours."

"Everything all right?" Joe asked.

"Oh yeah. Mom and Aunt Shirley are a little over-excited about the babies. Aaron asked them to back off a bit, and Mel declared the café a Mom and Aunt Shirley-free zone."

"How's the Riley and Taylor show?" I asked.

"We're up to episode six or seven. I just hope we can skip a disaster scene."

I patted her shoulder without comment. She rubbed her belly and left.

The door opened behind us, and Sierra stepped out. She gazed after Angie and tucked a few bills in her pocket.

"I guess that saves me a delivery tip. Good morning, Joe. And Kath. How nice. I'm so glad I planned for extras. You can take that on up to the gallery."

I yawned my response and felt we were even. "I wasn't exactly invited, was I?" I asked Joe as we climbed the stairs.

"Will you watch my booth for an hour on Friday morning?"

"I can probably do that. Why?"

"That makes you staff. Let's eat."

Five or six of the merchants were already there, looking uncomfortable. Martha and Floyd stood near a table set with plates, cups, and napkins. We opened the boxes there.

"From Mel's," Joe announced.

Mel's reputation did its magic. Her spinach-and-egg muffin cups broke our fasts, and her wedges of apple kuchen renewed our spirits. Her coffee broke the ice. Between sips and mouthfuls, we talked and shared a few laughs. When I was on my second muffin, I heard Sierra coming up the stairs with more people: Simon and Nervie.

"I'm glad to see you've already started," Sierra said. "I did want to say a few words about Belinda, though."

"You still can," Martha said.

"And we'll toast her memory with coffee," Floyd said.

"Someone give me coffee, *please*," Simon said, "and I'll do the toast." He blew on the cup Joe handed him, tested it, and then raised it. "In Belinda's memory, kind thoughts, thoughtful prayers, enduring sorrow. Rest in peace."

Sierra looked up from her phone. "Lovely. Thanks, Simon. I wanted to say something about coming together over food in fellowship, too."

"You just did," Martha said.

Floyd clapped, everyone joined in, and then went back to eating and talking. Joe and I mingled. Talk mingled, too, ranging from "Mmm" to discussions of sales, to the expected, "It's still such a shock." I ate a slice of kuchen slowly so that listening with a full mouth appeared more polite than nosy. My mind wandered a bit, too, wondering what "the expected" talk might be after introducing a friend to a ghost he couldn't see or hear. Joe hadn't said anything, and I hadn't brought it up.

Martha dropped a few platitudes into conversations while she sipped her coffee. When she put down her cup, she checked the time and muttered, "I hope we aren't making a habit of gung-ho fellowship."

Joe showed the scan of the sketch on his phone around, saying it was someone at the grand opening. "I lost the scrap of paper with his contact info and can't get it to him."

"Display it in your shop," Simon said. "Maybe he'll come back through."

No one recognized him.

Not surprisingly, Russell didn't attend. A few people

mentioned him being in their thoughts and prayers and wondered about the shop space.

"He plans to keep it open," Nervie said.

"We're still discussing it," Sierra said. "I told him not to rush it."

"He's ex-military, like my late husband," Nervie said. "Having a plan isn't rushing. It's how you do things."

"He's coming in tomorrow morning," Sierra said. "Nothing's been decided." She sidestepped further discussion by turning around and joining Floyd and Simon.

"I've been wrong before," Nervie said with a shrug.

"Was Belinda local?" I asked.

Nervie shook her head. "Russell's mother's family was, a ways back. He and Belinda retired here, and for some reason Belinda saw fit to stay after the divorce. She stayed in the house, too. Said he never cared for it."

"You knew her well?" Joe asked.

"Well enough to know she stayed in that house out of spite."

Martha, listening from a few feet away, moved closer when Nervie went back for more coffee. "To be efficient, I'll let you know that Floyd and I can give each other alibis." With another show of efficiency, she called goodbye with a full-arm wave to cover everyone in the room and then headed down the stairs.

"Were we that obvious?" Joe asked.

"I didn't think so. Being suspicious makes it hard to be friends, though."

After Martha took off, others trickled away. Nervie circled back around before she left to let us know she regretted speaking ill of the dead.

"It isn't my way," she said.

"I'm sure you didn't mean—"

"But speaking ill of her as she was in life doesn't bother me a bit. She spit at me like a cat that afternoon."

"Which afternoon?"

"Friday. After she found the tablecloth ripped to shreds."

I tried not to stare. "I didn't see you here."

"And I didn't see *you*. Although I've seen you more often than I'd expect, so I'm sure we'll bump into each other again." And she dashed away.

I sent a text to Ardis asking her to change the question to Nervie's students—*when* did Nervie leave the Cat, not *if*.

A text from another textile colleague had come in. I skimmed it and started to get excited. She'd heard about a collection of Arts and Crafts textiles at an estate sale in Alexandria and thought she'd also heard that part of the collection went missing. But that's where my excitement died (and truth be told, relief set in for the sake of those textiles). "Not the textiles," she wrote. "They're fine." They'd been sold to a museum in Massachusetts.

Joe walked me to the Cat after Sierra's breakfast, suggesting we take the long way. Breakfast at seven, no matter how slowly we ate or how long we chatted, still gave me loads of time before work. Joe's long way included a walk up Vestal Hill.

"Is that Belinda's?" I asked as we slowed our walk past a Carpenter Gothic. "Do you think Belinda was right, that Russell never cared for it?"

"Hard to believe he wouldn't."

"We didn't hear that from Belinda or Russell, anyway. We heard it from Nervie."

"It's quiet up here," Joe said. "Probably gets a nice breeze on the porch."

"Belinda got awfully quiet while Cole was around Friday afternoon. Then she told him to drop the search. But I can believe she did spit at Nervie like a cat. It seems like there was more real animosity between Nervie and Belinda than between Cole and Rogalla."

"Unless Cole hit a fatal nerve with the new nickname. Possum fits, though. I like it. Does Geneva have a nickname?"

"She said her daddy called her Ginger, not because of her hair, though. She must have loved ginger. She can't touch or taste or move anything, but oddly enough, she can still smell ginger. I thought, over time, I'd be able to make sense of 'ghost.' In some kind of scientific way, I guess. It's been seven months, though. I could say *only* seven months, but by now it makes sense that Geneva just *is*, even if I don't know why. When it comes down to it, I don't know why any of us *are*."

"Works for me," Joe said. "I'm not the Dunbar with the badge. I don't have to understand everything in terms of possible and impossible."

"That's an interesting take on law enforcement. Huh. Works for me."

GENEVA ENJOYED HEARING about Darla's reaction to the sketch. She drew her imaginary rapier from its scabbard and cut a Z in the air. She was less happy to hear that, so far, no one recognized the man or remembered seeing him. Rapier forgotten, she watched me feed Argyle and then followed me to the front room.

"But villains return to the scene of the crime," she said as I opened the cash register.

"Not always."

"But if he does, I might be the only one who will definitely recognize him." No swirling or pulsing bravado.

"This guy might be too smart to go back, Geneva. But I'm going back tomorrow morning, to see if I can talk to Belinda's husband. Do you want to come with me?"

"If he's smart, my plan will have to be smarter. I'll stay here and work on it."

"Okay. Oh, before I forget, Darla wants to know how tall the guy is and what he was wearing."

"Dark suit. White shirt."

"Height?"

She puzzled over that.

"Compared to me or Ardis?" I prompted.

"I don't know."

I SPENT THE rest of a busy day talking knit and purl, fingering weight and worsted, roving and in-the-grease wool. Some customers needed reassurance that buying patterns and supplies was a fine hobby on its own, regardless of how many projects they completed.

In between sales I wondered what it meant when people didn't behave as expected. Sierra had been quieter, less frantic, when Clod arrived to see the vandalized tablecloth. But maybe she put her best professional foot forward for the deputy and the fireman. Belinda had also been subdued instead of exploding when the tablecloth shreds disappeared. But maybe she was in shock, the disappearance one blow too many.

"Or Belinda discovered something," Ardis said when I ran my thoughts past her. "Or she heard something that shut her up."

"Like what?"

"You've got me. As for Sierra clamming up when Coleridge arrived, that's not so unusual. I tend to do the same when he's around."

I waited for a laugh to follow that statement, but it didn't come. She went to help a customer pick out embroidery floss.

"If she believes that, she's living in an alternate universe," Geneva said, appearing on the mannequin's shoulder.

The door jingled with incoming customers, or I might have told her that odd beliefs seemed to run in the family.

One of the new customers said she was on "a crochet-cation," stopping in as many yarn shops as she could along her route. "May I take pictures to document this stop? I'll identify the shop when I post them."

"Sure. Upstairs, too. Let me know if I can help you find anything."

Geneva posed in each of the pictures the woman took in the front room and followed her into the next, which set me thinking about photographs.

Belinda hadn't wanted pictures taken of the table-cloth. Was that so odd? As Ardis had pointed out, plenty of craftspeople didn't allow photos at shows or in shops because they didn't want copycats. Of course, all the copycats had to do was buy the pieces and then copy to their heart's content. They would have paid for that privilege, though. And if someone had bought the tablecloth, Belinda couldn't have stopped the new owner from taking boatloads of pictures and posting them anywhere and everywhere. But what if Nervie was right and the tablecloth was stolen? Pictures could lead back to Belinda. Although, again, once sold, she'd have no control over who saw the tablecloth or who recognized it. *If* it was stolen. Big if.

I went back to thinking about people behaving in ways I didn't expect. Had Belinda discovered something or heard something? A threat? Nervie *was* there Friday afternoon. Who else? Our mystery man?

"CAN I RUN something else by you?" I asked Ardis while we closed shop for the day.

"You know you can."

"What did Nervie's husband look like?"

"I didn't know him well, and it's hard to picture him after all these years."

"Could he be the guy in the sketch?"

"Oh, now." Her eyebrows were skeptical of the idea, but she thought about it anyway. "Peter was rounder."

"He could have lost weight."

"What's put this idea in your head? People do change, but Nervie would know him, wouldn't she?"

"What if she did?"

"And they did this together? Why?"

"We don't know why *anyone* would do it. Why should that rule them out? No one's seen the guy in the sketch since the murder. What if he came to town, did this for—or with—her, then left again?"

"Are you even listening to yourself? Or worse, have you been listening to Spiveys?"

That acted like the bracing slap of a cold, wet washcloth. "Thanks, Ardis. I needed that."

"Anytime, hon. Keep your wits about you when you talk to Russell in the morning. What did John say? Little byways are fine, but don't get dumped in the drink. That's close enough."

"Yes, ma'am."

TWENTY-ONE

SIMON SMILED FROM behind the Vault's information and sales desk when I arrived the next morning. "Kath, nice to see you today! You're becoming a regular customer. Do you know how nice it is to think we already have regulars?"

I didn't tell him I'd yet to buy anything; it was only a matter of time. "You make a great old-time shopkeeper, Simon. The bowler and sleeve garters are just the right touch."

"Leftovers from a production of *The Music Man* a few years ago. When Sierra asked me to fill in for her here, I couldn't resist looking the part."

"Perfect."

Customers came in behind me, so I told him I'd see him later and moved on. Classical music played in the background. I let the strings and piano carry me past Joe's booth. He wasn't there, but a couple of customers chatted while they leafed through his watercolors. As I climbed the stairs, I saw Floyd walking a customer toward the sales desk, each of them carrying a straightback chair. Someone coughed up ahead. Someone else laughed. Happy sights and sounds as the Vault settled into a comfortable pattern of commerce.

I stuck my head in Martha's shop to say something friendly and not at all suspicious-sounding, but she wasn't in. Russell was in Belle's, though. So was Nervie. Had I jumped when I saw her?

"Kath might be just what you need, Russell," she said. "She's some kind of textile wizard."

Russell didn't show any sign of recognizing me. Why would he, out of all the people who'd passed through Belle's Saturday morning? He also didn't seem to recognize Nervie's sarcasm.

"I'm so sorry for your loss," I said.

"I'm sorry for hers," he said. "This place gave her something to look forward to." He lifted the corner of an embroidered hanky and let it drop. "I hate to see all this go to waste."

"I'll see you later, Russell," Nervie said. "You have my number?"

"You gave it to me yesterday." When she'd gone, he added, "And the day before. Do you know how many single women have given me their numbers in the past few days?"

"Really? So soon? And haven't you been divorced for a while? It seems kind of insensitive."

"Nothing says it's over like death, I guess." He stared at nothing for a few moments, then touched the embroidery on the handkerchief. "What's a textile wizard?"

"Nervie's joke." I gave him the abridged job description of a textile preservationist—caring for historic fabrics, usually in a museum or conservation lab setting. Not too lecturey; Geneva would approve.

"You might be interested in this, then." He bent, brought a deep, flat box from under the display table, and handed it to me. "Take a look. Think you can preserve that?"

I swallowed. Probably gulped like a brown trout. I'd

held this box before. To be sure, I lifted the lid enough for a peek.

"Are you OK?" he asked.

"Yeah, yeah." The lid settled back down. *Be cool. Don't ask leading questions.* "When did this turn up?" *Probably leading.*

"Sorry?"

"This box. Friday afternoon, it was…missing. First Belinda found the tablecloth in it cut to shreds, and then the whole thing—box and shreds—disappeared. Belinda didn't tell you?"

Definitely leading.

He shrugged. "We were exes for a reason."

"But you were helping out in the shop on Saturday."

"Exes but not enemies," he said.

"Do you know anything about the tablecloth?"

"Only that it doesn't look like one now."

"Do you know if she kept records or notes about any of the pieces? Like where she got them?"

"You make it sound like she was organized or something. To tell you the truth, I don't know."

"If you find records, will you let me know?"

"Why?"

"I may not be a textile wizard, but I'm a full-fledged textile fool, and this tablecloth was something special." I might have stroked the top of the box a few times. "Um, can I have it?"

"A box of rags? Do you know something about it I don't?"

"Only that it can't ever be fixed, but I can't stand the idea of it being thrown away."

"Whatever. Look, I told Sierra I'm happy to keep the shop open until the stock sells down. But I don't know crewel work from a crawdad, and I've got zero interest in learning."

"Where *did* the box turn up?"

"Martha somebody, the woman across the way, gave it to me."

"When?"

"This morning."

"Did she say anything?"

"Something about a storeroom."

"Thanks."

I carried my treasure across the gallery to Martha's shop. Still no sign of her, but she'd conveniently left a stack of business cards on a table near the door. I took one. When I turned to go, I nearly ran over Nervie. That time I *did* jump.

"In a hurry?" she asked.

Like a pro, I made use of her leading question. "I am, so I'll make this fast. Do you have any idea where the Arts and Crafts tablecloth Belinda showed us came from?"

"No." She eyed the box.

"You said it was stolen. How do you know that?"

"I heard Belinda say so."

As soon as the Vault's front door closed behind me, I tried Martha's number and started walking. The call took less than thirty seconds.

"Hi, Martha, this is Kath Rutledge."

"What can I do for you?"

"Have you got a minute? Am I interrupting anything?"

"Go ahead."

"Did you really find the scraps in the storeroom?"

"What scraps?"

"The box of scraps you gave to Russell Moyer this morning."

"I didn't *find* anything. Sierra handed me a box on her way out. She asked me to give it to Russell and tell him she found it in the storeroom. I didn't ask her what was in it, and I didn't open it. I'm hardly ever that nosy. I have another call."

She disconnected before I could tell her about all the fun she missed with a Spartan attitude like that toward nosiness. Then I found Sierra's card and called her. That conversation lasted less than twenty seconds.

"Hi, Sierra, it's Kath Rutledge. Martha told me you found the box with Belinda's shredded tablecloth in the storeroom. That's amazing."

"Not really. It was sitting on a shelf."

"Russell said Martha found it."

"Russell's confused. Belinda must have been confused, too."

"Confused about what?"

"Where she left them. Sad to say, but that shop might be the Vault's first fatality."

We disconnected, and I wished she hadn't used the word "fatality." By then I was only a block and a half from the Cat, but I called Ardis, anyway.

"We didn't cover all our bases," I said. "We need to add Martha the enamelist to the list, and Sierra. As sources, but it won't hurt to look at them, either."

"What's happened?" she asked. "Where are you? Is Joe there with you?"

"I can take care of myself, Ardis. But thank you for worrying. I'm on my way back. Almost there—and I have the shredded tablecloth. Sierra said she found it in the storeroom."

"You don't believe her?"

"It's convoluted, but I think we should look at her and Martha the way we're looking at the others on our list. Look for connections to Belinda, to Gar, to whatever we had on the whiteboard." I ran up the Cat's front steps and opened the door, still speaking into the phone. "Do you mind if I take the box up to the study? I won't be long."

"I'll contact the posse with an update," Ardis said. "Take your time."

I pocketed my phone, waved, and carried my treasure to the attic. Geneva and Argyle, hearing my feet running up the stairs, were upright and alert in the window seat when I arrived.

"The shredded tablecloth," I said a little breathless.

I set the box on the desk, and curiosity brought them over. Geneva sat on a corner of the desk, and Argyle hopped up beside her. When I took the lid off the box, Argyle sniffed delicately above the shreds and then jumped down.

"He didn't hiss," Geneva said, "but he isn't impressed."

"It isn't much to look at anymore."

"We can't all look our best. What does it *feel* like?"

"I held some of the pieces at Belinda's, the day she found it like this, and I didn't feel anything." I didn't really want to feel that nothing again, either.

"It's okay," Geneva said. "Argyle and I are here."

I brushed a shred with a fingertip. Nothing. I picked up a handful. Nothing. Not even a ghost of the feelings remained, and I felt as though I was in mourning. The tablecloth had had a life, a story, and I'd missed my chance to know it. I laid the shreds back in the box, closed it, and went downstairs.

"Were the shreds in the storeroom all along?" Ardis asked.

"I don't know. I don't how we'll find out, either."

John sent an email to the posse later that morning. He'd located an interview with Sierra in an alumni newsletter and summarized it for us:

She loves the job and the apartment—low salary but no rent. When asked if choosing artists and merchants for the limited number of spaces was difficult and how she'd avoided hard feelings, she replied, "I assumed anyone applying for a space was professional enough to deal with rejection." Notable quotes: "It's a small beginning, but it's my show."

"I can make it terrific."

"It'll be a stepping-stone or a launchpad. I am going places."

"She sounds enthusiastic and professional," Ardis said.

I agreed. "But I wonder where she plans to launch herself to? And how soon?"

"And how do you suppose it'll look on her résumé that someone was murdered on her watch? Or two people? That would hardly be fair, though." After a moment she added, "Of course, it was less fair to Gar and Belinda."

I agreed with that, too.

"Where does this put us in regards to the man in the sketch?" Ardis asked.

"Maybe it's time to shake things up. See what falls out."

FRIDAY MORNING, WHILE ARGYLE and I spent quality time with belly rubs and rumbling purrs, I asked Geneva about her plan to catch the killer.

"It's an excellent plan," she said. "If I weren't terrified, I would go to the Vault this minute to put it in action."

"What part of it scares you?"

"The catching the killer part."

"But that's—"

"I know. A tragic situation."

"I was going to say that's the whole point of the plan. But it *is* kind of tragic. This isn't really like you. You've been ready to take on bad guys over and over. You *have* taken on bad guys." The only things I'd ever heard her say really scared her were the dark and ghosts… ghosts…a ghost? Oh my goodness. "Geneva, did you know that we haven't heard anything from the deputies about the man in the sketch? You're the star witness—the only one who saw him—and no one's seen him since."

"Vamoosed, did he?"

"That's a reasonable conclusion."

"So my plan to catch him in another evil act is useless."

"But that means you can go to the Vault and not worry about him. And revisiting the scene might trigger your memory, bring back more details. It would be a different way to catch him. What do you think?"

"Why, if I had a horse, I'd say saddle up."

"Let's hold our horses until Ardis comes in."

WHEN ARDIS CAME IN, she raised a skeptical eyebrow. "This is your plan for shaking things up?" She watched

Geneva pretending to examine the mannequin with a magnifying glass. "Is she likely to remember anything else useful enough to crack the case?"

"I'm willing to try," Geneva said. "What more can you ask of your ghost, stout-hearted and true?"

"It can't hurt," I said. "Do you mind being the responsible shopkeeper, again, while we go sleuth?"

"You know I don't. And I won't *think* of suggesting you aren't careful by telling you to watch your step and be careful."

She did, however, call Joe. He met us at the Vault.

"How's this going to work?" he asked.

"I'll follow her and 'talk' to her when I can." I held up my phone. "You stick with us and act natural."

"Sounds easy enough." He squinted, peering to either side of me.

"If you're wondering, she's beside *you*, mimicking every move."

Geneva hooted. I winced.

"What just happened?" he asked.

"She thinks she's hilarious. She's serious about this, though."

"And it's working already," Geneva said. "I know where I saw him before."

I put the phone to my ear. "Hi, Geneva. Who?"

"The killer. He didn't look evil then."

"Where did you see him?"

"In the antique shop."

"Do you remember when?"

"Before."

"Okay, that's fine. We'll see you in the antique shop."

I looked at Joe. His face showed an interesting mix of bemusement and shell shock. "See? Easy enough."

"I've heard you two 'on the phone' before, haven't I?"

"This ain't our first rodeo," Geneva said. "Git along, cowboy."

"Morning," Floyd said when he saw us. He stuck the feather duster he'd been using in a vase. "What kind of damage can I do for you today?"

"What kind of damage does he go in for?" Geneva asked. "Tell the cowboy to keep an eye on him."

"We're fine, Floyd," Joe said. "We might be meeting a friend."

"I saw the killer looking at the rolltop desk," Geneva said. "Opening drawers."

A memory flashed of Clod and Rogalla opening those drawers. And Bruce more interested in a "possum." Rogalla had showed up almost immediately after we found Belinda, too. Coincidence? But I was working on a different theory of Geneva's suspect, one that made more sense and less at the same time.

"This is a gorgeous desk," I said.

"Used by the first bank manager and every one since," Floyd said.

"Cool."

"The killer thought the desk was cool," Geneva said, "but this is drop-dead cooler." She floated over to the square, marble-topped table I'd wondered about on Saturday. "You'll like what's in the drawer."

"What is this table?" I asked Floyd.

"A biscuit table."

"Open the drawer," Geneva said.

I pulled it open. A damask towel, white with a Turkey red band of oak leaves and acorns looked up at me.

"Go on," Geneva said. "I dare you."

I looked at her, looked at the towel, and took her dare. My fingers tingled when I picked it up.

"What do you feel?" she asked.

"I can smell warm biscuits and taste the butter melting on them," I said.

"Well, you've got a better imagination than I do," Floyd said. "I wish I could pipe that aroma in here. It might help sell the table. I have something else you might appreciate, Kath." He brought over a small, lidded basket. It was dark wickerwork, about eight inches around and, with its domed lid, about four inches high.

Joe took the towel (and gave it a surreptitious sniff) when Floyd handed me the basket.

"Victorian sewing basket?" I said.

Floyd lifted the lid. "Complete with thimble, threads, etui, scissors, awl, and an embroidery project forever unfinished. A handkerchief, do you think?" He took it out and held it up. Someone had begun stitching a small heart of French knot forget-me-nots in one corner.

"It makes me want to make one of my own, Floyd." I stirred the tools around with a finger. "I don't see the awl, though."

"It's a beautiful silver thing," Floyd said. "An embroidery stiletto. It should be there."

"He just came in," Geneva whispered.

"Where?" I saw a couple browsing nearer the door.

"There," Geneva whispered. "Returning to the scene-before-the-scene of the crime. Time to ghost-up."

"In the basket," Floyd said. "Let me look."

I shoved the basket at him and stumbled over his foot to get to Geneva. What was she doing?

"Why I oughta...lemme at 'em." She blustered toward the desk. Toward...no one.

I caught a glimmer, a shadow. Not much more than the ghost of a fruit fly. And then she screamed like she'd seen a ghost.

TWENTY-TWO

Is she all right?" Floyd asked.

With my hands slammed to my ears, I probably didn't look all right. And looking around wildly, when the screaming no one else heard stopped, didn't help.

"Might be a migraine," Joe said. He put his arm around my shoulders and pulled me close. "Can you tell me?" he asked quietly.

"I will. But first I need to find her. I hope she's gone back to the Cat. I'll call Ardis."

"And I'll call Cole. I'm pretty sure he needs to find that embroidery stiletto."

"Call him. But outside."

We thanked a concerned Floyd and went outside and around the corner of the building to Postage Stamp Park. I stopped in front of the trompe l'oeil mural. Bruce had stared at it the first time I saw him do his jazz hands routine. Had he stared at the mural, though, or at the bricked-up door now painted to look open and inviting? Or had he watched someone float in and out through that ghost of a door, no possums involved?

I called Ardis and asked her to look or listen for Geneva. She said she'd call back, and did a minute later, puffing from the climb to the attic.

"She's in the study, hon. Moaning. Oh, my word."

"It can be hard to take, but she'll be okay. Thanks, Ardis. I'm on my way."

"Where's Ten?"

"Calling Cole. I'll tell you about it after I calm Geneva."

Joe said he'd wait for Clod. I kissed him and almost, but not quite, ran back to the Weaver's Cat.

BY THE TIME I got to the study, Geneva had stopped the worst of her moaning. Argyle waited on the landing outside. He came in with me and jumped up on the desk. I sat next to Geneva on the window seat. She hunched in the corner, rocking.

"When you scream at the sight of someone, and then flee in terror, it creates the wrong impression," she said. "Even if that person is a ghost. It puts a damper on the possibility of having a ghost friend."

"Why are you afraid of ghosts?" I asked. "I'm not afraid of *you*; I didn't scream when we met. Argyle isn't afraid. Ardis and Joe aren't. And do you know who else isn't afraid of ghosts? Rogalla's dog, Bruce. He must've been tracking that ghost the whole time Rogalla bragged about possums."

"I don't have the bravery of a beating heart."

"I don't think that's what makes the difference, Geneva. We have an advantage over you, but it isn't that our hearts are still beating. It's that we're lucky enough to know a ghost. So we know that ghosts are people, too. Not *were*, but *are*."

"Thank you." She sat up straighter. "My mama never liked a sad-faced so-and-so."

"Neither did my granny. They probably didn't have someone with your situation in mind, though."

"No, but there's no use crying over spilt bones."

"That's good advice. It has a ring to it."

"Or a clatter."

"What did the ghost at the Vault do when he saw you?"

"Before I shrieked like a banshee, I'm sure he thought I'd be a lovely person to know. That was your first impression, wasn't it? And you and I have been inseparable ever since."

"Think carefully, Geneva. Did the ghost give any indication he knew you were there?"

"He didn't. Not today or any other time. He just kept going about his business. How rude."

"Maybe not rude, but unaware. I think he's caught in a loop, and I think Bruce proved that when Deputy Dunbar and Rogalla had him sniffing for the tablecloth."

"Stuck on endless repeat and can't interact with a colleague? The poor thing."

"Colleague is a nice way to think of him, Geneva. You have a good heart."

Argyle nudged the tablecloth box an inch closer to the edge of the desk. I told him to cut it out. He nudged it again, then before I could get to it, he pushed the box off and watched it take a nosedive. It sprang open on impact, and he made himself into a neat loaf, paws tucked, looking smug.

"Thanks a heap, buddy boy. Thanks *for* the heap."

I didn't like the idea of scooping the shreds with my hands and feeling that nothing…but *why* couldn't I feel it anymore? Why couldn't I interact with this ghost of a tablecloth?

Geneva nudged my shoulder with hers. "I'm sorry it doesn't feel the same anymore."

The same anymore. "Geneva, that might be the answer. What if it *isn't* the same? What if the feelings aren't gone, because they never were? What if this isn't *that* tablecloth?"

"Can't you tell?"

"I haven't looked that closely. I tried to *feel*, but I didn't really look."

"Then what are you waiting for? And be sure to thank Argyle."

I rubbed Argyle between the ears. Then I scooped up some of the shreds, sat down at the desk, and spread them out in front of me. I went back for some of the singed pieces.

"It's brown linen. That part's right." I took a magnifying glass from the kneehole drawer. "The stitches aren't... I didn't study the stitching when I first saw it. But where they shouldn't have been obvious, they weren't. These *are*. The colors...these colors and materials and the workmanship are...pale. Watered down. I'm not sure that makes sense."

"Is it a copy?"

"Maybe. I'd have to put it together like a jigsaw puzzle and compare the two."

"Two," Geneva said.

"Two. I'm pretty sure Belinda was duped into thinking her treasure was destroyed."

"If she was a good actress, could she dupe everyone else into thinking it was destroyed?"

"Good question, Detective."

When I went back downstairs I outlined my theory of the two tablecloths for Ardis. Then I told her about Geneva's encounter with the "villain," and the awl missing from Floyd's sewing basket. She groped for the stool and sat down.

"An embroidery stiletto," she said faintly.

"Silver filigree." I glanced toward our display of needlework tools—utilitarian scissors, awls, and stilettos. "Why does the silver filigree make it sound worse?"

"It's an abuse of an elegant tool," Ardis said. "An abuse of art. And Geneva's mystery man isn't the killer? He's a ghost? You do know how craz—no, I won't say that."

"It feels crazy, though, doesn't it? Ardis, did Granny see ghosts?"

"I honestly have no idea. Have you ever seen anyone besides Geneva?"

"I saw a bit of a flicker where this guy was, but otherwise no."

"How is Geneva? Is she pulling herself together?"

"She's resilient."

"I'd expect nothing less from Daddy's side of the family." Ardis took pen and paper from the drawer in the counter. "We'll have a lot to cover at Fast and Furious this afternoon. I feel an agenda coming on. Incomplete information, hon—our investigation is drowning in it. Do you mind?" She pointed to the office door.

"Dive in."

I sent Joe and the rest of the posse a text letting them know, in brief, that we no longer had a suspect. Then, between customers, I mulled the problem of incomplete information. I'd contributed to it by not asking followup questions a few times. No point in crying over spilt bones, though, and maybe I could get an answer to one of those questions by calling Martha the enamelist.

"Martha, hi, this is Kath."

"More questions?" she asked.

Living right by being nosy. "Just one, if you don't

mind. The other morning, at Sierra's breakfast, you said you and Floyd can give each other alibis."

"And you took me seriously? How could we possibly give each other alibis? Our shops are on separate floors."

"You might've slipped away together."

Martha's immediate and deep belly laugh told me where Floyd stood in the slipping-away department. "I hope you know what you're doing. I'm pretty sure the police aren't interested in me as a suspect, but go ahead and throw me into your pool, if you want. I had no reason to kill Belinda, though, and no opportunity, and I just plain didn't."

"What about Floyd?"

"Floyd's on his own."

DEBBIE CAME IN for her afternoon shift, wearing a loose cotton top she'd embroidered with Jacobean flora. I told her how much I liked it; I didn't dampen her spirits by telling her about the embroidery stiletto.

"I've got something to ask Nervie," I said, "and I'd like to catch her before her class."

"Call and ask her to come early so she isn't in her usual mad dash." Debbie looked at my face. "Ah. You don't want to tip her off?"

"That sounds so—"

"It's okay. You don't need to explain." She really *didn't* want me to explain. Debbie knew about the posse's activities but didn't want to be part of them. She helped logistically, though, giving Ardis and me time away from the business. "Keep your phone handy," she said. "If I see her and you don't, I'll call you."

We were both busy with customers when Nervie

dashed in. Luckily, Ardis emerged from the office in time to take over for me at the cash register. I caught up to Nervie on the back stairs.

"Nervie? Have you got a minute?"

She stopped and turned around. "I need to get ready for class."

"I know." I closed the gap between us so I could keep my voice low. "Do you mind telling me again how you know Belinda's tablecloth was stolen?"

"Oh for—I heard her say it. You don't get much better than the horse's mouth."

"Did she say it to you?"

"No, I heard her…okay, fine, I *over*heard her."

"I'm the last person to judge anyone for overhearing, Nervie. Who was she talking to?"

"I don't know. She was on the phone."

"What did she say?"

"You know how loud she could get, right? Not for that phone call. She was in her shop with her back to the door. At first I didn't see she had the phone. Then I heard her say, 'It's stolen.' Those exact words." With a thump, Nervie sat on the step. "Did this get her killed?"

Geneva materialized beside Nervie. "So many wonderful actresses."

"She said 'stolen,' again," Nervie said with a tremor, "and 'took' and 'taking,' but I didn't hear the rest. I left. I really do have manners."

"How did you know she was talking about the tablecloth?" I asked.

"She said something about Arts and Crafts, so she must've been."

"Thanks, Nervie."

She pulled herself up by the railing and looked a little rocky climbing the rest of the stairs.

Geneva floated down to me. "I've changed my mind," she said. "Nervie could never act that well."

Ardis finished her agenda and sent it to the posse so they'd have it ahead of our Fast and Furious meeting. I printed a copy, and when Ardis and I went up to the workroom shortly before the meeting started, I put it on the sideboard for Geneva.

"Will she join us?" Ardis asked.

"She might."

"Ten?"

"Probably not." I could have said *probably fishing*, but I didn't want to stir her up. Joe had let Clod know our witness made a mistake about the man in the sketch. Fishing was a good antidote to Clod's reaction.

The others arrived in short order, Mel bearing a square pan of brownies. "Because we're back to square one," she said as she cut them and passed them around.

"Aren't we further back than that?" Thea asked. "We haven't developed any other suspects. We put our eggs in one basket and then threw the whole basket at W's mystery man. What happened?"

"The mystery man's a dead end," I said.

"W is mortified," Ardis added. "But not dispirited."

"We shouldn't be, either," I said. "The mystery man turned out to be extraneous. That's the whole point of gathering information and looking at connections—to figure out what fits and what doesn't."

"Why aren't we leaving it up to the deputies at this point?" John asked. "Not that I'm not enjoying myself."

"Because they seem to think the two murders are

connected, but I don't think they're looking at the right connection."

"And we have our pride," Ernestine said. "We do excellent work, whether we're nabbing bad guys or knitting baby hats." She tossed three hats with teddy bear ears on the table.

"What *is* the right connection?" Mel asked.

"The tablecloth," I said. "I don't know how, and the connection might be tangential, but it's there. And I think the deputies are overlooking it."

"You don't think you're just obsessed, Red?"

"I *know* I am. But that doesn't mean I'm wrong."

"Good enough for me," Mel said.

"Agreed?" Ardis asked. The others nodded. "Then let's hit the agenda. Item one: Developments."

I wrote *Developments* on the board, and below that, *weapon—embroidery stiletto*. "Not confirmed yet." I told them about that part of our visit to the Vault.

"Did Floyd engineer that discovery?" John asked.

"Does Nervie use an embroidery stiletto?" Ernestine asked.

"Excellent questions," Ardis said. "We don't know the answers, but this is why we have the posse."

"I'm guessing yes to both of them," Thea said. "Here's a new connection: things missing, presumed stolen. The tablecloth, a couple of Simon's books, a couple of the Main Street scarecrows, including ours from in front of the library—did I tell you that?" She shook her fist. "And now the stiletto."

"Which brings us to this." I wrote *tablecloth* under *Developments* and told them about the reappearance of the shreds. "They're the shreds Belinda showed me. I'm positive of that. And at first glance, I believed it was the original tablecloth. But it's not, and that's a bona fide expert opinion."

"Why the deception?" John asked.

"And deception on the part of whom?" Ardis asked.

"Good questions," I said. "Let me get them down. Keep asking."

They did, and I wrote:

Did Belinda know it wasn't the original?
Did she shred it herself?
Why would she shred it?
A cheap publicity stunt?
To cause trouble for someone else?

"She accused Nervie," I said, "but only to begin with. By the time Cole got there, she was so quiet I thought she might be in shock. Now I wonder if she'd realized there'd been a switch."

"Destruction, disappearance, reappearance," Ernestine said. "How interesting. Why do you suppose that sequence reminds me of Shirley and Mercy?"

"I don't like it when I see them too often," Ardis asked, "but I don't like it when I don't know what they're up to. They stirred things up from the get-go. Where are they now?"

"Spending too much time at Angie's place," Mel said. "Hence, Angie's spending a lot of time at the café. I put a futon in the office in case she needs a lie down."

"That's good of you, Mel," Thea said. "Now let's forget the twins again. If Belinda realized there'd been a switch, she might have wanted the shreds back to prove it."

I wrote *Theory* on the board, and under that, *Belinda went to the storage closet to get the shreds back.*

"She went to get them and someone snuck up on her?" Ardis asked.

"Or she went with the person, or to meet the person, who told her where they'd find them," I said.

"Who?" Ernestine asked.

"This is where we're back to square one," Mel said. "It could be anyone. I don't know what's next on your agenda, Ardis, but this means another square of brownie is on mine. Anyone else?"

While she handed seconds around, my phone rang. "The best laid agendas," I said, looking at the display. "Spiveys."

"Don't answer it," Ardis said.

But I already had.

"A body! Floating in the pool!" the fevered twins shouted into the phone. "It's him! Come quick!"

TWENTY-THREE

CHAOS. THE CALL was pure, blithering Spivey chaos, with the twins snatching the phone from each other and a dog barking in the background. And barking and barking.

"Slow down. Slow down, please," I said. "Whose body? What pool?"

"The swimming pool!"

"Al Rogalla's!"

"Rogalla's pool?" I said.

"And his body!"

"Did you call 911?" I asked.

"We can't!"

"We're on the phone!"

"With you!"

"Then for God's sake hang up and call 911!" I said, catching their fever at last.

"I'm going in!" one of them said.

I heard barking, a scream, a splash, more barking, another splash, another scream, silence. I looked at the posse. They stared at me, all mouths open. "One of you call 911," I said. "Tell them people are drowning in Al Rogalla's pool. And can one of you give me a ride over there?"

Thea, John, and Ernestine immediately pulled out their phones. I ran down the stairs, with Ardis and Mel on my heels. We squealed out of the parking lot in

Ardis's daddy's Honda. I texted Joe along the way and then set my phone on the dashboard.

Rogalla lived in a late-Victorian, two-story brick house with wraparound porches and beautifully kept gardens and lawn. Ardis left the driveway, careened over the lawn, around the house, and pulled up beside the pool, two wheels resting on the concrete apron and passenger-side doors closest to the water.

Mel and I flung the doors wide, took the few steps to the pool, and dived in. Mel went for the nearest twin. I reached Rogalla and—tore off his arm? A *scarecrow*, not a floating body. *Spiveys.* I flung the arm aside and went for the second twin. She whimpered when I put my arm around her. As I towed her to the side of the pool, Clod arrived, siren blaring. I heard Ardis and Mel telling him the body was a scarecrow, but he leaped in anyway. He'd seen what we hadn't—Bruce losing the struggle to stay afloat, carried down by his sodden fur.

Rogalla and another EMT arrived in a screaming ambulance as Joe's truck bumped across the lawn. They converged on the scene as Clod brought Bruce out of the pool and crouched over him. In a voice so devoid of deputy starch as to be a coo, Clod implored Bruce to open his eyes. At a whistle from Rogalla, Bruce jumped up and trotted over to him as though nothing had happened.

"Who let you out, huh, Brucie?" Rogalla asked. "How'd you get out?"

Clod harrumphed and marched over to the twins. Ardis, on her phone, narrated the pandemonium for the posse back at the Cat.

"Mercy's arm is broken," Mel told the EMT. "The

dog tripped her. She fell on the edge of the pool, onto her upper arm, and then into the water."

Clod didn't coo over Mercy, but his harrumph softened as he watched the EMT check her over.

"Would you like transport to the hospital, Ms. Spivey?" the EMT asked.

"Would you like to press a charge of negligence against the homeowner?" Clod asked.

Meanwhile, Rogalla took blankets from the ambulance. He put one around each of the twins and handed one to Mel and one to me. The last one he used to dry Bruce, leaving Clod to drip.

"Shirley can drive me to the hospital," Mercy said, her voice as pasty as her face.

"But our keys." Shirley pointed at the pool.

"Mel and I will take you," Ardis said.

They helped Mercy into the back seat of the Honda, and then got Shirley in the other side. Mel handed my phone to me and said, "Call us."

In deference to her injured passenger, Ardis drove sedately back across the lawn.

"Did the Spiveys say what they were doing here?" Clod asked.

"I didn't stop to ask. I'm sorry," I said. "They were in such a panic over finding Rogalla dead in the pool."

"That's all right. I know where to find them." He gazed across Rogalla's newly rutted lawn after Ardis. "Good job getting here and getting them out the way you did." He turned to Rogalla, with a nod at Bruce. "What's his problem? I've never heard of a dog that can't swim. He sank like the *Titanic*. The last thing I saw was his nose going under."

"Scotties aren't meant to swim," Rogalla said.

"Maybe some do, but Bruce is one of the modern breed of non-buoyant Scotties."

"I gotta hand it to him, though," Clod said. "He had faith he could save someone. Even underwater, he was paddling away. Where was he, and how *did* he get out?"

"In the kennel around the side. Not locked, but he's never gotten out on his own."

"Need me for anything else?" the EMT asked.

Clod and Rogalla waved him off. Then Clod followed Rogalla and Bruce around the side of the house. I turned to see Joe stripping down to his boxers.

"Well this is interesting. Wait, are those little sloths?"

"They are. I thought I'd look for Shirley's keys."

"That's sweet of you."

"Or anything else of interest."

"The water's cold."

"I won't take long."

I stood by the side, helping by watching, and only metaphorically wringing my hands. He brought the parts of the scarecrow over to the side. I fished them out and laid them on the concrete apron. He dived and swam along the bottom, came up, and went down again. He brought Shirley's keys up after the third dive but went back in several more times, until he'd covered the whole bottom. Clod and Rogalla came back as he climbed out.

"Did you get the keys?" Rogalla asked.

I held them up as I handed Joe my blanket.

"Anything else?" Clod asked.

Joe shook his head.

"What else were you looking for?" Rogalla asked.

"I wasn't sure," Joe said. "Maybe an embroidery stiletto."

My shoes squelched as I crossed the lawn to Joe's truck. I called Mel as we put another rut in Rogalla's lawn. She relayed a request from Mercy.

"She'd like you to run out to Angie's and tell her what's happened. Let her know in person, so she sees you mean it, and there's no undue worry."

We went by my place, then Joe's, so we could get into dry clothes. Then we took a road that started winding as soon as it left town. We followed it into the hills and turned onto their road, which wound even more. Angie and Aaron lived a few miles along, a mile beyond a bridge over a branch of the Little Buck River. Joe's truck crunched gravel as we turned up the drive to an old Tennessee farmhouse with a tin roof and deep porch.

"Well, hey," Aaron said when he opened the door. He called over his shoulder, "It's Kath and Joe."

"Ask them in." Angie's voice came from a muffled distance.

"We could use your help," Aaron said. "Come on in." He took us through the living room and down a short hall. "They're in here," he said, stopping at a bedroom door. "Go on in, Kath. I'll bring you a chair."

The bedroom was only just big enough for the bed, a chest of drawers, and a wicker rocker. Angie sat in the rocker crocheting something pink. A younger woman with bare arms and the name *Riley* tattooed on her right shoulder sat cross-legged at the foot of the bed, reading a paperback. A gray-and-white tabby snoozed beside her.

"Hey, Angie. Sorry to barge in when you have company," I said. "We have a message from your mom."

The younger woman sneaked a look and went back

to reading. Aaron brought in a dining room chair, and I slipped it into a clear space at the end of the bed.

"Joe and I'll go on out to the kitchen," Aaron said.

I would have gladly joined them, but I sat down, smiled at Angie, and hoped the cat didn't wake up. It looked cozy and sweet, but if it was like every other cat besides Argyle, it would see me and hiss.

"This is Aaron's cousin, Taylor," Angie said. "Taylor's going to stay with us for a few days. Taylor, this is *my* cousin, Kath. Mom sent you all the way out here, Kath? Why didn't she call?"

I told Angie the bare details of the accident—what and where—and that Mercy didn't want her to worry. Angie leaned her head back and stared at the ceiling. She might have been counting to something higher than ten. Taylor, who hadn't turned any pages, let her book close on her lap.

"Are you all right, Angie?" I asked.

"Oh, yeah."

"Any idea what your mom and Shirley planned to do this afternoon? Why they went to Rogalla's?"

"'Not a clue' covers both."

"They left because of me," Taylor said.

"No, they didn't," Angie said.

"They left as soon as I got here."

"They were leaving anyway." Angie sat upright again. "Kath, Taylor needs advice. Taylor, Kath solves problems. All kinds."

Taylor hugged herself.

"Good book?" I asked. "May I?" I picked it up. *Wild Ayes: A Time-Travel Scottish Romance.* I opened it, and out of the corner of my eyes I saw Angie roll hers.

"That's the only thing I have left, after I left the only man I ever had." Taylor started crying.

Angie handed her a box of Kleenex. "Okay if I tell her about it?"

Taylor nodded and sobbed into a wad of tissues.

"She left him," Angie said.

"Riley?" I asked.

"How do you know Riley?" Taylor snuffled.

"She read your tattoo," Angie said. She rolled her eyes again. "This has been coming on for a couple of weeks. Aaron and I thought it was his drinking."

"I never said it was his drinking," Taylor said.

"I know, and I'm sorry we didn't know what you were going through all this time."

"I couldn't tell anyone."

Angie reached over and rubbed the cat's ears. "When Riley left for work this afternoon, Taylor came over here. The book's the only thing she brought with her. She feels more comfortable sitting in here. She's afraid of him."

"Of what he's done," Taylor said. "He told me where he got the book when he gave it to me."

"You said he threw it at you," Angie said.

"And I caught it, like a bouquet at a wedding. He knows I like a book with a bare-chested man in a kilt on it. He shouldn't've taken it, but he did it for me. And now I don't know what to do."

Angie told me the rest of the story, with hiccupped corrections, between sobs, from Taylor. Riley worked in his uncles' body shop in Shady Spring. Over the summer, he started taking afternoons off, lying about why. Then, a few weeks back, he got freaked out by someone who did what he'd been doing, but not as carefully.

"He says he never once broke a driver's window," Taylor managed to say. "He didn't want anyone having a bad time driving away. It rains a lot in the mountains."

"He freaked out over someone breaking the wrong window," Angie said.

"Over the body, too," Taylor said. "He *totally* freaked over the body."

"But he still took the book?" I asked.

"It was our anniversary," Taylor said.

"Scoot over," Angie said. She set her crochet aside and sat next to Taylor, an arm around her shoulders. "You already know you need to turn him in, don't you? So let's ask Kath the best way to do that."

"Anonymous tips work wonders," I said.

We didn't stay long after that, and Aaron saw us out. At the door, I asked, "Are Riley's uncles members of the Tennessee Herpetological Society?"

"Could be," Aaron said. "I don't keep up on their doings."

In the truck, Joe said, "Give her twenty-four hours. If she doesn't call it in, we will."

"You don't think Riley had anything to do with Gar's death?"

"No, I think Cole got that one right, and the killer's still out there."

"How will we know if Taylor calls the tip line?"

"Pretty sure Cole won't let news like that go unannounced."

On the way back into town, I sent an update to the posse.

TWENTY-FOUR

"I MISSED ALL THAT?" Geneva said when I gave her a recap the next morning at the Cat. "Why did you let me foolishly mope the afternoon away?" She flounced up to the ceiling fan and sat in an aggrieved heap.

"Are you going to mope this morning away, too?"

"Why? What will I miss?"

"Have you noticed we're short on dull moments lately? In fact, look who's waiting for me to unlock the front door. That's Belinda's ex-husband, Russell."

"He's staring. If you knew ventriloquism he wouldn't see your lips moving as you talk to thin air."

"Good idea. But if he's rude enough to comment, I'll tell him I was talking to Argyle."

She beat me to the door, floating through the glass and straight up to Russell. As I unlocked, she floated back in and whispered, "He has a calculating look in his eyes."

"Good morning, Russell. How are you?"

"All right. You?"

"Fine, thank you." I checked his eyes for the calculating look but wasn't sure I saw it.

"Conniving," Geneva said. "He wants something." She took up her post on the mannequin's shoulder.

I went back behind the counter and set my phone in easy reach next to the cash register. Ardis wouldn't be in for another hour.

"If you really want to know," Russell said, coming over to the counter, "I'm exhausted. I had no idea—being executor—it's more than I ever knew I'd have to deal with. *Nervie's* more than I can deal with. I hide inside. I don't dare sit on the porch or she'll stop by. Bring me a casserole. Want to talk. Everyone wants something."

"I'm sorry to hear that. Are you here because *you* want something?"

"Heh, yeah. Fair enough. I do. Someone told me that you're someone who meddles enough to get things done."

"Yeah, fair enough," Geneva said. "Heh."

"That isn't exactly complimentary. Do I want to know who said it?"

"Shirley and Mercy Spivey."

Figures. "So, what is it you think I can get done?"

"I have a proposition."

"I'm listening."

"Sierra wants a commitment for the shop," Russell said, "or she'd like me to vacate. That seems both reasonable and unreasonable at the same time. I need to know what Belinda's got there, what it's worth. I've gotten feelers from some of the people she bought from. Simon wants the books he found for her. A woman in Chattanooga and one in Asheville asked if I'll sell back to them, at cost. But the way Belinda kept records, I have no way of knowing if I'll be cheated. I told them all they have to wait."

"Good. Why does Sierra want a decision so quickly?"

"She mentioned expanding the gallery space before Christmas. If the shop goes."

"If Belinda still had it, that wouldn't be a question, would it?"

"No. My accountant is sorting through the mess of her records. He says as long as I keep the shop open, and sell according to the prices Belinda set, there shouldn't be a problem."

"And that should give you time to figure out the scope of the merchandise."

"That's what I want to ask you about. Can you help with that?"

Thank you, Shirley and Mercy. Could I help? Sure. I might even discover more treasures. But it would be a considerable time commitment. And the thought of sorting through hundreds of pieces of vintage cra— Inspiration struck. "Did you ask Shirley and Mercy if they'd do it?"

"It never occurred to me."

"They'd be perfect. They know embroidery. They're interested in old pieces. They have the time." And it would give Angie and Aaron breathing room.

"Genius move," Geneva said. "They'll be so pleased."

"Do you think they will?" Russell asked.

"I know they will."

"Now that we have that squared away," Geneva said, "why don't you tell him about the tablecloth and see if he turns into a raging killer?"

I squinted at her and went with a safer question. "I'd be interested in seeing the books Simon found for Belinda."

Russell blew out a breath. "Another headache. He says she told him she didn't want them after all. Too dry and academic. That sounds like Belinda."

"Too lecturey," Geneva said. "That sounds like you."

"He said he found another buyer and gave back Belinda's money," Russell said. "Before she could give him the books…this all happened. But considering how much he says they're worth, he's not getting anything until Rogalla finds transaction records."

"Wouldn't Simon have copies?"

"Doesn't matter. I told him not until we find Belinda's or find out they don't exist. Then we'll negotiate."

"Can *I* see the books?"

"I gave them to Rogalla for safekeeping."

After Russell left, I updated the posse on Rogalla's involvement with Belinda's estate. Ardis arrived soon after I sent the text, still on a riding-to-the-rescue high. She even greeted the twins and didn't immediately bolt when they dropped by. Mercy, her arm in a sling, looked on the edge of pain.

"She isn't supposed to do too much too soon," Shirley said.

"But we wanted to thank you again for yesterday," said Mercy.

"Why did you go to Rogalla's?" I asked.

"We followed that bearded so-and-so," Mercy said.

"The one we saw sitting in the truck out there by Angie's," said Shirley.

"And we followed your advice," Mercy said.

"What do you mean?"

"Not too closely, though," Mercy said, "the so-and-so, I mean. We followed your advice to a T, but we stayed back so he wouldn't spot us, and ended up at Rogalla's."

"If we hadn't been so shocked," Shirley said, "we would've seen it was a scarecrow and not Rogalla's body in the pool."

"Also, in our shock, we lost the so-and-so," Mercy said.

"Where did you follow him *from*?" I asked.

"We spotted him outside the Vault," Shirley said. "His movements were highly suspicious, so we did our civic duty and followed."

When they left, Ardis asked, "Why did you tell them to follow that so-and-so, and what was he doing at Rogalla's?"

"First, I didn't, and second, that's another piece of incomplete information."

Just before lunch, I dropped an armful of amber and amethyst skeins in the front window display. I'd meant to arrange them more artistically, but the sight of an approaching Clod stopped me. I snatched my phone from my pocket and texted Joe:

Cole about to crow? Stay tuned.

Geneva tsked over the heap of yarn.

"Quick," I said, "if Ardis isn't with a customer, tell her the deputy's here."

She saluted, whisked away, and she and Ardis flapped back together before Clod had a chance to cast his usual leery eye around.

"That was a fine thing you did, rescuing the dog yesterday, Coleridge," Ardis said. "No one else even noticed him going down for the third time. Have you learned anything more about that rather odd situation?"

"The Ms. Spiveys are still recovering from the ordeal," Clod said. "They might be able to tell us more in the next day or two."

"I imagine they're home and resting," Ardis said.

"You'll find this interesting," he said. "We made an

arrest in the smash-and-grab robberies. And do you remember those two rat-faced McDougals? We also found out the real reason they were in town last week."

"That *is* interesting," I said.

"Congratulations—and do tell," said Ardis.

Clod was happy to and generously gave credit for their success to an anonymous tip. The McDougals (Calvin and Burt Nave) were with their nephew Riley (Riley Nuckols) when Clod and Shorty went to pick him up. Calvin and Burt had received a tip of their own that Riley's jig was up, but that he might need help recognizing that himself. Riley hadn't been ready to confess when the deputies arrived, but Calvin and Burt helped him there, too. They'd suspected Riley was the "gang," and they'd told him to stop. He hadn't. Then Gar was murdered, and Riley threatened to go into Blue Plum and find the SOB who'd jeopardized his operation. Calvin and Burt came to town looking for Riley.

"Because in their assessment," Clod said, "Riley's as dumb as a box of rocks and he might just find the SOB and get himself killed."

"Why did Riley think he'd find the SOB in Blue Plum?" I asked.

"No comment," Clod said, and left.

"So now," Ardis said, "does that mean Coleridge is operating on a deficit of information, too? Or is he just not telling?"

"And why did the bearded McDougal go to Rogalla's yesterday? Things missing, things found, incomplete information. A lot of pieces to juggle. And that reminds me—I left something out of my text about Russell's visit this morning. He said Sierra wants to expand the gallery and wants Belinda's space."

"Is that a motive?" Ardis asked.

"Maybe. It's information, anyway." I sent another text to the posse and one to Joe telling him Clod crowed, as predicted. Then I scrolled through messages wondering what else I'd missed, hadn't shared, or hadn't asked. *Pesky unasked questions. Like this one.* The colleague who'd told me about the estate sale textiles she thought had gone missing in Alexandria had written "Not the textiles. They're fine." Did that imply something else *was* missing? I hadn't asked, but that was easy enough to fix with another text. And then it was easy enough to get lost in the world of fibers, customers, and earning a living.

Debbie and Abby came in for their Saturday shifts, but Ardis and I stayed through the lunch hour. After lunch, Ardis left to do her weekly shopping, and I dithered between taking paperwork up to the study and going home to do laundry. Thea saved me from both.

"I did it. I confess," she announced as she came through the door. "I tried to stop myself, but I was helpless." She put something loosely wrapped in tissue on the counter, then carefully unfolded the tissue, exposing the Briggs Myers mystery. "I couldn't resist. I've come to apologize, because this means *far* less money for yarn for months. But I'll let you hold it, if you want. Are your hands clean?"

I wasn't sure I should even breathe near it, but her eyes expected me to admire her baby. As it lay in its tissue swaddling, I opened the cover—and stopped. Someone had lightly penciled a design inside the cover, in the upper left-hand corner. I pointed to it.

"Used bookseller's code," Thea said.

"I saw one last night in a book Aaron's cousin had. The one she said her boyfriend took from Gar's truck."

"It's a common practice," Thea said. "Some are price codes, some are dates, some are a bookseller's own mark."

"Mind if I take a picture of it?"

"Get one like this, too." She held the book next to her beaming face.

I sent that picture to her and the picture of the mark to Angie. I asked Angie to compare the mark to the one in Taylor's book. Then I went up to the study to do a different kind of paperwork.

"Screen time?" Geneva asked when I opened my laptop.

"Come read over my shoulder. See if you can add anything."

I opened a document and gave it a heading: *things missing, things found, incomplete information, and things we forgot to ask.* Then I started typing.

Deputies found used romance paperbacks in Gar's truck
Twins followed a McDougal to Rogalla's
Why did the McDougal go to Rogalla's?
Who let the dog out?

"Is this supposed to make sense?" Geneva asked.

"Not yet."

My phone pinged with a text, Angie saying she'd check the book when she got home from work. I put down the phone. It pinged again, my colleague getting back to me.

2 books missing. Studies of A&C textiles, embroidery.

This time I knew the next question. My colleague anticipated me, though, and before I started typing, a follow-up text pinged in with the titles, publication data, and identifying marks of the missing books.

"Ooh, Geneva," I said, "lovely, lecturey books."

While she swooned across the laptop's keyboard, I called Rogalla to find out the titles of the dry, academic books Russell had given him for safekeeping.

"Sorry, I'll have to get back to you," he said. "Someone tried to break into my office. I'm on my way to meet the deputies there, now."

"No, ooh?" Geneva asked when I disconnected.

"Just more irritating incomplete information." I went back to typing.

Unsuccessful break-in at Rogalla's office
Rogalla safekeeping Belinda's books
Simon sold Belinda those books, wants them back
Riley thought he'd find the killer in Blue Plum
Nervie heard Belinda say, "It's stolen"
Belinda traveled to estate sales, used to live in DC area
A&C textile, embroidery books missing from Alexandria

"You should call the darling twins and ask them who let the dog out," Geneva said.

I did. Shirley answered—whispering, she said, so she wouldn't annoy a fussy, uncomfortable Mercy. "The dog was already out," she said. "It ran at that hairy so-and-so and scared him off. You know the rest."

I stared at the screen for a long time after that. I *didn't* know the rest. Didn't know how to *find* the rest. Too many holes, like a moth-eaten sweater. But, no, it wasn't even as solid as that.

Then Angie's text came in.

TWENTY-FIVE

Match, ANGIE'S TEXT SAID. She attached a photo of the mark in Taylor's paperback so I could see for myself. Definitely a match. But what did it prove?

That I'd been wrong about the tablecloth being the connection between the two murders. Except for the part where I was right.

"You look confused," Geneva said. She'd grown bored with the static screen, and my silence, and floated over to settle with Argyle in the window seat. The sun, coming in at its autumn angle with a yellower light, made her look less like a patch of fog and more like a scrap of lace, like an antique lace mantilla.

Lace—full of holes, but substantial enough to throw around my shoulders and dance a tango. Netting—also full of holes, but a net can snare. "I might be confused, Geneva, but when have I ever let that stop me? We're going to need a trap."

We'd need the posse, too. But I didn't want to give away the answer I'd come to; I wanted to see if they'd leap the same holes I'd leapt and land in the same spot. To that end, I gathered my exhibits—photos of our whiteboard work, copies of our "investigation" texts, Angie's photo and mine (with brief information about the marks and where and when the books were acquired), and the document I'd tapped away at that afternoon (to which I added my thoughts on lace and netting). I attached all that to a group email and wrote a note with simple instructions: *Open book test: Read the attached. Name the killer. Text me. Go.*

"You're leading them, a little bit, by calling it an open *book* test," Geneva said. "Hit Send anyway."

I did.

"How long do we have to wait?" she asked.

"People are busy. It might be hours. It might be to-morrow before we've heard from everyone."

"We should plan a cunning trap while we wait."

"I should go home and do laundry."

"Which is more important? Clean socks or snaring criminals?"

"For that matter, I could knit a pair of clean socks while we plan."

"A two-fer," Geneva said. "Except your knitting is slow and painful to watch. You can take notes while I plan. I know about traps and snares. My grandpappy trapped bobcats."

Rather than take notes on her grandpappy's skills, I pulled the box of shreds over and started knotting them together into one length.

Geneva interrupted herself to ask, "Isn't that evidence tampering?"

"It'll be just deserts when I'm finished."

Sooner than I expected, though not sooner than I or the poor bobcats would have liked, my phone pinged with a text. Thea—mad as a trapped bobcat. "My baby is a stolen book. Verified on stolen book database. He is toast."

A few minutes later, John wrote, "Motive for *you* to kill *him*, Thea. Doesn't prove he killed anyone. For re-cord, I agree. It's Simon."

Mel sent: "Thanks. Spoiler alert next time?"

Joe: "His motive?"

Ernestine: "Why kill in those locations?"

Thea: "He left cheap romance in Gar's truck? Why?"

Ardis: "Stage setting. Same with leaving our scissors at scene. Simon loves sets, playing a part."

John: "Need to wait and eliminate other suspects?"

Ardis: "Wait and he eliminates one of us if we get too close."

Mel: "LOTS of holes here. None of this is proof. Need more info."

John: "Give info we have to deputies?"

Ernestine: "Are we credible after W's mystery man crashed and burned?"

"I'll never live it down," Geneva said, reading over my shoulder. "How lucky for me, I'm already dead. Tell them about the trap."

I wrote, "Two-fer. Give info to deputies. Get ultimate hole-plugger—self-incrimination. Set a trap."

Joe: "Sycamore trap."

Ardis: "Ahem."

Joe: "Gar's favorite fly, called it sycamore fly. So tasty you have to hide behind sycamore tree to put it on your line or fish crawl right up your leg to get it."

Thea: "Use a book for bait."

Ernestine: "Fancy book on fancy stagecraft. Make him drool while he bites."

Joe: "Better—Gar's 1st edition script 'Who's Afraid of Virginia Woolf?' autographed by Albee and original Broadway cast."

Ardis: "Heart just stopped. Gar had that?"

Joe: "No, but Simon doesn't know that. Bait and switch."

I wrote, "You all appear to be free for oodles of texts. Are you free to plot and plan?"

Ardis: "On Daddy duty. Make it my place?"

Mel: "Almost suppertime. I'll bring Hot Browns."

"And when we catch him," Geneva said, "Let's hope he doesn't crawl up a leg and bite."

OVER MEL'S TASTY SANDWICHES, we devised our tasty, three-part plan: 1) Lure Simon to the script. 2) Trip him—literally—in the act of snatching it. 3) Turn him over to the deputies. Then, to make the nonexistent script as irresistible as Gar's legendary sycamore fly, we wove a story around it. That Gar, a fan of the play and Albee, bought the script and put a good bit of effort into getting it autographed by the author and original cast. The crowning jewel was Uta Hagen's signature. Gar had carried a torch for Uta since seeing her in the play opening night.

"Did he carry a torch?" Thea asked, looking dewy-eyed.

"Probably not," Joe said. "Remember, we're making this up."

Ardis would be our storyteller, using her repertory chops to convince Simon of the script's glory, glamor, and unguarded condition. "I am appalled," she would tell Simon. "And as a true booklover, I know you'll be appalled, too. I overheard Joe laughing to Kath about the script, because he borrowed it before Gar died. He figures it's his, now, because no one knows he has it. But in Gar's 'honor,' he has it in his shop, in the bottom of the box where he keeps his overflow stock of brown trout paintings." She promised to sound extremely disappointed in both Joe and me. Then she'd tell Simon that she'd confronted Joe and told him to find out the name of Gar's executor and turn the script over. Or else. "But now I'm even more irritated," she would say, "because Joe said it has to wait. He's leaving for Asheville and won't be back until tomorrow."

"Will Simon bite?" Ernestine asked.

"If he killed Gar over a book, he'll believe the script exists," Joe said. "He'll know Gar collected rare books on flies and angling. Gar didn't have many, because he had expensive and eclectic taste, but the Albee script fits in with that."

"The good thing is," John said, "if he doesn't rise to our sycamore fly, we haven't lost anything but time."

"And time spent fishing doesn't count," said Joe.

JOE DOCTORED AN old manila envelope to make it look full. "It's bulked up with paper," he said when he gave it to me Sunday morning, "along with a few subtleties to give it tension."

"The way Albee does in Virginia Woolfe?" I said. "Wily work, Dunbar."

Ardis stopped by the Vault Sunday afternoon, shortly after it opened, and played her role for Simon. I sent our collected information to Darla, as the safer deputy. Then I took the box with the knotted together shreds and spent the afternoon "working" in Joe's shop. Geneva came with me and hung around the teller's cage kicking her ghostly heels. The envelope went into the bottom of Joe's box of brown trout paintings.

Sierra waved from the information and sales desk. Midafternoon, Simon ambled over to say hi and ask if Joe would be in.

"Tomorrow or Tuesday," I said. "He had business in Asheville."

The afternoon wore on. I hadn't seen Martha, Russell, or Nervie come in at all. Geneva grew bored or bold and floated off toward Floyd's. There weren't any screeches, so I assumed all was well. Sierra offered me a bottle of water. When Simon waved goodbye at the end of the day, I sent a text to the posse. Then I puttered, pretending to restock displays, wondering where Geneva was, until Sierra asked how long I'd be.

"Oh, look at the time. Sorry. On my way."

"Good, I am, too. After I change. Hot date."

"Great! Have fun." *Bonus!* No need to worry about the resident on the third floor while we sneaked around on the first.

She let me out the front, and I went around to the back, where Joe, Mel, Thea, Ernestine, and John waited in the shadows.

"No Ardis?" I asked.

"No sitter," Joe said. "But she sends her best wishes for big fishes."

We waited a little longer, until Sierra came out and hopped in her car. Then Joe let us in to take up our positions. Thea went straight to Simon's shop to scan the shelves for other potentially stolen books. Joe unlocked the storeroom where Belinda died.

"You two don't mind being in here?" I asked Ernestine and Mel.

"It will be an honor," Ernestine said.

"Thanks. The hall light switch is by the back door. I'll bring the rope."

Lights were still on in the front of the building so that patrolling deputies could see any shifty charac-

ters wandering where they shouldn't. John and Joe sat
in the front corners, out of view of anyone looking in,
unobtrusive to the unobservant inside. Trying to keep a
low profile, I retrieved the knotted length of tablecloth
shreds I'd left in Joe's shop and took it to Mel and Ernestine in the storeroom.

"Text when it's time," Mel said, and closed the door.

I needed to take up my position, but I went to Floyd's
first, to look for Geneva. She'd said the other ghost
hadn't been aware of her. But if she *could* make a connection, what would happen? Could it change her situation?

I heard her before I saw her, sitting on the biscuit
table, singing her mother's song, and felt a wave of relief. "Everyone's here," I whispered. "Now we wait."

"Waiting's only hard when you're waiting for biscuits."

We had no way of knowing when Simon would make
his move, or if he would. But we'd waited like this once
before (last time, in the woods, near a sinkhole), so we
settled in with knitting needles flashing to pass the
time. *Mine* didn't flash. They steadily clicked, though,
until Geneva flew to me and said she heard the click
of the back door opening. I finished the row, stuck the
free needle in my back pocket, and set the rest aside. I
sent a text to the others: He's Here.

We let him come. Simon didn't expect anyone to be
there, so he didn't see the two men sitting in the front
corners or the woman behind the potted palm. Nor the
ghost who hung nosily over his shoulder as he rummaged for the right box in Joe's shop, and then the envelope in the box.

"Unbearably smug," Geneva said. "He's wearing gloves."

I sent the text letting Mel and Ernestine know it was time to tie the rope to the doorknob opposite their hiding place, stretch it across the hall, turn out the light, and wait.

"Point for the killer," Geneva said. "He put everything back neatly."

Envelope in hand, Simon headed for the hall. Joe and John quietly took up new positions at the front door in case he turned and went that way. I followed Simon down the hall. He swore when he saw the light was out but kept going. When he turned the corner, I made my footsteps obvious to spook him. He stopped. I stopped.

"Sierra?" he called. "Hello?"

"Try this," Geneva said. She made a moan I'd never heard before.

Simon started walking again. I did my best to imitate Geneva's moan. Simon hesitated. I moaned again. He took off running for the door—and that made his trip over Mel and Ernestine's rope that much more spectacular. He did a full-body plant on the terrazzo. He probably lost his breath—if not then, definitely when I jumped on his back. And there, in the spot where he'd stabbed Belinda, I pressed the tip of my knitting needle.

"You don't want to move, Simon. This is the biggest, baddest pair of scissors you've ever seen, and I *will* pound them straight into your heart."

He wriggled. I pressed harder until John and Joe came and tied him with a sailor's and a fisherman's precision. When Mel turned on the light, and they flipped Simon over, he looked at my knitting needle. I blew on its tip, like it was a smoking pistol, and holstered it in my back pocket. Ernestine called 911.

"Nice wounded-bobcat imitation," Joe said.

Thea, conducting her inventory in Simon's shop, only came out when she heard the sirens. "Couldn't help it," she said. "I got lost in a good book."

TWENTY-SIX

THE SIRENS BROUGHT the full deputy treatment—Clod, Shorty, *and* Darla arrived. "Sometime it would be nice if you didn't try to show us up," Darla said as she walked past me.

Simon, full of fury, demanded they arrest all of us for false imprisonment, me for assault, and Joe for theft. The deputies untied Simon. Geneva wrung her hands. Neither of those actions bothered me, but a furrow showed up between Joe's eyebrows, and then deepened, and our plan suddenly skittered.

"Do you need medical attention, Mr. Grace?" Shorty asked.

"I'm sure I do, but I'd like to see this settled first."

Clod and Shorty herded us up to the gallery where some of us had sat with them before.

"I received a tip," Simon said, before sitting down, "from a reliable, responsible source."

Geneva hooted and then clapped her hands over her mouth.

"The source told me your brother took a valuable script from Garland Brown, and that I would find it hidden at the bottom of a box in his shop. And I did find it. It's the envelope the deputy is holding."

Darla, wearing gloves, held up the envelope. Clod pulled on gloves, and she handed it to him.

"Tell them he wore gloves while he prowled," Geneva said.

"First, what are you all doing here after hours?" Clod asked, connecting the rest of us with a slash of his finger.

"Knitting, mostly." John saluted Clod with his needles, and we followed suit.

"Ms. Rutledge has only one needle," Clod said. "And no yarn."

It was such an obvious observation, I ignored it. "If Simon looked for that envelope in a box in Joe's shop," I said, "shouldn't his fingerprints be on whatever he touched while locating said box and on whatever else might have been in it?"

Shorty and Darla exchanged looks I couldn't quite decipher. Then Clod held up the envelope, and my attention zeroed in on it.

"All right if I open this, Mr. Grace?" Clod asked.

"Absolutely." Simon sat back—a posture of confidence.

"Mr. Dunbar?" Clod said.

Joe's posture didn't reveal much. Refusing to meet Clod's eye, and Clod using their surname, said more.

"This wasn't part of the plan," Geneva said.

I shook my head a very little bit.

"You say no, Ms. Rutledge? Don't open it?"

"What? Oh, no, I was just asking myself if I believe Simon's story."

Clod opened the envelope and looked inside. "Bring a chair over, Shorty." Chair in place, Clod took out a sheaf of paper. "Exhibit A. Paintings," he said.

"Those are pastels," Darla said.

Clod counted them. "Ten *pastels* by…someone illegible, priced at—" He whistled and put the pastels on the chair. He dipped back into the envelope and brought out Belinda's art embroidery pillow cover with the gold-finches, and then a sheaf of paintings. "Another ten or twelve, this time by the more legible and even less affordable Mr. Dunbar. I knew you were good, Ten, but I didn't know you got this much for them."

"I don't if someone steals them," Joe said.

"Is this a brother game?" Geneva asked.

I didn't try to answer. Clod took one more item from the envelope and handed the envelope off to Darla. I sneaked a look at Simon—rigid. And what Simon might not have noticed—I certainly hadn't—while Clod captivated us with his show-and-tell: Shorty had moved. He stood directly behind Simon.

Now Clod held a folded handkerchief—the unfinished forget-me-not hankie from Floyd's Victorian sewing basket. Carefully, almost tenderly, he opened the folds to reveal a silver filigree embroidery stiletto.

"That's not possible," Simon said.

"What's not possible?" Clod asked.

"I mean—I meant I don't recognize it," Simon said.

"Recognize what?" Clod asked.

"But the *script*," Simon said, turning to Darla. "It's in the envelope."

Darla peered into the envelope. "Nothing left but scrap paper."

"Ask Ardis," Simon said. "Ask her. Call her. Call her now."

"Here's Ardis." Ernestine held up her phone. "She says there is no script, this is all ad lib. She says Simon likes to rewrite lines and ad lib and thinks he's being a creative artist, but he's wrong. He's a murderer."

Simon's ad libs, after that phone call, proved Ardis right.

"IT WAS ALL there in the stage settings," Ardis said the next morning at the Cat. "His cleverness, the clues, and his comeuppance."

"You were lucky that stunt with the envelope worked," Clod said.

Joe had stopped by with four cups of coffee—one for me, one for Ardis, and one for himself. The fourth, sitting on the counter, seemed to conjure Clod from thin air and caffeine.

"We're lucky," I said, "and not without skills."

Clod snorted but took a sip of coffee rather than rebut. "Anyway, the poor guy cracked, confessed, and then collapsed. But you took a real chance. He could've gone ballistic. You all didn't have to go after him—it was only a matter of time before someone else caught on to him."

"You already had," Ardis said, "when you refused to believe the gang killed Gar. His stage setting there was good enough for the casual eye, but it didn't hold up to expert inspection."

"That's what happened with Gar," Clod said. "Simon offered him an extremely rare book on angling. But Gar, being an expert and a collector, knew the book wouldn't be available outside of private collections unless it was a fake or stolen. It wasn't a fake. Simon said Gar wanted to meet with him, that Gar was going to give him a chance to make things right, return the book, turn himself around. Simon agreed to listen, but he asked if Gar would meet him somewhere away from the prying eyes and ears of Blue Plum."

"Too bad Simon didn't know the gang never broke driver's-side windows," I said.

"How do *you* know that?" Clod asked. "That detail still hasn't been released."

"But you told us there was a missing detail," I said, "so we made use of those skills we're not without."

"What about Belinda?" Joe asked.

"Same thing. She recognized a book, something about it, and threatened to expose him. We're still working on whether he's the guy who tried to get into Rogalla's office. Maybe prowled around his house, too, and let Bruce out."

"Which one of the rat-faced McDougals has the beard?" I asked.

"Calvin," Clod said. "Why?"

"Ask him if Simon let the dog out. See what he says."

"Did Simon throw the scarecrow in the pool?" Ardis asked.

For a brief moment, Clod looked shifty-eyed. Then he ignored her question and asked his own. "The stiletto wrapped in the hankie was a nice touch. Is that another one from Floyd's?"

"We borrowed it from Nervie," Joe said. "It belonged to her grandmother."

"We haven't found the one Simon used yet," Clod said, "but Floyd gave a photograph and full description to the medical examiner. The ME says it sounds like a possible match. Oh, and the scissors—Nervie told us she had a pair of yours at the Vault and they're missing."

"When you finish with them as evidence," Ardis said, "we don't want them back."

"Simon might've used them to shred her tablecloth," Clod said. "The shredding and singeing were supposed to be a warning to keep Belinda from talking. She'd shown him the tablecloth, so he knew where to find it.

He lured her to the storeroom with the promise of getting what was left of it back."

"Did he say anything about switching the tablecloths?" I asked. Clod looked blank, so I told him about the substitution.

"Huh," he said. "Her initial reaction—calling us, getting quiet while she processed the threat—that might've been what he expected. But then if she figured out it wasn't her tablecloth, and blew off his threat, that could be when he decided to kill her."

I thought of Thea making her inventory of suspect books. "Was he going to kill everyone who figured out what he was doing? That wasn't a sustainable business model."

After Joe and Clod left, Ardis asked, "Did *Coleridge* put that scarecrow in Al Rogalla's swimming pool? And who did switch the tablecloths?"

"If Cole is responsible for the scarecrow, it makes you wonder how Rogalla will retaliate. As for the tablecloths, I might have an idea."

I called Russell and asked if I could come talk to him about Belinda's linens. He said he was at the house, clearing it out.

"I could use a break," he said.

A bit of autumn mist hung in the air, muting the colors, as I climbed Vestal Hill. Russell waved from the porch when he saw me. We sat in a couple of rockers there, looking out over the town.

"You aren't hiding from Nervie today?" I asked.

"No, hiding wasn't going to work. I flat out told her I wasn't interested. I don't think she really minded. It was a shame she lost Pete the way she did. He and I were buddies in the service. Nervie and Belinda never did take to each other, though."

"I heard Pete left her," I said.

"Only in the final way. He's buried at the VA in Johnson City. I help the Boy Scouts put flags on the graves every Memorial Day and make a point of putting Pete's flag on myself."

We rocked for a while, and then I told him I knew the shreds he let me have weren't the real tablecloth. "This might be a jump, Russell, but you said you didn't know crewel work from a crawdad. But you used the term 'crewel work.' I think you know more than you're letting on."

His rocker squeaked, and he appeared to ponder that.

"Russell, please, I just want to know if the tablecloth is all right."

He nodded. "It's safe. It's in my mother's cedar chest."

I closed my eyes for a few seconds.

"It was hers," he said. "It belonged to my mother, made by my grandmother. It's something, isn't it? She was magic with a needle. I lost it to Belinda in the divorce." He looked at me. "I think you know how much that hurt."

"I think I do."

"When I saw she planned to sell it—I couldn't let her do that. And then I thought I could teach her a lesson. So I took it, and I got back something I cherished more than I ever cherished our marriage."

"What did you substitute? It's very close, but—"

"My mother's copy of the original. It wasn't nearly as good. She made it when she was a girl. It was sweet, though, and I'm sorry Simon destroyed it. I'm sorry about Belinda, too."

"Can I buy the original from you?"

"Maybe I'll leave it to you in my will."

THEA STOPPED BY on her lunch hour and told us Darla had asked her to help them with a complete inventory of Simon's books, in the shop and in his house.

"His position as director of Outreach and Distance Learning at Embree took him to campuses and libraries all over the southeast," she said. "It had him hobnobbing with college presidents, deans, academics—you know, people who might also have nice *private* libraries."

"A guest on their campuses and in their homes," Ardis said, "and he stole from them?"

"And from other bookstores," Thea said. "He has legitimate stock but felt no qualms about adding stolen books. Maybe he felt en*titled* to them."

GENEVA FLOATED DOWN from the ceiling fan after I'd finished ringing up a sale of crewel yarn. She stopped directly in front of me and said, "What?"

"Sorry?"

She traced a giant question mark in the air. "The question you keep almost asking. The one that makes you look at me and then look away. What?"

I took out my phone. "Last night, when you were gone so long in Floyd's, I got worried. What happens if sometime you *do* make a connection with another…"

"Let's call this hypothetical being my boo-som friend. Are you worried we'll disappear into a misty gray sunset together and you'll never see me again?"

"Is that any more unlikely than seeing you in the first place?"

"As with so many questions concerning ghosts, I'm in the dark."

"Did you see your friend last night?"

"Sadly, no. The rolltop desk was gone, and so was he. Happily, I think whoever bought the desk has a new houseguest."

OVER LUNCH LATER in the week, I went to walk around the Vault. I went first to Nervie's shop. She wasn't there, and that was fine. She'd arranged her patterns in baskets. I flipped through them, looking for any evidence she'd copied other designers' work. If she had, I couldn't tell. Maybe someday I'd ask the twins about it. More likely I wouldn't.

When I went back downstairs, Sierra and Martha stood looking into Simon's shop.

"It's a bit more than I wanted to pay," Martha was saying.

"But the location's worth it," Sierra said, "and having jewelry in the actual vault will be perfect. Don't you think so, Kath?"

"Absolutely. Your work is gorgeous, Martha, and the vault's a perfect setting."

Martha looked pleased and told Sierra she'd give it serious thought. I asked Sierra if the rumor about classes at the Vault were true.

"Not any time soon," she said. "Not before Christmas, anyway."

That wasn't exactly the answer I was looking for, but there'd be time to worry about that later. I went across the hall to look around Floyd's. He'd sold the

Victorian sewing basket with the half-finished hankie, but the biscuit table was still there. Floyd came over to help me admire it.

"It's a genuine East Tennessee piece," he said. "Came from the Harmon family, out along the river. That's the original piece of marble, too. Nothing fancy, but neither are biscuits."

Back at the Cat, Geneva hummed her mama's biscuit song, and I offhandedly asked if she'd known a Harmon family. She stopped humming and without hesitation recited part of a child's bedtime prayer:

"And God bless Aunt Lou, and bless Ada, Lydia, Laura, and Clara, too. Amen."

"Who are they?" I asked.

"Aunt Lou Harmon and her little four-part harmonies. My mama's sister and her girls."

I called Floyd and told him not to sell the biscuit table to anyone else; I'd be right there. I ran the whole way back to the Vault, and later that day Joe brought the table home to the Cat in the bed of his pickup. We found the perfect spot for it in the kitchen.

"Daddy used to say that Mama's biscuits were so good they'd make you take back something you didn't steal," Geneva said.

"Do you remember the recipe?" I asked. "Can you teach me?"

"I remember the most important part."

"What is it?"

"It's what you say when you eat them—mm-mmm."

* * * * *

MEL'S PEAR-AND-GINGER SCONES

*Makes 6 or 8 scones, depending on
how big you want them.*

*2 o r 3 firmish pears (about 1 pound), peeled, cored,
and cut into 1-inch chunks
1½ cups all-purpose flour
¼ cup granulated sugar
1½ teaspoons baking powder
½ teaspoon ground ginger
½ teaspoon salt
6 tablespoons cold unsalted butter, cut into small
cubes
¼ cup chopped crystallized ginger
¼ cup heavy cream
1 large egg*

1. Heat oven to 375°F.

2. Line a large baking sheet with parchment paper.
   Arrange pear chunks on parchment and roast (no
   need to stir) until they feel dry to the touch and look
   a little browned on the bottom, about 20 minutes.
   Slide parchment with pear chunks onto a cooling
   rack and cool to lukewarm. Leave oven on. Line
   baking sheet with another piece of parchment.

3. Whisk flour, sugar, baking powder, ground ginger, and salt together in a large bowl. Add butter cubes and cut in with a pastry blender until the cubes are about the size of baby green peas. Stir in cooled pear chunks. Give the mixture three or four quick mashes with the pastry blender (to break a few of the pear chunks, but leave most intact). Stir in crystallized ginger.

4. In a small bowl, beat cream and egg. Stir into flour mixture with a fork, just until you can bring the dough together in a ball. Don't overmix.

5. On a well-floured board, pat dough into a 6-inch circle. Cut into either 6 or 8 wedges. Arrange wedges, two inches apart, on parchment-lined baking sheet.

6. Bake scones until firm and golden, about 30 minutes if you're making 6, about 22 minutes if you're making 8. Transfer to a cooling rack. Serve warm.

7. Unbaked scones freeze beautifully, and you can put them straight into the oven from the freezer. They'll take only a few minutes longer to bake.

EMBROIDERED HANKIE CORNER: FORGET-ME-NOTS FOR A GHOST

Pattern designed by Kate Winkler for
Crewel and Unusual, *Designs from Dove Cottage, 2018*

Materials:
Cotton or linen hankie
Cotton embroidery floss in light orange, medium blue, medium green
Embroidery needle
Small embroidery hoop

Instructions:
1. Use two strands of floss for all embroidery.

2. Lightly pencil heart shape on hankie corner.

3. Make dots at top center and bottom point of heart, then 4 points on each half of heart, to roughly outline shape.

4. Secure hankie corner in hoop; adjust tension as needed while working.

5. With orange, make a French knot at each dot, working around outline of heart.

6. With blue, make 5 French knots surrounding each orange knot, again working around outline of heart.

7. With green, complete outline of heart shape by working straight stitches between flowers.

8. Add lazy-daisy stitch leaves in green, ad lib, some inside and some outside the heart.

Loop Start Tip:
To avoid extra tails (which must be woven in) or knots on the back of your work, start with a single strand of floss twice as long as you need. Put both ends through the eye of your needle and bring the needle up from the back of the work—without pulling the loop through to the front. Then, put the needle down through the fabric two threads over from where it came up, and pull it and the thread through the loop, neatly securing the thread.

ACKNOWLEDGMENTS

THANK YOU PEGASUS BOOKS, Claiborne Hancock, Katie McGuire, and Cynthia Manson for bringing the Haunted Yarn Shop Mysteries back to life. Katie, you're the editor every writer needs. Thanks to you, Geneva the ghost is sitting pretty on the mannequin's shoulder at the Weaver's Cat, waiting to see who comes through the door and what happens next. Thank you, Esther Pawlowicz, for consultation on late October colors in northeast Tennessee. Thanks to colleagues past and present in Tennessee and Illinois, for lending your names to citizens in Blue Plum—Aaron Carlin, Darla Dye, Thea Green, Debbie Keith, and Mike Rogalla. Thanks, also, to Mike and Val Rogalla for letting their Scottie Bruce come play with me in Blue Plum. Special thanks to Janice Harrington and Betsy Hearne for careful reading and thoughtful, valuable feedback. The ever-generous Kate Winkler has designed another pattern for this book. Thank you, Kate! My own Mike gets the biggest thanks of all. Not only do you put up with my long hours of typing and provide expert information about flyfishing in the creeks of eastern Tennessee, but you've moved beyond making the best grilled cheese sandwiches in the world and now also make the best chef salads.

ReaderService.com has a new look!

We have refreshed our website and we want to share our new look with you. Head over to ReaderService.com and check it out!

On ReaderService.com, you can:

- Try 2 free books from any series
- Access risk-free special offers
- View your account history & manage payments
- Browse the latest Bonus Bucks catalog

Don't miss out!

If you want to stay up-to-date on the latest at the Reader Service and enjoy more Harlequin content, make sure you've signed up for our monthly News & Notes email newsletter. Sign up online at ReaderService.com.

RS19